Joan of Arkansas

Madeleine Herrmann

ISBN: 978-1-63210-038-2
Library of Congress Number: 2018949759

Disclaimer: This is a work of fiction. Any resemblances to real people and events are coincidental.

Cover art courtesy of creative commons at pixabay.com

Acknowledgments

My fondest thanks to Thomas French for his artistic support and personal care throughout the process of writing and publishing.

Joan of Arkansas

Awakening to the World

Madeleine Herrmann

Plain View Press, LLC www.plainviewpress.net

1101 W 34th Street, Suite 404 Austin, TX 78705

For all who love the natural world

and long for peace.

"The purpose of a writer is to keep civilization from destroying itself."

—Albert Camus

Contents

Chapter One: A Girl Called Joan

Joan Larousse could hear her parents arguing downstairs. Her father, Henri, spoke loudly and sounded angry. Susan, her mother, responded in a timid whimper. Joan was too far upstairs to understand what they were saying, something about the trip to Washington that her father had just come back from, and him being late because his jet had almost missed the runway upon landing. He kept repeating, *This lousy life… this lousy life!* And *It's all your fault! You push me all the time.* Joan wondered what her mother had done. *Pushing how? And what if her Dad had crashed and died?* Thoughts kept running through her head as she tried to make sense of her parents' conversation. She pulled the blanket lightly over her shoulders and snuggled into her bed, feeling sad and apprehensive.

A summer moon was shining between the bedroom curtains. It was a crescent moon playing hide and seek with the clouds. The gentle breeze made the curtains dance and brought a scent of wild mint inside the room. Joan took a deep breath. It felt good. A barn owl was hooting in a tree nearby and it made her smile. *But, why did her dad say that? Why did he call life lousy? Why? Life is good,* she thought, closing her eyes and breathing in slowly as she tried to persuade herself that life was good.

Joan woke up early the next day. She would walk to the park, her favorite place, before anybody woke up. She slipped on her jeans, a yellow t-shirt and a pair of sneakers, then hesitated for a moment in front of her cell phone. *No,* she thought, and left it on her bureau. She liked the silence of the woods and being alone with herself, away from any other voices except the warbling and trilling songs of birds. Joan tiptoed downstairs silently. The house was still. She quickly walked out the front door.

The park was part of a large old estate which her father bought when she was a baby. He had special trees, flowering bushes and fruit trees planted here and there. A pond was strategically placed adjacent to a stream with real fish in it. A large section of the park was left wild, untouched. Joan liked that part the best. She called it the hidden woods, *le bois cache*, her French tutor, Mademoiselle Giroud, liked to call it. It was a special place full of mystery and surprises, among old trees and mossy rocks, where a fox could occasionally be spotted coming out of its den. Joan headed for that part of the woods, wondering what kind of birds she would encounter today. She felt free, mischievous, happy, and excited as she skipped beneath the trees toward her favorite place.

She reached the cave, stopped and looked around, as if a voice was telling her to wait. She carefully inspected the surroundings, and then stepped slowly under the pine tree which overshadowed the entrance. A ray of early sunlight filtered through a small crack by the opening, faintly illuminating the interior. It warmed her heart. Joan felt confident. No one could keep her away from this special place that had been a refuge for her since she had discovered it when she was a little girl. It felt like home, a special home of her own.

There was a rock in the form of a chair that she sat on inside. It was comfortable and familiar. She touched the moss and ran a finger along the small drip of water which came down from the side of the cave, as if she had completed the ritual she needed to be welcomed inside. Her heart was beating with joy and anticipation. Here, at last, she was safe; she could think and answer all the questions she had. She felt welcome and happy, as if the place cradled her in some sort of a loving blanket. Joan didn't understand why this always happened to her in the cave, why this was a different place, a peaceful place, as if she were in another world or something, but she did not question it, and abandoned herself to the feeling of awe. She knew, deep inside, that in this cave her thoughts would flow clearly.

Of course, she didn't talk to anyone about this feeling for fear of being called weird. Her parents, knowing them, would certainly call a doctor. "My daughter prefers to hide in a cave rather than being with friends her own age, Doctor. What is the matter with her? Please tell us.," she could hear her mother say. Joan laughed at the idea. *But there is someone who perhaps could understand*, she thought. *Yes, Mademoiselle Giroud would understand.*

Joan thought of her parents fighting again. *What did her father mean by, "It's all your fault?" What had her mother done?* Joan brought up the image of her lovely mother: her blonde hair floating in the wind as she was hitting a tennis ball, her smile, the way she walked, bouncing lightly through the garden. Her mother liked her tennis teacher; it was evident. He had even kissed her hand once. Susan liked people, talking, and gossiping. She could spend hours on the phone. *Open-minded, for sure, curious, but too intrusive? True.* She probed into everything Joan was doing. *Flirtatious? Definitely. Did that have anything to do with the fight?* Joan preferred to stay with the first image of her mother running through the garden. It soothed her. A cute little newt coming down the cave's wall, brown and slimy, suddenly caught her attention. Joan caressed it softly for awhile.

Joan's mind skipped to her father's face. He looked stressed lately, tired. *He is always on a trip here and there when he is not in Washington, always flying in his stupid jet. So dangerous to land in bad weather on a small strip,* she thought. *Being a senator is much more pressure on him than when he was in the oil business. Now he has to travel so much. He's always away somewhere. Always!* Joan thought about how nice it was when she was a little girl and he took her to the pond and showed her the frogs and ducks. Joan let herself go back to the feeling of being with her dad, holding his big hand. It felt secure and warm. There was no rush. Nature was all around, cradling her softly; the birds talking to her in their funny language and she felt so close to her father then. *Why had things changed so much? Why? Maybe the best thing would be to ask her parents what was going on. Maybe…*

Joan had a hard time understanding what her parents were all about nowadays, and she didn't like what had been happening at home: fights and a thick atmosphere which made her feel uncomfortable. She mostly avoided thinking about it for fear of destroying all of her good memories, but she had begun to dread being home, especially when her parents had those big parties. The parties were very lavish affairs, with lots of alcohol and perhaps also drugs, noise, confusion, and ugly decorations. Men with red faces staggered all over and giddy women rubbed her hair, saying how beautiful she was and asking whether she had a boyfriend. She grimaced at the idea of those gatherings. *Were those people faking happiness? Just faking?* Their smiles didn't look right, kind of forced. Joan pondered on the idea for awhile. *What is happiness?* she asked herself.

Thoughts of those parties brought sad feelings into her heart and she could feel for sure that happiness was not to be found there, at least not for her. She decided that she would ask her parents later whether they were happy. *Happiness? What is happiness anyway?* she pondered.

Slowly, the cave brought Joan back to the blanket of love which nature provided for her earlier, and she felt the peace it created. She breathed in the moist air as she stepped out into the sunshine and headed back into the woods. *There is happiness right here,* she thought. *I know. I can feel it.* She scampered joyously on toward the house.

She arrived as people were sitting at the breakfast table. She apologized for being late and quickly took a seat next to Mademoiselle Giroud, who had come early for Joan's French lesson, since it was Saturday. Joan's parents thought French and European history were essential, considering that Henri's grandparents had come from Europe to start farming in the U.S. in the early 1900s. When Joan turned fourteen, her parents decided that the high school curriculum was not enough, so they hired Mademoiselle Giroud. French and European history were two disciplines which Mademoiselle, a foreign exchange student at the local university, was well-qualified to teach, since she was French and majoring in European history.

Joan looked at her mother, who seemed like she hadn't slept much, her eyes encircled with dark shadows and the kind of expression that tells you things are not going too well. Her dad was quiet and looked tired. *Probably the trip,* Joan thought. The maid brought Joan her orange juice and a plate of blueberry pancakes.

Joan liked their maid a lot. She called her by her first name, Martha. Martha had been with the family since Joan was born and served as a nanny for her when she was little. Both she and her husband, Claude, lived in a cabin behind the main house. Claude did garden work and occasionally chauffeured the family when they needed him. It seemed to Joan as if they were part of the family. They had been there forever. Martha was sweet, funny sometimes, and Joan would never forget how her comfy soft arms hugged her when she picked her up from elementary school.

"Where is your phone, Joan?" her mother inquired. "We bought you that thing so that you could stay in touch with your friends and with us too."

"It's in my room. I left it there when I went for a walk."

"Why didn't you take it with you? Make sure you get in touch with Kristin. She called me earlier to ask where you were. Something was urgent, she said."

"Okay, Mother, I will."

"I wish you didn't always disappear into the woods at your age. I wish you were more normal, Joan. Did you hear what I said? *Normal*," Susan added angrily. "What's so great about that place anyway? You have your own veranda here. Why hide in a gloomy cave? Why?"

"I feel happy there, Mother. Real happy, like, at peace. Are you happy, Mother?"

Susan's eyes fixed on her daughter, glaring with total surprise at the reply. Caught off guard and unable to answer, she got up and proceeded to leave the room, looking angry. Mademoiselle was breathing deeply and Henri finished drinking his coffee.

"You can clean up now, Martha," Susan said as she quickly opened the glass dining room door. "And don't forget the luncheon at 1 o'clock. Eight ladies, one vegetarian. Tell Claude to pick things up at noon. I ordered food at Pascal's."

Chapter Two: Kristin's Urgent Message

Joan went up to her bedroom. She opened the curtains and made her bed neatly. *One less thing Martha will have to do,* she told herself, shaking her head. Her phone was on her bureau with a text message from Kristin which read: *I have to see you today and talk. The shit is hitting the fan. It's about Mr. Silver. Call me.*

Joan dialed Kristin's number, curious to hear what had happened with her favorite science teacher, Mark Silver.

"You won't believe what happened to Mr. Silver. There's a petition to fire him from the school. Imagine! The best science teacher we've ever had!" Kristin blurted into the phone.

"Whoa! That's awful! How did that happen?"

"A senior girl's mother started the petition and it's signed by a lot of parents, including your mother, if you want to know. I saw the petition on my mother's desk."

"What? Kristin, let's get together and talk about this. Okay? Listen, I have a French lesson with Mademoiselle this morning so could you come over like 2 or 3 this afternoon?"

"Okay, I'll come over at 3. We've got to do something!"

Still puzzled by the urgency of Kristin's announcement, Joan headed for the library, where she and Mademoiselle Giroud usually met for her lesson. Mademoiselle greeted her with an inquisitive look. "Everything's okay, Joan? You seem concerned."

"I am… actually, I'm worried about something Kristin told me. Someone started a petition to get our favorite science teacher fired from the school. I don't know the details yet, but she said my mother signed it too. Can you imagine?"

"Really, Joan? That's pretty serious. Do you know what happened?"

"No, I don't. He's very intelligent and articulate. I think his degree is from U.C. Berkeley. He makes things easy for us to understand and repeats them different ways if we can't follow what he is saying, just like you do! I would say he is creative and keeps up with what is new and challenging, perhaps things that are controversial at times but important enough to investigate. Oh, and he is very good-looking, you can't miss that, dark hair and beautiful blue eyes. Probably in his thirties. We love watching him explain the hardest subjects!"

Mademoiselle Giroud was smiling at Joan's enthusiastic description of her teacher.

"So, what do you think these parents would have against him? Are they jealous? Afraid he would seduce his students? Or is it simply a case of generation gap, when the older generation expresses a dislike of new things they don't want to accept because it means change, and they don't want their kids exposed to it? That's the usual story, I suppose. We had this happen in the '60s in France as well, when things started to change radically. We had a real student revolution as a result. The French like revolutions, as you very well know," Mademoiselle Giroud added, laughing. "Try to find out more about the real reason for this petition, Joan. See if the teacher did something to alienate the parents, and we can talk about it later. Do you know if your science teacher has tenure in the school?"

"I'm not sure. He started teaching there two years ago."

"Hmm… this may be a problem," Mademoiselle sighed. "Okay. Joan, let's get to our French lesson now."

Joan was still having a hard time with the subjunctive. They had spent several sessions on it. She could not see why you should use a different verb form when the clause would be the result of a possibility or a mood instead of a fact, like, *Je vois qu'il pleut*, which was a statement of fact that meant, "I see that it is raining", and *je souhaite qu'il pleuve*, which was a statement of desire that meant, "I wish that it would rain."

"But Joan, it's the same with all the languages derived from Latin, and you have some left-over forms of the subjunctive in English as well. For instance, you don't say 'I wish I am rich' but 'I wish I *were* rich,' right? It makes sense. Doesn't it?"

"Yes. But that's easy! This is nothing compared with all these present, past subjunctive tenses that you have in French with all the different forms for all the different persons!" Joan sighed.

The grammar part of the lesson was tedious for Joan, of course, but they never lingered too long on it, and Joan, on the other hand, had become very good at speaking French after the two years spent bi-weekly with Mademoiselle, talking about daily life, international events, French history, and reading French literature, all this in French, of course. Today, they were reading and discussing Camus' *La Peste*, in English *The Plague*.

"Next week, I'll have a surprise for you, Joan. We'll talk about some famous women in the history of France. Women can make big changes, as you know from American history, and there are some great French women also who made a big difference. Maybe women have a special inner wisdom," Mademoiselle added with a wink. "Don't you think? Now, go make use of that wisdom with your friend Kristin and you'll tell me later what the story is. I'm very curious!"

The lesson had been very interesting, but long, and Joan was tired when Mademoiselle left. Joan liked the way Dr. Rieux dealt with people stricken by the plague in the story, while knowing that they were condemned to die. She admired his great humanitarian side, but she had a very difficult time understanding the concepts of existentialism and the theory of the absurd, which were the reason Camus had written the novel. *An interesting way to look at life!* Joan thought. Someday, she would sit in her cave and ponder over the ideas, alone and in silence. She would try to make sense of it in her own way.

In the meantime, she ran to the kitchen to fix herself a sandwich. She was hungry. Martha was bringing the dishes back from the dining room, mumbling about how some people were leaving half of their lunch on the plate. "What a waste," she repeated, while throwing the leftovers in the garbage. "What a waste!"

"Great sandwich and great dessert!" Joan commented, tasting some of the leftovers on the silver platter and licking her fingers. "You are the best pastry chef, Martha. I love your chocolate truffles."

It was 2:45 p.m. and Kristin would be there soon. The last guests were leaving the dining room, thanking Susan profusely. "And I hope your project will go well," one of them added, winking in connivance. Joan waved at them while walking toward the veranda, her head buzzing with questions. *What was this "project" her mother had been undertaking? Was that just a lunch those ladies were having, or did it have to do with the petition that her mother had signed, according to Kristin? But Kristin's mother was not at the meeting. Why, then?* It looked like something fishy was going on. Joan was very puzzled.

What the family called the veranda was a magical place, and Joan relaxed the minute she opened the door. A waft of warm tropical air flooded her face and she let herself breathe in the sweet fragrances which emanated from everywhere in the greenhouse. Because he knew that his daughter loved nature, her father had this special room built adjacent to the dining room. He had been creating a beautiful warm place for Joan to take her away from the capricious Arkansas weather and give her a permanent tropical site she could dream in. The variety of plants and flowers, from giant hanging ferns, ginger trees and philodendrons, to colorful Birds of Paradise and climbing orchids, lined a gravel walk leading to a mossy rock waterfall. Joan immediately looked for Victor, the resident parrot, and said hello to him. He answered in his throaty voice, "Hullo, hullo, hullo," fluffing his feathers. The few items of furniture were a couple of large wicker double-seats painted orange, and Joan sat in the one nearest the waterfall. Kristin would know where to find her. She had been here before, and it was their favorite place for a private conversation.

Kristin arrived punctually at 3 o-clock, anxious to see her. Unlike Joan, who resembled her blonde mother, Kristin was a brunette. A tall, good-looking, vivacious girl. She was wearing a revealing top which accentuated her athletic shoulders and her tanned chest. She immediately sat next to Joan, adjusting her tight green shorts on the seat.

"God, Joan, you are so fortunate to have this place! It's so, so incredible, like being in another world!" Kristin whispered, leisurely stretching her arms on the back of the chair. "Some people have all the luck! I can't imagine having a father who would build such a place just for his daughter! Really, I think you are much loved, but also very spoiled, my friend!"

"You are right, Kristin, I am spoiled, and I know it, and I try my best to share it with you, right? With others also, when I can. You like to come here, don't you?"

"Sorry Joan, I guess I'm a little jealous," Kristin added, smiling. "But we have some important matters, you know. We have a big problem on our hands, Joan."

"Yes, about Mr. Silver. What do you know about the petition you mentioned?"

"Well, they say Mr. Silver presented a taboo topic to his senior science class last week. Something about global warming and its effects on the planet. He talked about catastrophic events which could result from it and one of the students freaked out when she heard of the dire consequences. She told her parents about it later and then her mother started a petition to have him fired from the school."

"Whoa! And you said that my mother signed the petition already?"

"Yes. I saw her name on the list on my mother's desk. There are already 20 names. My mother has not signed it yet, but she must be thinking about it. Most names are from the mothers of seniors, I think, and three from the juniors. It's serious, Joan. They are going to pass the list on to all the parents they can reach and get him in trouble. Would you believe? Such a great teacher!"

"Bad stuff! I wish I had been in the classroom when he gave that talk. I don't know that much about global warming, but it sounds serious. Do you know who the mother is that started all this?"

"Mrs. Field, I think. She is the wife of a very powerful businessman and Ellen is her daughter."

"Well, I'm afraid for Mr. Silver if she has a lot of power. Let's put our heads together, Kristin, and see what we can do, okay? But I would like to know more about global warming and its consequences first, wouldn't you? I once read about it on a website on the Internet. Some scientists were predicting imminent dangers for the future if it is not dealt with. I didn't understand everything, but it sounded awful. I can understand why Ellen freaked out! Global warming, global, that's big, global... think of it, Kristin, global!" Joan repeated, accentuating the word while closing her eyes.

Behind the philodendron, a guttural voice was repeating the word global, gargling the sound joyously in its red-feathered throat while fluffing its variegated green coat. "Global... global... global," Victor repeated, obviously enjoying the sound! The two girls laughed and laughed, taking away some of the seriousness of their conversation and the tension which had fallen over the room, leaving two giggling girls hugging for comfort by the chanting waterfall.

"Okay, Kristin, I have a great idea. I think Mademoiselle Giroud liked my description of Mr. Silver. You know, good-looking and intelligent? Perhaps we could arrange a meeting for them, under the pretext of introducing them to each other, and then ask him for the scoop on global warming. He would explain it well, I'm sure. I am very curious. And this way, I could introduce Mademoiselle to a very charming man she could sympathize with, don't you think?"

"Hmm... hmm... not bad! Two birds with one stone!"

"Kristin, please, I hate that expression! What do you have against birds? Victor would not like it. Don't ever say that anymore!"

"I won't, Joan. Promise! Now, please, let me know when you get your plot all figured out, and preferably soon because of the petition, okay? I'm looking forward to it."

The two friends parted with a look of conniving and smiles on their faces as they walked out of the veranda. It had been a productive visit and Joan felt very good about it. The problem could be tackled in an interesting way with Mademoiselle as an intelligent helper. It would be fun to get her and Mark together, Joan reflected, smiling inside. *Life is great and full of surprises!* she thought, taking a deep breath.

Chapter Three: Lunch with Dad

Joan was still puzzled by the fight her parents had a couple of days before, so she decided to take her father up on an offer he made some time ago. "I'll take you out to lunch one of these days, sweetie," Henri had said. Great! Maybe she could ask him why he said that life was "lousy" and that it was her mother's fault. Joan could not figure that whole thing out, especially the "lousy" part. She also was curious to know why Henri wanted to take her out to lunch. Usually, these meetings had a special purpose. *What could he want to talk to me about?* she wondered.

Henri needed to return to Washington, so lunch was set for the first day Joan would be able to leave school around 1 o'clock. Henri picked her up in his black Lexus and kidded her as he opened the passenger door. "*Entrez mademoiselle*, today we are going to your favorite seafood restaurant. Do me the honor," he added formally, as he took her bag and set it on the backseat.

"Your French accent is not too bad, Dad," Joan responded, chuckling. "And thank you for taking me to Marius'; he has the best mussels. I love his *moules marinière*. And I'm starved!"

When they arrived at the restaurant it was full, but the *maître d'* recognized Henri and told them that he would have a table available soon. He directed them to the waiting area. Joan sat next to her father, feeling at ease and excited.

"Thanks for taking me out, Dad. I'm happy you are safe after the landing scare the other day. I was worried. I don't like when you fly, especially when the weather is bad."

"Don't worry so much, Joan, I know what I'm doing, and I love you and your Mom too much to do something stupid. Can you understand and remember that?"

"Yes, I suppose I can try. Dad, forgive me for bringing up something I overheard the night you came home and had a fight with Mom. I was upstairs and could hear some things you said. Do you really think that life is lousy, Dad? Is it because of all this traveling you do? You are gone so much."

"Maybe I felt that way at the time, tired from the trip and from the Washington scene. But you should not have heard that, little miss snoopy. Adults have the right to be upset."

"Yes, Dad, I guess, but why did you also say that it was Mom's fault?"

"Now you are treading on dangerous ground, Joan. This is between your mom and me, and I don't want to talk about it, okay?" Henri added, looking very upset, as if he had been caught. It completely changed the conversation and he didn't know how to deal with it.

Fortunately the *maître d'* relieved them from Henri's embarrassment when he walked in, announcing that their table was ready. Joan followed her father to a table next to the window. The tablecloth was carefully decorated with seashells, and a single red rose in a glass vase stood in the middle. It was cheerful and sunny. They both sat down.

"What a lovely setting, Dad! Thank you. I can't wait for those mussels now!" Joan exclaimed with a large smile. Henri was slowly relaxing his forehead and mouth from the deep lines that appeared while they were talking in the waiting room, and Joan felt sorry for her father. Had she been too blunt?

"I'm sorry, Dad, for having asked you such personal questions. Will you forgive me? But I was so sad when I heard you say that life is lousy. I want you to be happy, Daddy. I think life is good, can you see that?"

"I *am* happy, Joan. Most of the time," Henri punctuated slowly. "But life is not the easiest thing to deal with, especially when you have lots of responsibilities. Someday you will understand, sweetie. But now let's celebrate and order, okay?"

Henri ordered a glass of white wine for himself and a Shirley Temple for Joan. Both settled on a large plate of mussels with croutons, the house specialty. Joan's eyes were shining with expectation! Henri had totally relaxed by now, and the ambiance was happy.

"I'm sure you wonder why I asked you out to lunch, Joan. In fact, I have something important to discuss with you. You got your driver's license a couple of months ago. Was it just after your birthday, sometime in March, maybe? Anyway, at the time you didn't want to get a car. Now school is almost out and you probably could use a car for the summer, right? So what will it be? Let's see," Henri said, happily pursing his lips. "I can't buy you a Ferrari and I'm sure that you don't want a Jaguar, but what do you think about a white Mercedes, Joan? Or perhaps a new model Mustang? I'm sure you would be the queen of the parking lot at school. Imagine all the envious boys who would love to ride with you! You could take your pick!" Henri added, smiling.

The waiter was bringing their order and Joan took a whiff of the plate of mussels he placed in front of her.

"Heaven," she said, closing her eyes.

Henri sipped his wine, delighted about his generous offer to his daughter as he admired his plate of mussels, and waited curiously for her answer. Joan raised her head and looked at her father. She took a deep breath.

"Dad, I don't know what to say. It seems as if you want to spoil me again. I don't mean to disappoint you, but I have no desire to be the queen of the parking lot. Actually, I would prefer a small economy car which doesn't use too much gas. Would you buy me a Prius, Dad?"

"A Prius, Joan!" Henri laughed, shaking his head. "That's the last choice I expected from you, sweetie. You certainly are different from your mother. She always picks the very best and the most expensive when she's given a choice. I can't imagine why you would choose a stupid, common, cheap car when you have your pick of other great ones. Joan, what kind of girl are you? You've got me confused here. I guess I don't know you very well, and I will have to learn what makes you tick. Let's eat lunch and we'll finish our conversation later."

Henri became silent as they started eating their lunch. They obviously were both very adept at gathering the mussels in their shells and covering them with the garlic and wine sauce before putting them in their mouths with the greatest gusto. Except for some slurping, the lunch was very quiet. Father and daughter were lost in their thoughts and delighted with the taste.

"Were you thinking hard, Dad?" Joan asked when they finished their last mussel and soaked up the remaining sauce with the few croutons left on their plates. "I guess you are still wondering why I want a Prius instead of an expensive, showy car. Maybe I can explain why, Dad, so you can understand."

"I certainly do want to know. It's incredible to me that a beautiful teenager like you, who could have anything she wants, would make such a choice! Why, Joan? Tell me."

"You know I love nature, Dad. What I want is a small car and my reasons are simple to understand. I belong to a new generation and I'm looking at the future of this world, this world I hope to live in for many years to come. I want to do my small part to prevent overconsumption from destroying nature. I'm worried that big cars and fossil fuels are slowly taking us down the drain, producing too much carbon dioxide. So that's why I want a small car which doesn't use so much fuel and is better for the environment. Dad, do you understand?"

Henri was taken aback. He took a deep breath, trying to assimilate what he had just heard. The logic of his daughter's explanation was simply so unquestionable that he became aware he could not argue with this new perspective. He remained silent for awhile. His conscious mind fought with subconscious emotions that popped up, ready to explode, but he didn't say anything. He took another sip of his wine and decided to change the conversation. "Joan, would you like some dessert?"

"Of course I would, Dad. Maybe the French pear tart?" Joan accepted, licking her lips. "If you share it with me, it will be super."

"Great choice, Joan, and very economical. First you want a Prius, and now you want to share a dessert," Henri responded laughing. "Don't you think I can afford two servings of dessert?"

"Of course you can, Dad. I suggested sharing just because their portions are big and I would prefer to eat a small piece of the tart."

"Maybe there are great ideas in this funny head of yours," Henri replied, shaking his head with a puzzled look on his face. "Okay, let's go for the pear tart, but I want some chocolate ice cream on my half."

Father and daughter finished their lunch on a sweet note. The tart was perfect. Of course, many things were left unsaid after this meeting which they both came to with strong expectations. Joan would have to wait to find out what was going on in her parents' relationship. Henri would have to search deep to accept his daughter's generational concepts, but seeds had been planted in each other's minds about unexpected new perspectives. At any rate, there had been a lot of love exchanged between father and daughter, and they left the restaurant with good feeling in their hearts.

Chapter Four: Mademoiselle Giroud to the Rescue

A lot had happened and Joan didn't know how to deal with all the thoughts churning in her mind. Okay, she was going to get a car, which probably would make things easier for her and give her more freedom. Okay, her Dad didn't want to speak about why he said that life was lousy, and blamed her Mom for it. How could she deal with this gently, but still find out? Okay, she and Kristin had a big job on their hands if they wanted to stop that petition against Mark Silver which was moving quite fast. Okay, okay, okay. And what else? Yes, there was also something in the back of her mind which she would have to decide soon: What about the junior prom she had been invited to by two different guys? She didn't know which one to choose. Joan was overwhelmed by questions and decided she would spend some time in a quiet place to think all this over. In her cave, of course, which always worked miracles for her!

Tomorrow morning would be the best time, she thought, as she could get up early and no one would notice. Sleep would help sort things out and her mind will be clearer. Joan sighed with a sense of relief. The evening dinner was spent with her parents acting as if they were total strangers. Little conversation was exchanged, except that Henri mentioned to Susan that Joan decided she wanted a Prius. Susan started laughing out loud, adding that she was not surprised, since Joan was "not normal, really."

"Where does this girl get all these crazy ideas? The cave, the Prius, what else? Can't you do anything about it, Henri? I give up. Can you, please? Maybe we should have a therapist look at her?" Susan added, looking at Joan while shrugging her shoulders.

"Mom, that was a lousy thing to say. I don't need a therapist," Joan interjected, humiliated. "I think I'm able to make good choices for myself, and if you don't understand me, then perhaps it's because we don't have the same view about life. What's normal for me is different from what is normal for you, right? And maybe I'm happy about it!" Joan added, while rising angrily from her chair. "Okay? Now I'm going upstairs and do my homework, if you don't mind. Goodnight, parents."

Joan left the dining room quite upset. *That was a terrible way to be treated,* she thought. *What is "normal" anyway?* she questioned, and ran up the stairs. *Normal. What is normal for Mom, really? And what did Mom do to make life feel lousy for Dad?* Maybe there was something there to think about.

The homework didn't take long. It was just correcting an essay that she wrote about Thoreau for her English class. Getting into her warm, comfortable bed calmed Joan down from the bad vibes she got from her mom downstairs. Then she thought, *Why go on resenting her Mom for what she had said, anyway? I am normal in my own way, and she is normal in hers, right?* She laughed, relieved. *That's all. Someday I'll try to say this to her calmly!*

Joan's sleep was shorter than usual, and it was still dark when she woke up. She decided to wear a jacket and took a flashlight to walk to her cave. A full moon was still shining in a clear western sky, lighting the pond with soft glimmers. It was peaceful and beautiful. Joan felt the energy of a new day slowly dawning with promise and it filled her with happiness. When she arrived at the cave entrance she realized that she had never come to visit when it was dark. She shone her light toward the entrance. It was somewhat spooky. *Will an animal be asleep in the cave?* she wondered. *What kind of animal?* She hesitated, but then lit the entrance fully, taking a deep breath. A great horned owl flew out with its wings flapping loudly, making Joan back out with her heart beating fast. "Just an owl," she said, flashing her light to calm down. Then she walked toward her favorite seat on the rock.

Now I have a lot to think about, Joan said to herself, sitting comfortably and turning the flashlight off. *Where will I start? Okay, the thing about Mom and Dad, the word "lousy," right, which I used yesterday at the dinner table... I don't think Dad wants to talk about it. I tried at the restaurant yesterday and it didn't work. Maybe Dad has some reasons to blame Mom for making life difficult for him? I got a sample of that last night, but what were his reasons? If I only knew, perhaps I could help. Is she too demanding? Does she push him? He hinted that she always wants the best and most expensive things. Could that be it? Does that make him work harder to earn more money?* It didn't seem to Joan that she could answer this first question, so she decided to wait. *Adults are so complicated sometimes,* she thought. *Oh yes, and there is the tennis teacher who likes Mom and kisses her hand. Are they having an affair? Is Dad jealous?* Joan felt frustrated at her inability to understand her parents, so she decided she would wait. *Maybe I could talk with Mademoiselle Giroud,* she thought, pursing her lips.

"The car business now, no problem," Joan said aloud. *Dad has already accepted the choice in spite of his surprise, and it will be great to start driving my own car in the summer, even if I'm not the queen of the parking lot!* She laughed, imagining herself parading around with a crown on her head, sitting in a white Mercedes!

The third problem was a difficult one, however. How could she organize a meeting with Mark Silver, Kristin, and Mademoiselle Giroud, so they all could discuss the climate change question together in depth and hear what he had said in the senior science class that started the problem? Then they could organize something to counter the petition. *This should be done very soon,* Joan thought, feeling its urgency. *And it should be done well.* She was excited and afraid at the same time. *What if they failed?* The people they would go up against were well-established in the community, some of them powerful and a teenage protest might have very little weight in their decision.

It took awhile for Joan to answer her own question. *Of course, we will not fail!* She remembered her Dad's reaction when she explained that she wanted a small car that didn't use much gas because, in a small way, her future depended on it. Joan got it, and snapped her fingers. *Yes, that's it… the explanation has to be unquestionable, obvious, simple, and so logical that nobody could find anything to object to… Dad could not find anything to say, right? So they will not find anything to say either!* Joan decided to wait until the next French lesson to ask Mademoiselle Giroud to call Mark Silver and tell him of the urgent need to meet and come up with a plan to counter the petition that she was sure Mark was aware of by now. They would have to come up with something totally logical and irrefutable. Joan took a deep breath, reassured by her own belief. A line of morning light filtered into the cave, uncovering the baby ferns growing along the rock wall. A familiar newt was showing its head behind a grayish stone. "Come here, baby," Joan called, advancing her index finger toward it. "Let me caress your slimy back. You are so beautiful."

Ah! And the last question, Joan thought. It was not an easy one, either! Which of the two possible escorts would she choose to take her to the junior prom? They both offered to take her with great expectations. She felt honored in a way, but also wondered why it had to be the guy who asked the girl. *Well, let's chalk it up to long-established customs,* she said to herself. There was Roger, the tall one, somewhat handsome and always well-dressed. He was intelligent and one of the best students in her class. Some girls called him a nerd because of his sophisticated language and because he already had been accepted at a prestigious university. He probably had a great future ahead, and Joan was sure her parents would love him, especially her mom! Joan liked his intelligence and smart manners, but the superior way he talked with his peers turned her off. Phillip, the other candidate, always had a twinkle in his eyes when he spoke. He looked as if life agreed with him and he felt *bien dans sa peau,* as Mademoiselle Giroud would say, which meant "at ease in his own skin." He was not the best student and was somewhat critical of teachers he didn't like, but he came out on top in English class because of his talent in writing poetry. Joan liked that, especially when he wrote poems about nature, which she related to. He was not as handsome as Philip, nor as tall, but there was something about his friendly approach and uninhibited conversation Joan found attractive. She knew intuitively that her parents would not like that he was the rebellious type, but that was a trait Joan did like. He was someone different and artistic. She decided again to talk to Mademoiselle Giroud about her preference. Maybe her tutor could help Joan make the final decisions to all the questions she had brought with her to the cave. *Great,* she thought. *My French lesson is coming up!*

Joan felt like she had been thinking too much. A sense of urgency prompted her to get up and leave as the warm morning light seeped in and flooded the mouth of the cave. It was time to get home before everybody got up. But no, there was something else she still had to do. Something important. The thing she had invented to relieve her mind when it was racing or cluttered. Something like a mini-meditation, as she called it. Joan sat down and closed her eyes. There was a place she had discovered inside herself that she could always return to, her center or maybe what was called the soul. Maybe it was the place she had been before she was born. A place of peace within herself and out in the wide universe, where everything was just right and perfect. Joan abandoned herself to the feeling of that peace for awhile, immersed in serenity. It was very soothing.

The walk back home was enchanting, among the trees, along the pond, and across the meadow bathed in morning dew. Joan was delighted to find that no one was up when she arrived home. She snuck quietly into her bedroom.

She called Mademoiselle later in the day and asked her whether she could stay awhile after her French lesson on Saturday. She needed her advice on some very important matters. Mademoiselle was delighted to hear that one of the questions involved the science teacher whom she would meet, and agreed to spend another hour with Joan. *It's a good sign*, Joan said to herself, smiling. *Am I becoming some sort of a matchmaker? My description of Mr. Silver must have made a definite impression on Mademoiselle… great!*

Chapter Five: An Uncommon French Lesson

Kristin sent Joan a text message in the evening while she was eating dinner with her parents. It was brief, but exciting.

"Guess what? I arranged everything for our meeting! You won't believe our luck. Call me tonight!" Joan read the text over, breathing a sigh of relief, while Susan looked at her curiously.

"So, you've been using your cell phone a lot lately, Joan. Isn't it great to have such a gadget? Texting is such a fast way to communicate. We didn't have that when I was your age."

"Yes, Mom, the phone is really handy I must admit. Kristin keeps in touch by texting, but I still need to talk to her to get more details. So if you will excuse me, I'll go to my room and catch up with her."

"What about your dessert, sweetie?" Henri called to Joan as she was hurrying away from the table.

"Maybe I'll come back down for it later," Joan replied, running out of the dining room.

After she closed the door to her bedroom, Joan fell into her favorite chair, holding the phone next to her heart, shutting her eyes.

"Now what, Kristin? What have you been cooking up, my friend?" she whispered, opening her eyes and punching Kristin's number. "Hi, miss organizer, so we are lucky, you said. What kind of luck? What's up?"

"Well, Joan, I beat you to it. Mark Silver's telephone number was at the bottom of the petition and I knew that your French lesson was tomorrow morning, so I took a deep breath and I called him."

"You did?"

"Yes, I did, and I explained that we wanted to talk to him because there was a petition going around to fire him and we wanted to do something about it. He was very receptive and curious, but didn't ask too many questions. I didn't have any problem asking him to meet us tomorrow morning during your French lesson. This way, he can also meet Mademoiselle Giroud. I did a great job, don't you think?"

"Great job indeed, Kristin. Wow, you amaze me when you want to do something! Now, when and where should we meet? I suppose at my house… in the veranda, perhaps? And what will I tell my parents? My mother is so intrusive! If I bring you and a strange man to the lesson, she will ask questions for sure. I don't think she has ever met Mark Silver. Well, I'll just say that you are coming with a friend you want to introduce to Mademoiselle. That sounds good, don't you think?"

"Sounds perfect. I told him to meet me and I'll bring him over at 10 o'clock, okay? In the veranda, right? Now, I have to run. See you tomorrow, Joan. We've got it made, you'll see!" Kristin hung up before Joan could reply.

Joan was overwhelmed. Things happened so fast. She decided to sit and imagine the next day and how it would work out. Then she went back down to the dining room where her parents were finishing dessert.

"So, you decided to have dessert after all," Henri said.

"Yes, Dad, I couldn't miss Martha's *crème brulee*. I see you enjoyed it already."

"Not only enjoyed it, but we had seconds," Susan added, stretching the waistband of her pants away from her stomach. "It's addictive. So, what was the exciting news you had from Kristin that you ran away from the table for?"

"Mmm… mmm… she's stopping by tomorrow during my French lesson and is bringing a friend to meet Mademoiselle."

"A man or a woman?" Susan inquired, curious.

"A man. I told her it was okay. Don't worry. I can handle it, Mom. It will be interesting. We'll meet in the veranda."

"Trying to find a beau for Mademoiselle? I'm sure she could do this for herself. She is attractive enough. I hope he's not a teenager. At any rate, don't forget it is your French lesson, Joan, and it should be spent learning French, not socializing."

"It will be okay, Mom. It was Kristin's idea for a short visit. I'll make sure to do the whole lesson and I'm sure I'll learn a lot tomorrow."

Joan left the dining room after wishing her parents good night. She spent two hours finishing her French homework—a composition on existentialism and how she would define it in a few words. It was difficult for her to write that kind of stuff in French. The philosophical ideas had been hard enough to grasp, and defining them in a few words, was a monumental task, let alone doing it in French! After reading steadily over pages of sophisticated language, she finally settled on a simple definition, regretting that she had not had the opportunity to think about this quietly in her cave where inspiration came to her more readily. But it made sense to her as it was. She finally wrote, "According to Jean Paul Sartre, existence comes before essence. Man is an accident of nature who comes into this world without an essence. It is by living on this Earth, by working hard and making something of himself, that he keeps defining who he is, therefore creating his essence as he goes along." *Right? Okay, that sounds good enough!* Joan took a deep breath. She felt exhausted and sighed, thinking about how hard it is to explain and sum up such difficult concepts. She closed her notebook and went to bed.

Sleep did not come easily to Joan. She was still pondering the assignment. *Why is it that I have only lived a few years and yet feel something like an essence inside myself?* she thought. Why was it that when she was in her cave and looked deep within herself, she felt there was a place that had been with her since she was born and probably before she was born? A place which made her feel that she was part of the whole universe? Was it her essence? *Is there an essence? What does that mean? And does the essence come before existence, unlike what Jean Paul Sartre says?* Maybe she could talk with Mademoiselle about this. Joan decided it was too much to answer these questions and she was too tired. She closed her eyes and drifted to sleep.

Joan's parents left the house early the next day to run errands in town. Henri needed to stop by a lawyer to have conjoint papers signed for a real estate deal he was working on. Joan was told they would probably return in the early afternoon.

"It sounds like you'll be busy with your friends, Joan, and with your French lesson too, don't forget," Susan added. "Make sure you keep socializing to a minimum. You will have enough of that in the evening anyway. Remember, we have a big party after dinner for our friends who are moving to Washington, D.C. soon. Martha may need some help in the kitchen. Ask her."

Joan sighed as her parents left the house. The thought of another of those boring parties she had grown to hate was horrible to her, but the thought of being alone in the house for the whole morning with Kristin, Mademoiselle, and the important visitor was comforting. It made her jump for joy.

"Great! We have some important work to do! And questions to ask!" she exclaimed, smiling.

Joan decided that talking about whatever got Mark Silver in trouble would be the most important part of their visit. Then, when things wrapped up and Kristin and Mark left, she could resume her French lesson with Mademoiselle Giroud. Sounded like a good plan. She went to her room to get her notebook, then walked into the veranda to arrange seats for everybody by the waterfall. It sounded like Victor was as excited as she was, judging by his animated parrot language. *He sure likes company!* Joan thought. *Victor must be lonely all this time by himself in there! Maybe I should get him a nice mate*, she added, blinking her eyes.

Mademoiselle arrived somewhat early for the lesson. Joan smiled at her eagerness, noticing the elegant new dress she was wearing for the occasion. "You look so beautiful, Mademoiselle! Not your usual serious French teacher's outfit! I like it, I like it!" Joan repeated excitedly, causing Mademoiselle Giroud to blush.

"It is just an old summer dress, Joan. Something for the tropical veranda, right?" Mademoiselle explained, looking a little embarrassed. "But thanks for the compliment."

Joan led her toward the waterfall, where she had arranged chairs in a circle for the meeting. Victor flew to the top of the banana tree to get closer to them. He looked interested.

"Since you are here early, Mademoiselle, there is something I want to ask you. Maybe you can help me make a decision."

Joan explained her dilemma regarding the two candidates she had to choose from for the prom, describing their different qualities. Mademoiselle listened carefully to the young girl's hesitations alternating with enthusiasm, trying to decipher her real preference.

"Joan, I think the best way to choose is to listen to your heart and how you feel!" Mademoiselle concluded, as Joan nodded pensively. "It is the best way, Joan. You'll see!"

"I guess you're right," Joan agreed as Victor flapped his wings and repeated "Right, right, right…" in his guttural, imitative voice. The two started laughing aloud.

Just then Kristin entered the veranda, followed by Mark Silver, who walked in as if he were stepping into some kind of new world. He stopped in complete amazement.

"Whoa! What do we have here? The tropics in Arkansas? I can't believe my eyes," he said, following Kristin toward the two women.

"Mr. Silver, this is my friend Joan, whom you know from science class, and this is Mademoiselle Giroud, her French teacher."

"Nice to meet you, Mr. Silver, and you can call me Monique."

"You can call me Mark," he replied, shaking her hand. "My French is very poor, I'm afraid, but I love the language and I can read it better than I can speak it!" he added, with a large smile.

After the four sat comfortably in the circle, adjusting to their respective positions, there was an awkward moment of silence. It seemed as if the group had gathered together for an important discussion which no one knew how to start. Kristin was holding her breath, but finally broke the stillness.

"I'm sorry I sounded in a hurry to get this group together, Mr. Silver, but when I found out about the petition, it seemed urgent and maybe we can help resolve this. As I mentioned to you in my call, some of the parents at school have signed a petition to get you fired. We think you are a wonderful teacher and don't understand why. Could you explain what you think might have happened?"

Mark Silver took a deep breath, looking at his captive and receptive audience. He shook his head, and with a thoughtful expression addressed anxious Kristin, closing his eyes for a moment. "It was probably my presentation in senior science class about the urgency of dealing with global warming, which is potentially irreversible. I spoke from a scientific perspective, but it can be difficult to comprehend. Most of the students had never heard about global warming and looked somewhat bored. The subject didn't get their attention until I brought up the catastrophic effects of global warming, and the dire effects on our future."

"I guess that's when that student Ellen Field freaked out," Joan said. "Then she told her mother about it, and her mother started the petition. I can see it all now." Joan pursed her lips in a thoughtful and curious expression. "Mr. Silver, can you explain more about global warming for us? I have heard about the excess carbon dioxide, the melting ice caps and the pollution caused by fossil fuels, but how bad is it? What situation are we facing in the world? What dire catastrophes did you tell the class about?"

"I can sum up briefly some of the scientific facts I told the seniors in my science class," Mark answered. Looking very serious, he sighed as he continued with the difficult task. "Young people today are not living in the same climate their parents grew up in. In the atmosphere, the CO_2 level reached record proportions last year. The CO_2 is trapping atmospheric heat, causing record temperatures around the world. The effects are heat waves, rainstorms, hurricanes, flooding, and melting of ice caps and glaciers, causing rising sea levels. And 94% of the atmospheric heat settles in the oceans. The heat and CO that get absorbed in the water are beginning to kill the coral reefs where the fish and other sea life live. Wildlife and human health are being affected already. This is at a critical stage. If action is not taken soon to reduce global warming, the whole planet could be seriously affected in unprecedented ways. "

Mark stopped for a moment, looking at the eyes fixed intently on him. "The deforestation of rainforests all over the world makes it worse, and the CO_2 and methane gas produced by fossil fuel consumption keeps accelerating with human use. We are at a turning point. It is serious. If immediate action is not taken to reduce global warming—something which many people still deny—then its impact will continue to intensify. Some people even talk about the possibility of a sixth mass extinction of life on Earth if we keep the status quo, and it could happen faster than we think."

Mark stopped. He was visibly shaken by the words he had just spoken. Joan, Kristin, and Mademoiselle Giroud were silent. In the lush beauty of the veranda and its relaxing warmth, the passion Mark showed in stating his knowledge to his attentive audience caused them to lean forward, listening intently. He made his point, a point motivated by his belief in the scientific facts he had carefully studied. His intelligence, and the intelligence of his listeners, had been fashioned by millions of years of evolution into the apex of today's consciousness, expressed sometimes so eloquently in human invention and understanding, but threatened by its own destructive impulses and desire for material things. Life in this moment, with its beauty and its hopes—our marvelous blue planet Earth—suddenly seemed endangered by an elusive enemy created by mankind and, like the sorcerer's apprentice, was incapable of being stopped from replicating itself. But what could bring this dilemma out of the fog of gloom? Was there a solution? This is the question on everybody's mind.

Mademoiselle Giroud broke the silence. She got up with a sense of confidence and resolve. "Well, I can see why Ellen's mother started this petition! It scared Ellen, so her mother took a defensive posture out of fear. It's easier to deny something when the truth is not bearable, isn't it? We all do this to avoid things we cannot face. The idea that we are destroying the Earth we live on is frightening. We bury our face in the sand, but this time Ellen's mother is trying to eliminate the bearer of the news rather than face it. I feel for you in your situation, Mark. Is there a way to fight this petition? There must be a solution, right?" Mademoiselle Giroud, feeling very concerned, sat down, breathing deeply. "I have been reading about this issue on my own, Mark. I even talked to a French professor on the subject last year. The whole world is aware of it, and of its dangers, but some still deny it."

"There is something I want to understand," Kristin intervened. "Something so obvious to me. Why is it so hard to find a way to stop the pollution and the CO_2 emissions? Why can't people see what is happening right in front of their eyes with the weather and the way it has evolved lately? Why? Why do we keep going on as if nothing were happening, when there is such a threat right in front of our eyes? Why?" Kristin stopped, obviously angry.

"Kristin, unfortunately the solutions are refuted by special interest groups who distort the evidence," Mark continued. "The groups are funded by the fossil fuel industries and companies who don't want to convert to clean energy. They intentionally misrepresent science in the media to deny the problem to the public. These are very wealthy and powerful organizations which profit from the way things are. The economy is based on an endless consumption of goods and the public has grown accustomed to this consumption. The public is afraid of the changes it would take, and they know it."

"But what good will it do for anyone when the Earth and the environment are on their way to destruction? That is *so* stupid. That is incredible!" Kristin shouted, waving her arms. "How can't people see that? We are all in the same boat, right?" Kristin continued, angry and agitated. "Those industries are probably run by old fogies who don't care whether they go on living. They don't think about future generations, they are just plain egocentric."

"Kristin, I'm afraid a lot of these people who are in denial are very familiar to us," Joan sighed. "I'm even thinking of my own parents," she added, with a sad expression. "You should have seen my dad's reaction when I told him I wanted a Prius instead of the big, fancy, gas-guzzling Mercedes he offered. I had to explain why and I'm not sure he really understood. But he is he thinking about it now."

"Maybe there is hope in what you did, Joan," Mademoiselle Giroud intervened. "Maybe it is our job to make people think. Our voices can be heard if we are convincing enough and very logical. It's hard to refute logical evidence! But the first step to take now is to counter this petition and figure out how we can reestablish Mr. Silver's reputation as the best science teacher your school ever had."

"Thank you, Monique, thank you very much," Mark replied, touched by Mademoiselle's vehement statement. "We may be going against a tidal wave as David against Goliath in this case, I'm afraid. However, if we do this on a small scale all over the world, then we have a chance to save our planet. It's a wonderful undertaking and words can be powerful!"

Mark closed his eyes for a few seconds, as if dreaming the impossible dream, the far-reaching goal he had decided to follow. "I can't tell you all the positive energy I feel right now from this group," he added, with a smile. "This puts faith back into my heart. Thank you, all of you. Thank you so much!"

Now that the decision was made and the task was evaluated as a possibility, the logistics of how to realize a countering of the petition was brought up for discussion, and it seemed that posters and placards would be designed to that effect. They came up with a list of slogans to put on them:

"Learn the science of global warming before you deny anything!"

"The environment is our source of life and health… we must save it!"

"Be bold, seek the truth! The fate of our planet is at stake!"

"Teachers should not be afraid to tell it like it is!"

"Mr. Silver it the best science teacher this school has ever had!

"Firing Mr. Silver is anti-education!"

They were enthusiastic that putting these lines on posters would eloquently and sufficiently help. They would need to find students to help, a task both Joan and Kristin were willing to take on, feeling confident that they knew friends who would agree. They took notes to get the ball rolling forward to protest the petition.

Why is it that time seems to go so fast when exciting things are happening? The meeting had been heavy, emotional, fascinating, constructive, and conclusive. The participants were somewhat spent, but happy and confident. The warmth of the veranda and the soothing sound of the waterfall had sustained their focus, and now it was time to part. Joan remembered her mother's admonition that it was her French lesson, and not time for socializing! *Some socializing,* she thought with a grin, considering the work which had been accomplished.

Kristin was already getting up. Mark Silver looked at his watch and pulled a card out of his pocket, which he handed to Mademoiselle. "I would love to hear more about the French professor you talked to about this issue, Monique. Can I call you and meet you for coffee sometime?"

"I would be delighted," Mademoiselle answered, writing her telephone number on a small piece of paper she pulled out of her bag. "I'm usually free in the late afternoons. I really enjoyed meeting you," she added.

"And so did I," Mark Silver answered, shaking her hand as he got up to follow Kristin, who was already near the entrance teasing Victor as he perched on an oleander.

"We must go," she told Mark Silver. "I borrowed my mother's car today and she needs it back. I'll drop you off at the school, okay?"

Joan and Mademoiselle decided to stay in the veranda for the rest of the "lesson." Neither were very eager to proceed after the long meeting and the various feelings it brought up for them. Joan was pensive and tired; her parents would return soon.

"Can we just talk, Mademoiselle? I don't feel like doing grammar today. I have my assignment on existentialism ready for you. Here it is." Joan handed the paper to her with a sigh. "This thing about existence before essence is a hard one for me. I do feel some sort of an essence somewhere inside, which feels like it has always been there. But if birth creates existence and if your essence is created through what you do in this life, maybe at the end of your life, that defines your essence. But what about the part I feel inside already,without doing anything?"

"Joan, you are a beautiful human being. Someday we'll talk about this essence stuff. Right now we are both tired. This was an uncommon French lesson, I must say. It so happens that lessons can take a different turn sometimes and we learn more than we would if the lesson were simply the 'usual,' don't you think? So let's leave it there, Joan, and now we can go on living what our essence is for the rest of the day, okay?" Mademoiselle concluded, smiling.

"Mademoiselle, Mark Silver is adorable, isn't he?" Joan interjected, blinking her eyes as Mademoiselle walked toward the exit, chuckling. "Tell her, Victor. Adorable! Adorable!"

"Adorable… adorable…" Victor joined in, fluffing his colorful feathers as he flew to the door.

Chapter Six: Another Party

Joan was torn between a sense of relief and one of apprehension. The meeting had been great and productive. She was happy that Mark Silver seemed to like Mademoiselle and vice versa. She also appreciated the relaxed way in which her French lesson had ended, making her feel closer to her teacher as they both acknowledged the priority of an important project over the usual dutiful class time. Her perspective on her parents' return, however, and the idea of the party they planned for the evening was another story. What would the crowd be like? Could she be excused at one point, even though her parents liked her to be present at those gatherings? How would she handle the possibility of talking or hinting about the petition in progress, if the subject was brought up? All these questions ruminated in Joan's head as she left the veranda to walk toward the kitchen.

"Martha might need your help," Susan had said.

The kitchen was a disaster area when Joan walked in. Two of the caterers had already unloaded their boxes onto the counters, piling up pies, cut-up vegetables, salads, and trays of frozen *hors d'oeuvres*, one of which fell to the floor in pieces. The tall caterer, John, shouted at Martha to get the ovens started. Before long the decorator walked in with her aide and boxes of ribbons, colored paper, a streamer inscribed "*Au Revoir*," and loads of fancy yellow tablecloths and napkins. Joan didn't know where to stand, nor how to get to the refrigerator to make a sandwich for herself. She was hungry.

Poor Martha was looking at her kitchen with a horrified expression. She didn't dare to move. What should she do next? She was supposedly in charge of organizing this whole thing, but it all seemed out of her hands and she would probably end up with the mess afterward. Joan asked Martha if she could get her a sandwich and a glass of water and join her in the breakfast nook, away from the madding crowd, for a break. It was a great idea. They sat together for a little while, chatting quietly while the havoc continued for a good half hour in the kitchen. Martha was delighted to escape the commotion, but still concerned about her floor. All of a sudden, like a miracle, the noise stopped, the boxes were gone, and some pleasant scents indicated that the ovens were being used for a good purpose. The table settings and silverware had disappeared from the kitchen, only to end up elegantly placed in the dining room where the streamer was displayed. It looked like a great party was coming together.

"These people are pretty efficient," Martha said, walking into the kitchen and looking at her floor. "They even cleaned up the mess. They are better than the last crew we had here. I told Madame that I wanted her to get some better caterers. She sure did it."

Joan gave Martha a high five as they both laughed and brought their lunch dishes to the sink.

"Crystal clear, Martha. I can't see a single spot! But wait, I think I'm getting a message," Joan said, taking her phone out of her pocket. "It's probably my friend Kristin. You know Kristin, of course."

Martha nodded as Joan walked away from the kitchen and stopped in the hall.

A text from Kristin stated that she had wasted no time since she left the veranda. She dropped Mark Silver off at the school and already contacted two friends from the junior science class to ask for their help with the posters. Joan was astonished.

"But, Kristin, the petition is not signed and out yet," she texted back. "Can't we wait until it is finished?"

"It's better to prevent than to cure," Kristin replied. "We'll be ready before things get too hot!"

Joan marveled at her friend's insight, diligence, and energy, realizing that she almost single handedly organized this project to near completion. Joan wrote back, shaking her head, "Thank you so much, Kristin, I don't know what we would do without you. You are just amazing. All the world needs are people like you. Thank you."

"So, you are texting again, Joan. Good girl! I knew you would eventually learn to use your phone to communicate with the world. How was the French lesson?" Susan inquired as she walked into the hall, smiling.

"Great lesson, Mom. We talked about existentialism and I handed in my assignment on the subject, written in French," Joan replied.

"Existentialism. What's that?" Susan continued, grimacing as she carefully took off her designer coat. "Never heard of it. One of these days you'll have to explain it to me. One of Mademoiselle's favorite subjects, I presume. Is she luring you into philosophy these days?"

"Sort of. It is actually fascinating, Mom, but it is too long to explain right now. One of these days, as you said, I'll try to describe the philosophy of existentialism to you… in English, that is."

"Joan, can you help me look over the dining room and see if everything is okay? People are coming for a light buffet dinner at six, and there will be music later. I asked a jazz group to entertain us. I heard they were very good. We might also dance. Isn't that great? By the way, I invited somebody for you. He's coming with his parents. Roger Sarl." Susan stopped to look at Joan, trying to read her reaction. "You know him, don't you, Joan? He is in your junior class. A bright guy, very handsome, I'm told."

"Yes, Mom, I know him. He is handsome all right. He's one of the guys who asked me to go to the prom with him."

"Oh, yes, the prom! I forgot all about it. It's coming soon, isn't it? We'll have to talk about your dress, Joan. I'm sorry, I've been so busy lately that I almost forgot the prom. This is a big event for you! Did you say *one* of the guys, Joan? So, there are other guys who invited you?"

"Yes, Mom, there is another boy, but we can talk about it later, okay?"

Susan and Joan walked into the dining room. The lights had already been set up and a small dance floor was reserved in front of the music area. It was cheerful and bright with the yellow settings on the tables, very inviting for socializing. The streamer that read *"Au Revoir"* in cursive letters hung over the music platform and the curtains were already drawn. A perfect setting for a party! Susan could not contain her enthusiasm.

"This is going to be great, Joan. You must wear your new party dress, the green one. You know the one, with the soft pastel designs? You liked it when we bought it. Remember?" Susan stopped to look at Joan and said softly into her ear, "I think Roger Sarl likes you. His mother told me," Susan winked. "But I wasn't supposed to tell you! Okay, I did. Bad mom!"

"Yes, Mom, I'll wear my green dress. It is very pretty and thank you for getting it for me." After hesitating for a moment, Joan added, "Why don't I wear the green dress to the prom, too? You don't have to get me a new one, Mom. It is such a pretty dress. I would love to wear it at the prom!"

"Joan, you need a formal dress for the prom. Something long, sophisticated, exquisite, and worthy of your beauty! This is a special occasion in your life, girl, and you will remember it for a long time."

"Mom, can we can talk about that later? When we have more time," Joan said with a sigh. "But thank you for the compliment on my *beauty*," she said, accentuating the word. "Wouldn't I be *beau-ti-ful* in any dress?" she added, chuckling.

Susan rolled her eyes and let her go.

The day had been long and challenging so far—an emotional meeting, calming Martha's anguish about the party, trying to communicate with Susan, and now, getting ready for a party that she really didn't want to attend, for which she had reservations about the guests. It was time for Joan to relax and think quietly, away from the house. She had two and a half hours, enough time to sit in her cave for an hour and then get ready for the party.

As always, the walk across the park put her heart in a happy place. The birds were active in the afternoon and she also caught sight of two rabbits chasing each other. "Spring!" she murmured, smiling. "What a beautiful time of the year."

The talk in the veranda had left Joan with some questions she never thought of before. It bothered her. That thing about the special interest groups who got in the way of challenging the effects in the world from global warming, just because they didn't want to give up their profits from fossil fuels. That didn't resonate too well with her. What about her father? He was in the oil business once. Was that how he made all the money to purchase the luxurious place where they were living? Was he still benefiting from the proceeds from his days in that business? Did he not want to give up drilling and look for alternative sources of energy? This idea bothered Joan a lot, and she decided to talk to her dad about it soon. What else could she do? She felt helpless. She thought she could start by spending less money and consuming less. The Prius and the prom dress could be a beginning. She would help slow down the consumption of fossil fuels the best she could. She didn't want to move away from her parents, of course, she loved them too much, but perhaps she could sway them away from their expensive lifestyle. She would try to use irrefutable words of wisdom, like when she talked about the Prius with her dad. He seemed to hear some what she said.

Joan looked for her favorite newt on the wall of the cave. He had settled in a small crevice filled with water, looking perfectly happy. "You sure don't have to deal with the problems of the world, baby," she told him. "You are lucky, enjoy your freedom!" she added, gently touching the wet creature.

What about this upcoming party? Joan didn't like the idea, but decided she would make the best of it. She would be polite with the guests, yet she would answer their questions intelligently and not be afraid to speak her mind. Actually, she admired Kristin and wanted to emulate her. Kristin was straightforward, honest, and bold—unafraid to follow her heart. Joan decided that she would tell Roger, for instance, that she had not made up her mind yet about the prom, and that he was in stiff competition with Phillip. *That sounds straightforward*, she thought, laughing. But why did her mother have to invite him and his parents to the party? What a bummer!

Well, at least Mom forgot to ask about the mysterious guest that Kristin brought to the meeting in the veranda, Joan thought, relieved. *I'm so glad she forgot!* One less answer to be given; one which she was sure her mother would not have liked, to tell the truth. Joan hated to lie, and she wondered how she would have handled that one had her mother asked about it.

Joan was ready to return to reality now, after thinking about all these situations and dilemmas. Relieved and relaxed, she bid goodbye to the newt, which had not moved an inch, then walked out of the cave, toward the pond, where she stopped for a few minutes and did her ritual mini-meditation. She was ready to face the world now and run home to put on the beautiful green dress, something which she relished in her thoughts. It was so pretty, so cool! *It will be my lucky charm at the party*, she thought, while scampering happily home in plenty of time.

Kristin had texted her while she was out and Joan read her message when she got to her room. She was inquiring why she had not yet started calling friends about the petition. Joan decided to call Kristin to discuss the issue.

"I'm sorry, Kristin, but I thought it would be better to wait until we have more information about the petition. Right now, we just know that it is in the making, but it has not been finished yet."

"Okay, I'll talk to my mom about it. I don't think she will want to sign it after I tell her what happened with Mark Silver today. My mom is usually good on social issues, and I don't think she likes Mrs. Field very much. They had an argument one day about the school lunch when my mom told her that they should remove the soft drink machine from the cafeteria the sugar in the drinks is not good for us. Mrs. Field's husband works for a soft drinks company. Imagine! Anyway, they never did remove the machine, but my mother made her point. Okay, I'll find out where the petition goes from here."

"I'll see you at school tomorrow, Kristin. Pray for me. I have to go to a stupid party this evening. Roger will be there with his parents and I think I'll tell him he has some competition. Did you get your prom escort lined up yet?"

"Yes. It will be Charles. He likes me because I'm straightforward, as he says!"

"That makes two of us, sister. Straight as an arrow, and I appreciate it a lot. See you soon, my friend."

It didn't take long for Joan to get ready. She looked at herself in the mirror, wearing the pastel green dress with some lacy white flats and she smiled in approval. No makeup, just a little lip gloss finished the picture of a beautiful sixteen-year-old young woman. *Not bad*, she said to herself, smiling. *Now I'm ready to go act my part!*

When Joan arrived at the party, the music was already playing and some guests were lined up at the buffet for their dinner. The sommelier was going from table to table, offering varieties of wines and champagne. People sounded cheerful and the atmosphere was joyful. Many heads turned when Joan made her entrance. Notably a young person in the room full of adults, she also provided a note of beauty and lightness the older group could not miss. Joan's eyes searched for Roger and his parents among the crowd. She finally located them in a back corner, talking with an important-looking gentleman in a tuxedo.

Susan walked in with Henri, holding his hand and waving at the group. Everybody applauded. She was wearing an exquisite red designer dress, showing a lot of cleavage. Her blonde hair was tucked back into a comb decorated with pearls, which matched the red shoes she was wearing. She looked radiant. *Mother at her best,* Joan thought, knowing how these parties gave her mother the ultimate feeling of what happiness is all about. *I am happy that she is happy.* Joan sighed. Henri seemed proud of his escort. Handsome in his white tuxedo, he radiated the image of a man who is successful, a man who has made it in the world.

My parents! Joan thought with mixed feelings, looking at a scene out of a Hollywood film from the fifties, with all its glitter and beautiful music. *I should be feeling on top of the world, too.* She smiled and took a deep breath. *Is life a dream? Something we have to live through in order to grow? A school we don't know we are attending on this Earth? Dad said a few days ago that life was lousy, but it does not look lousy for him today,* Joan reflected, raising her eyebrows. *I must not forget my own role in the play today, and I love this green dress that I'm in, my costume.* Excitement filled her heart. *Let's go for it!* Joan walked in resolutely to meet the joyful crowd.

"Hello Joan, how beautiful you look!"

"Hello, hello." Smiles and the word "beautiful" were showered liberally as she walked slowly through the crowd, acknowledging each couple with a large smile or polite greeting. She chuckled as she remembered that her father wanted her to be the queen of the parking lot! *I sure feel like the queen of the crowd today,* she thought as the people cradled her in warmth and compliments. *Actually, it feels quite good.* Their greetings seemed genuine and she abandoned herself to the feeling. *Is this the way a queen feels?* she asked herself, laughing. *Maybe that's why Mom likes these parties, being enveloped in admiration and love for awhile, forgetting life and its ups and downs. I can relate.*

Joan made her way slowly toward the Sarl family. No wonder Roger was so tall! His parents must have passed the tall gene on to their son, as they were both around six feet tall. *How lucky can a guy get?* Joan thought. *Not only are they tall, but also attractive.* The trio was definitely good-looking and their conversation turned out to be intelligent and flawless. It focused around colleges and admission. "Something which was becoming more and more difficult these days," they accentuated, and how grateful they were that, "Roger was already accepted at M.I.T., along with other universities." They mentioned all the work they did to help him with his papers and applications. They seemed very proud of Roger, their only child, whom they had obviously pampered a lot. Roger listened shyly to the litany of compliments, anxious to get away from what the rest of the usual story would be. Joan could feel his impatience growing and she offered him a way out, suggesting they go to the buffet for some *hors d'oeuvres* and other goodies.

"I have some college applications in," Joan said. "But I'm not in a hurry. We have over a year before we graduate and I want to be surprised." She paused and added, "My parents act as if they are the ones who are going to college!" She put some shrimp *canapés* on her plate. "Congratulations on your admission to M.I.T., Roger. You must have a lot of talent in the technology field. You will probably figure out new ways to deal with some of the environmental problems. They need young, intelligent people to come up with solutions."

"Yes, Joan, but my interest is more with computer software for the medical profession."

"Like what?" Joan asked, intrigued.

"Like teaching young medical technicians how to use robots to help in surgery."

"Yuck… I wouldn't want a robot to operate on me, Roger. That sounds terrible," Joan interrupted in dismay.

"It's the future of medicine because technology can do so much and is so precise. More and more man's intervention will be advanced with technology," Roger clarified.

Joan was totally shocked. A robot! She added some cucumbers and greens to her plate while Roger helped himself to a large portion of quiche Lorraine with a watercress salad. She invited him to sit with her by the drum section, thinking music would change the tone of the conversation. *How am I going to tell Roger about the prom?* she thought with some anxiety. All her good, straightforward, *a la* Kristin resolutions had fallen by the wayside, and she hated to reject Roger. How would such a successful guy take a rejection? Could she do it?

They ate silently. Roger was obviously preoccupied. Mrs. Sarl stopped by to check on the two, wishing them to enjoy their meal and asking whether they had seen the gorgeous display of flowers at the entrance to the room. She also suggested that they visit the colorful array of non-alcoholic drinks which adorned a table to the right of the buffet. They got up to investigate and choose a refreshment. Joan knew that Roger had a pressing question on his mind, but he postponed it and asked her for a dance. The music was soft and suggestive, in contrast with Roger's stiffness, which Joan didn't understand. He danced as if he were made of wood! Was it his normal posture or was an unanswered question stiffening his whole body? Finally the music stopped and they walked back to their seat. Joan was relieved.

"I guess you are wondering about the prom, Roger," Joan said, taking a deep breath. She paused. "Thank you for inviting me. You're a good friend. I admire your intelligence and I enjoy our talks. I don't want to ruin our friendship, but I think that I'll let Phillip to take me to the prom," Joan concluded, happy to have delivered her answer so easily.

"Okay," Roger said, pausing and looking disappointed, "but I have one question, Joan. Can you tell me why you decided to pick him over me? I just want to know."

"Well," Joan replied. "It is more of a feeling than a logical decision. I like the poet in Phillip. The way he talks about nature and its beauty moves me to tears. We have a love for nature in common. Do you like nature, Roger?"

"I really don't spend much time outdoors," he replied. "My main interests are books and intellectual pursuits. The rest is a waste of time. I agree with the beauty of nature, but…"

"But you haven't grown to love it in your heart," Joan interrupted, feeling sorry for her brainy friend. "Well, sometime I'll take you for a walk in our park and maybe you'll change your mind about nature being a waste of time!"

"Yes, Joan, if you take me there, then it won't be a waste of time," Roger concluded with a flirtatious look. "I may have something to learn from you!" he added.

"How are you guys doing?" Susan interrupted as she walked by the table. "Don't you love this band? I'm so happy I chose the jazz theme for this party, and I noticed that you just danced together."

"Yes, Mrs. Larousse, and Joan just announced the lucky guy who will be taking her to the prom," Roger said in a disconcerted tone.

Susan got the message immediately and prepared to leave the scene, but Roger held her back with a smile. "However, I got a consolation prize, which may be even better in the long run. Joan invited me for a walk in the park!" he concluded happily.

Joan considered the cleverness with which Roger had taken the rejection and then turned the tables on the announcement. *Great strength of character; he just does not give up!* Joan thought. *Perhaps I should try to get to know Roger better… Life is a game, isn't it? Choosing the right words, playing with feelings, learning from failure to make it a win, keeping hopes alive when the dice are cast. Where does all this subtle energy come from? Roger could simply have walked out, insulted and whiny. He must have a good sense of himself,* she concluded. *This is a lesson for me!*

The party continued late into the night as parties always do, made up of glitter, music, dancing, loud conversations, flirting, eating, and a lot of drinking. Some guests even got downright drunk and had to be driven home. Susan looked tired, and Henri peeked at his watch several times. He called Claude, who was already in bed, to ask him to take two drunken couples home because they were unable to drive. Joan decided that this had not been a stupid party after all. She had played her part well; she'd had some fun. Above all, she'd learned something about human behavior from the composure of a rejected young man who gracefully turned the tables on his disappointment. She admired that! The next step would be to deal with Phillip. What would that encounter be like?

Joan went to her bedroom, exhausted and sleepy, took her good-luck-charm green dress off and folded it carefully over a chair. It had been quite a day. She sighed and put her nightgown on. *Sleep, restful sleep, to the land of dreams… is there anything more wonderful than sliding into that world?* Joan thought, as she gently pulled the blanket up and relaxed. "Life is good," she murmured, smiling. *But isn't it wonderful to wade into the field out there, with the stars and the rest of the universe?* Closing her eyes, she fell into sleep.

Chapter Seven: Keeping Hope Alive

Thank God, Joan's first class didn't start before 9 o'clock, so she could gather her thoughts before she met Kristin at school during the first break. She asked Claude to drive her since she did not have enough time to walk that morning. After quickly eating a bowl of fruit with nuts and honey, she jumped into the car with a sigh of relief. She would review her notes before the 9 o'clock math class and think of the questions she would ask Kristin while sitting in the library. Great!

"Thank you, Claude. I'm sorry for this last minute change of plans. I just could not have made it without you this morning! You are my savior," Joan kidded with a smile as she slammed the car door.

"I see you have some pressing school business today, Ms. Joan. Relax, it's always a pleasure for me to help you out. Will you need a ride back?" Claude started out of the property gate.

"No, thank you. Kristin can drop me off on her way home. She is using her mom's car these days. Claude, did you know that my dad is going to buy me a Prius this summer?"

"A Prius?" Claude repeated with great shock. "No, I didn't know. I'm quite surprised. I hear they are good cars though. Congratulations!"

"Yes, a Prius! And I talked Dad into it. I chose it, Claude, what do you think of that? You know, because of the gas consumption, global warming stuff. My dad couldn't believe my choice, but I explained why, and he got it! I'll miss my walks to school next year, though!"

"You're a wise young lady and a very smart one," Claude added, nodding his head as he turned in and dropped Joan off at the entrance to the school parking lot. "Have a great day," he added, as Joan was already running toward the library with her bag swinging by her feet.

The library was empty. Joan took a deep breath. *Great*, she thought, knowing that the quiet atmosphere was hers. She always liked this place, where knowledge and wisdom were sheltered safely in all the books lined up on the shelves. *So much to know.* Joan sighed, looking up and down the rows of books. *So much progress! Human beings sure have come a long way from their cavemen ancestors!*

"But, what about caves?" Joan whispered, giggling.

Caves? Caves are still very important! What would I do without "my" cave? Everything starts there for me when I need to reflect deeply and go inside. Strange thought! *Did the cavemen begin thinking deeply in their own dark places as I do, to get inspired?*

The math assignment Joan had to turn in was ready except for the last equation, which she quickly finished. Now she could focus on how to deal with the petition and how to ask Kristin some pertinent questions. She hoped that Kristin would know whether her own mother signed it, whether she passed it on to other parents, whether Ellen was still freaked out, and whether the juniors' parents were going to sign the petition, too. Joan took notes, including asking how the posters were progressing and when they should begin their protest in front of the school.

The librarian walked in and stopped next to Joan, smiling. "You look very busy, Joan. May I help you?"

"No, thank you, Ms. Stern. I have just about finished a list of questions to ask to my friend. We are doing a very important project together."

"Is there something I could find in the library that would help?"

"Not really, but you could answer one question for me, Ms. Stern."

"What is it, Joan?"

"How many years does a teacher have to be working in this place before he gets tenure?"

"I believe it is three full years. Whom do you think should be fired?" Ms. Stern added, puzzled.

"It's a long story which you probably aren't aware of, but some parents are petitioning to have Mr. Silver dismissed from this school right now."

Ms. Stern was taken aback. "But Mark is such a wonderful teacher! We haven't had a science teacher comparable to him in years… the students love him."

"Yes, most students love him, but some parents are upset because he brought up global warming and discussed the dire consequences of global warming. It scared a student, and some parents deny all of the science about it. It's a mess! They want him out."

"That sounds familiar," Ms. Stern answered, pursing her lips. "A few years ago, we had to confront the refusal of some parents to include the theory of evolution in our science program. Some religious parents were up in arms, accusing the school of challenging God and criticizing religious beliefs. Those parents believed in creationism, that God created everything. It was also a mess!"

"And how did it end?" Joan asked, begging.

"Well, we had to compromise, Joan. Compromising is always an intermediary step between accepting a new paradigm and clinging to the old one! We decided to include creationism as well as evolution in the science program, just to let the younger generation see both, and maybe disassociate from the old beliefs. It may take some time."

"Creationism? What kind of science is that?" Joan asked, frowning. "It's not science, is it, Ms. Stern?"

"No, Joan, it's a belief, more specifically a religious belief. Think of what would happen if we rejected this belief all of a sudden? Imagine the effect if we questioned one of the most cherished ideas of where life comes from and what life is all about… that people have believed for eons? Religions developed all over the world would have no way to explain themselves. These beliefs are anchored in the collective unconscious of humanity. Religions want to be the sole expression of truth."

"Yes, religions around the world fought against each other, and they still do today," Joan added, nodding.

"If we were to challenge the most beautiful spiritual visions of the stories created over the ages and their expressions—Adam and Eve, the Bible, all the avatars who tried to explain the human condition: Jesus, Mohamed, Buddha, and others—it would be as if we destroyed some of the most beautiful works of art in the world! All the temples of worship—Notre Dame and Chartres with their treasures, the Pyramids, the Wailing Wall, Mecca, the Taj Mahal, all the Saints, the seers, the Crusades—you know, all the human explanations which were ever given for the spiritual side of life we experience. Just being the humans that we are today, however, leaves us with questions. I think we are just now starting to reach a very different stage in our evolution, Joan. Something which has to happen as the state of the world shows us we need to take a different route. This is all part of our evolution. We need to expand into a new, higher form of consciousness. Let's hope we get there before we destroy ourselves."

Joan was totally stunned. In a few words, Ms. Stern had summed up what she had been trying to figure out about the evolution of life. She felt that something similar was happening in the growth process of humankind. She remained silent for awhile. Speechless. Ms. Stern noticed her strong reaction and wanted to make Joan feel at ease. She put her hand gently on her shoulder and told her that she would be happy to help her in any way she could, and that someday she would lend her a DVD to watch about evolution. Something she would resonate with. Joan thanked her and, overtaken by strong feelings, put her arms around the librarian and hugged her. It was a strong moment, as if a bond were created between the older one, full of knowledge, and the younger one, who'd just had an epiphany.

"And don't forget the compromise," Ms. Stern reminded Joan as she picked up her bag and left quietly for her math class. "Sometimes people are not ready to hear the truth yet!"

The math class was over before Joan could concentrate on what was said or written on the board. Her mind was somewhere else. Ms. Stern's overall view of civilization's evolution through the ages and their efforts to explain the human condition with the help of various religious establishments made so much sense. It was like one of the obvious, irrefutable truths that any logical person would understand, yet there were so many people still unable to get it! *Did it have to do with the state of their consciousness? Was consciousness evolving to a new level in the world these days? And at what cost, in the middle of chaos? Did it have to do with people's inability to look at global warming and what it entails, and reject it because of the state of their collective unconscious, as Ms. Stern called the long-established status quo of their mind?* Joan was stunned but happy that she had at least understood why all these problems existed in the world. *So, compromise before the paradigm changes was the answer. That's what Ms. Stern had said, right? But how long would it take?* She sighed.

Before she left the class, Joan got a bright idea. Maybe she could talk to Roger about this evolution to a higher state of consciousness. He was bright. He may know about it. They could have an interesting conversation. *Okay, sometime in the future, after the prom,* she thought.

In the meantime we have some work to do. She walked to the cafeteria to meet Kristin for the break.

It was a short break—only 15 minutes—and Joan did not think she could handle making a lot of decisions after the amazing talk she just had with the librarian. When she saw Kristin sitting seriously at the table waiting for her, she smiled and joked. "Kristin, forgive me, but let's just gossip right now. I want to tell you about the party last night," Joan said, with a mysterious look.

"Yes, how was it?" Kristin answered, curious to hear about it.

"Well, I danced with Roger. I was like dancing with a board! He was so stiff, you wouldn't believe it. But then he taught me a big lesson and that changed my mind about the guy."

"Uh oh," Kristin answered, even more curious this time. "Did he suddenly switch to another dancing style?"

"No. When I told Roger I would go to the prom with Phillip, he took it so well and I was surprised. He turned the tables on me by gratefully accepting my offer to introduce him to the love of nature by walking with me in the park! He was quite charming!"

Kristin started laughing out loud. She could not stop. "Joan, did I get it right?" she continued, giggling. "You said you wanted to introduce Roger to the love of nature? Does that mean you will invite him to lie in the grass with you? Maybe that is what he understood! He probably could give you some lessons about nature, also! You are something else, my friend, you and your poetic side! Anyway, let's meet at lunch. We have some work to do. Funny, funny," Kristin repeated as she walked out laughing, leaving Joan totally embarrassed and nodding her head.

Kristin met Joan for lunch in the cafeteria. The two friends ate their lunch quickly, avoiding an explanation about their previous conversation. Kristin felt that she had been too hard on Joan when she made fun of her and Joan was too embarrassed to bring up the subject. So instead, they cheerily toasted their glasses of water together to Mrs. Field, hoping that the soft drink machine would soon be removed from the premises, and thus help the students curb their sugar consumption.

"Let's do what we can to make this world better, in any way we can, slowly but surely," Kristin said, drinking her ice water. "Our bodies are 70% water anyway. We must keep them hydrated with something besides soft drinks!"

"Speaking of Mrs. Field," Kristin continued. "I found out that it wasn't the first time her daughter Ellen freaked out in class. She did it once in the lab when they had to dissect a frog, and again in PE class when she refused to wear shorts for a calisthenics session. It's her way to revolt if a teacher's ideas clash with what her authoritarian parents believe. She doesn't say anything; she just throws a tantrum and leaves the room. In this case with Mr. Silver, I heard that Ellen's dad talked about it at one of his church meetings, calling global warming nonsense, and said that we were just entering another age that was part of God's plan. Imagine how confused the poor girl must get when presented with something her parents reject! No wonder she freaks out! And these days so many things come into question with scientific exploration! I feel sorry for Ellen."

"Who told you all this, Kristin?" asked Joan. "It sure makes sense, and it's no wonder Mrs. Field started the petition. They want to oust someone because of the influence he may have on their child! Mr. Silver does not have tenure yet so they think they have a chance to get rid of him! You would think school is for freedom of opinion, where someone can listen to a lecture and make up their own mind. I guess that is more likely when we can listen without the background noise of our parents' opinions! Thank heaven this isn't the case with us, even though we still love and respect our parents. We have come a long way, my friend! Aren't we great?" Joan added, teasingly raising her head up with pride.

"I got the info from Sylvia, who is in Ellen's class. Her mother got the petition too, but refused to sign it. It looks like the parents who signed so far were in the same church groups as Ellen's parents. They heard Mr. Field's irate rendition of his daughter's account of the global warming lecture by Mr. Silver, and it was good enough for them. Some of the juniors' parents heard about it as well, and I think there are about 25 signatures as of now. Enough to present it to the school principal." Kristin continued looking at her notes.

"I still wonder why my mother signed it," Joan said, looking pensive and disappointed. "You said you saw her name on the petition, Kristin. Why do you think she did it?"

"Remember what Mark Silver said about the special interest groups who distort the evidence because they are funded by the fossil fuel industries? The distortion is perpetuated by the media, and the people who benefit from the profits are not about to change their views either. Fewer people really know the truth about the whole thing when it is distorted and *God* gets quoted! That's the biggie! Also, your mother may watch conservative newscasts and such, like the Fields do. Who knows?"

"I thought my mother was an intelligent woman. I'm very disappointed. I'll have to talk to her about this soon!" Joan concluded, with a big sigh.

It was time now to talk about the posters, to find out when the petition would be presented so they could start their protest campaign, to get the names of the volunteers, and unfortunately, it was also time to stop talking, because the bell that ended lunch just rang!

"Good work, Kristin. We are getting somewhere," Joan finished, with a smile.

"Bye, Joan. We'll continue later. Enjoy your English class and say hello to Phillip. I think you should let him know about the prom. He must be sitting on hot coals waiting! He is so sensitive and sweet. Don't make him wait!"

"I won't. I'll tell him today. Kristin, can you give me a ride home later? I'll meet you in the parking lot at 4:30, okay? See you there," Joan concluded, walking happily toward her English class. *Whoa, what a busy day! It's amazing how much I have piled up in a few hours. My mind is being challenged for sure, and this is not the end,* Joan thought, imagining Phillip's face when she told him that he would be her date to the prom.

Chapter Eight: To Kill a Butterfly

Joan always enjoyed English class. It was her favorite, along with science class, of course! The teacher had a lot to do with it. Mrs. Goldman was a little bit like Mademoiselle Giroud—very articulate, knowledgeable, patient, and interesting. She added her own comments to an author's work and she always remembered specific details from her students and their assignments. The whole class knew, however, that she had a special affinity for Phillip. It's probably not that often that an English teacher has the luck to end up with a genuine poet in her class, and everybody agreed that he was good.

Today, as he usually did, Phillip submitted a poem as his classroom assignment and Mrs. Goldman asked him to read it to the class at the end of the lesson. He walked up to the podium slowly, poised and composed. The class had recently read a novel about the uselessness of violence, so Phillip called his poem, "To Kill a Butterfly".

The poem dealt with the beauty of a butterfly, expressed in such poetic terms that they could almost feel its wings spreading out in a field of flowers. The colors and the delicate, paper-thin wings were there within their reach. They felt as if they were in the field with it, forgetting themselves as people, going back to the source of what beauty is. Then, a sad part followed:

Weed killer drips from green vibrant leaves

That will wither and die.

The poisoned milkweeds shrivel

Leaving a ravaged land for butterflies.

The metaphor of transformation is described next in the poem, creating an incredible image of the metamorphosis that takes place to make a butterfly, the difficult changes it experiences in the cocoon, and the pain that the transformation entails. Finally, the end of the poem exposed the long evolution of humanity to where it is today, in crisis, with the wars and all the violence which is done to our Earth, humanity squirming in the cocoon, trying to evolve, disturbing the butterfly's transformation. The ultimate question came last: whether we, as humans, would kill the butterfly.

The class was silent. Some of the students were in tears. Joan was extremely moved and thought about how good it was that Ellen had not been in the audience. She would have freaked out and disturbed the silence. Instead, you could have heard a pin drop. It was beautiful.

"I think all the students resonated in their souls with what Phillip read today," Mrs. Goldman concluded. "Now I'll let you go. And thank you, Phillip, for such a poignant and well-read poem."

Joan walked over to Phillip as he descended from the podium, thanked him, and asked whether he could walk back with her to the library. It would be a good place to talk for awhile, she said, as she wanted to tell him something important. Phillip accepted gladly, anticipating what her promising smile had in store for him, and knowing it was probably an answer to his offer to take her to the prom. *Things look good,* he thought, conscious of the way she responded. They walked together quietly and found a place to sit in the study area.

Joan decided not to make Phillip wait any longer and announced that he would be the one to take her to the prom. He was delighted and ceremoniously kissed her hand like a gentleman, saying, "Thank you, thank you, Joan, you are making my happiness complete," as if he were playing a part on stage. Joan giggled and congratulated him again on the incredibly moving poem he read.

"I really got inspired to write this a few days ago," Phillip explained. "I read on an ecological website that the monarch butterflies have almost all disappeared from the U.S. because chemical companies are destroying the milkweed, their main source of food with an herbicide. Chemicals have destroyed 80-98% of the milkweed in the Midwest, and the monarch butterflies are disappearing as a result. Imagine, Joan. The Agent Orange chemical was used in the Vietnam War and it defoliated the trees and plants and killed hundreds of thousands of people! And their chemicals continue poisoning plants and animals here in the U.S.! Can anybody stop this mass killing? Isn't it symbolic? The butterfly is the image of metamorphosis, the harbinger of change and transformation. Are we doomed to stop natural evolution? These corporations are free to poison us with their genetically modified food, and poison the butterflies with pesticides!" Phillip was totally upset, shaking his head in disbelief. "I'm so helpless, Joan. I feel like the world is sliding away into the abyss because we brought it to the brink. I don't know how to cope with this. This is our future, you know," he added letting his arms fall to his side.

"I feel the same way, Phillip. Some parents here are petitioning to fire our science teacher Mr. Silver, just because he discussed the dire effects of global warming with the senior class! Kristin and I are planning to fight the petition. Things are cooking, Phillip! We'll win, you'll see!"

"That's terrible, but I'm happy you are optimistic, Joan, that you can do something about it. All I can do myself is write poems! Not really much action. With what's happening, some days I feel that we'll never be able to save our planet Earth and its living creatures! I feel so sad and discouraged."

"Yes, your poem reflects that… it's very insightful, Phillip. But listen, maybe the butterfly has a lesson for us, don't you think?" Joan answered, trying to lighten things up.

"What do you think the lesson is at this point?" Phillip answered with a long sigh.

"You know, Phillip, the thing about metamorphosis… imagine the rumbling and churning and rotting which the caterpillar undergoes inside the cocoon before it emerges as a butterfly. Maybe that is what we are going through now. A metamorphosis! Maybe the chemical companies are rotting parasites right now, maybe obsolete dinosaurs making their last stands. Transformation is a powerful energy which has led the world through many changes over the ages. Maybe it is at work all around us now, trying to shake everything to pieces without us recognizing it, but we all feel it happening. This time we may be able to do it with wisdom, and get into a new dimension in our consciousness which we have only begun to explore. I'm not giving up, Phillip," Joan concluded with a deep breath. "Let's do it!"

"I admire you, Joan. You have a lot of guts for a woman!"

"What do you mean, 'for a woman,' Phillip? That sounds odd!" Joan exclaimed, laughing. "If I didn't know you better, I would think you are prejudiced against women!"

"On the contrary, Joan, I really feel that women will be the ones who will save the world at this point! The men have pitifully failed, it is so obvious," Phillip concluded, shaking his head. "Perhaps we can talk more about this later," he added, walking slowly toward the library door, looking down and depressed.

"Was I supposed to hear what Phillip just said?" Ms. Stern interjected as she walked by Joan, carrying a pile of books. "An astute man, he is. I was just talking with Mrs. Goldman awhile ago. She was raving about his talent with poetry. She told me about the one he read today, "To Kill a Butterfly." Remember, Joan, when we talked about evolution, changes, and the work it takes to get there? I think Phillip has been able to put it in images that speak to our soul. We feel all this in our guts as we look at what is happening to the planet today. Everybody senses it deep down, even if they deny it in fear. We resonate."

"Yes, Phillip is our artistic spokesman. I worry about his hopelessness, though. I would like to be able to help him."

"Just listen to him, Joan. Be there and take his foresight as a mission."

"What foresight, Ms. Stern? He didn't mention any kind of positive resolution to the dilemma, he just sees humanity killing the butterfly!"

"The foresight was his parting words when I overheard your conversation. When Phillip said that he felt women would be the ones who would save the world, remember? The poets and the artists are often the forerunners of what is coming in the future, Joan. They feel the vibes. There is a part of their brain, soul, or consciousness—something inside their hearts—which is tuned in to the whole."

Joan was silent, breathing deeply as she looked at this woman who had become a mentor for her. She thought back on Phillip's expression when he talked about women being able to save the world as a last solution to an impossible task. She closed her eyes for awhile and finally said, "Yes, I would like to help do this in my own small way. Maybe you will help me learn about the role of women in the history of the world and how this can happen, Ms. Stern."

"You have already started, Joan. You and Kristin are on a roll. Go and work on opposing the petition against Mark Silver, and the rest will happen. I will also help you with some books to read about women that will give you hope."

Joan looked at her watch. It was already 4:40 and Kristin had been waiting for her in the parking lot, she was sure. She excused herself, said goodbye to Ms. Stern with a lot of thanks, and hurried out of the library to meet Kristin. She felt tired, as though she were carrying a load of responsibilities on her shoulders and life were becoming more and more difficult. Her lightness was flying away. She was a woman. And women were supposed to help to save the world. *That's big,* Joan thought.

Chapter Nine: Lessons from a Little Prince

After the memorable day when Phillip had touched her heart about the caterpillar and its symbolic transformation, Joan often visualized its pain and hidden turmoil, and she internalized what it felt like to be a butterfly in the midst of a cocoon transition toward new beginnings. *It's like what the world is going through right now*, she thought, *when everything seems to be falling apart.* Joan could feel that crisis building within her. Forces fighting for recognition. It filled her with a sense of powerlessness and fear of the unknown, but also with the excitement of new frontiers to explore, beyond what she could ever imagine. She sat in the veranda, waiting for Mademoiselle Giroud, dreaming away.

Joan had not prepared any French assignment this time. The last lesson had been absorbed with the important meeting with Mark Silver and Mademoiselle left without assigning any homework for her. *It's time to return to some serious French studies*, Joan thought, thinking of what her mom would say if she only knew! Joan smiled at the idea of all that had been going on in the past few days, and how she would be at a loss to explain this to her mother! Instead of her usual daily routine at home, playing the role of the teenage daughter the way her parents saw her, she now had a mission as a young woman. A serious mission to save the world. Her parents would laugh, just like they laughed about the cave! Would they ever understand her?

Mademoiselle walked in with a large smile. She looked happy. She was wearing the same dress she had on at the meeting. She put her books down and sat near Joan by the waterfall.

"I think we have a lot of work to do today, Joan, but first you must tell me the news. We talk in French all the time, so nothing you say is a waste of time, and I will correct you when necessary," Mademoiselle continued with a smile.

Joan started relating her work on getting the protest going with Kristin, the way making the posters had been shared by volunteers of both senior and junior students, male and female. She told Mademoiselle that there were, at this point, 25 signatures. Probably enough to present to the principal. She also mentioned that the librarian told her it takes three years for a teacher to get tenure. Joan then talked about Phillip and that she had followed Mademoiselle's advice. She listened to her heart and picked him for the prom. She described how Phillip received the news.

"Good for you, Joan. I don't know Phillip, but I imagine he must be a good choice since you have similar interests in nature and poetry. Was Roger upset?"

"Not really. He was gracious and he took a rain check when I told him I would take him for a walk in the park to see nature! I didn't want to lose his friendship. He is quite intelligent, you know, and we may discuss some important subjects someday!"

Joan stopped for awhile, thinking, and then she spoke seriously to Mademoiselle about the poetry reading in English class, the discussion with Phillip about the butterfly and Phillip's depression about the world in crisis. His statement about the role of women to make change happen convinced Joan that she had a mission from now on. Joan looked more and more tired as she finished the story, now mixing French and English words, her head looking down.

Mademoiselle became concerned that Joan felt the weight of the world's problems too heavily on her young mind. "Joan, you are pushing yourself too hard. Let's get back to the present, okay? Can you see how beautiful this orchid is? It has grown around the tree with all its energy, searching for the light! It is still and beautiful. We too can be still. Can you feel the stillness Joan?"

Joan closed her eyes for a moment, her face smoothed down. "Yes, Mademoiselle... for awhile I felt just as depressed as Phillip when he was talking about the cocoon. I was getting lost in my thoughts. I'm sorry!"

"No need to be sorry, Joan, we all have these moments of doubt and sadness. However, I don't have any doubt right now that you can accomplish your mission in a beautiful way! Listen Joan, I have a great idea. Do you remember one of the first books we read when you began French with me, *The Little Prince?*"

"Of course I do, Mademoiselle, it was so cute and so deep at the same time."

"Okay, for your next lesson, I would like you to find some words of wisdom in the book which could apply to the state of the world and humanity today as expressed by *The Little Prince*. The book was written in the nineteen forties, at a time when the world was in a totally different place, but there are things which still apply to our days as well. They are eternal. This assignment will be easier than our other discussions, like existentialism. It will give you a break, Joan. You are a very mature and intelligent young woman but sometimes I sense that I ask too much of you. I often forget that you just passed your sixteenth birthday! You fool me with your wisdom young lady! Read *The Little Prince* again and we can talk about his travels through the cosmos in our next lesson."

Mademoiselle looked as if she was ready to leave, but Joan had something very important to ask her. She hesitated, but in a very timid voice she finally formulated what was on her mind. "Mademoiselle, can I ask you a question? I have been dying to know what happened after our meeting in the veranda with Kristin and Mr. Silver. Did he contact you after you gave him your phone number? He seemed interested in seeing you again."

"Well, if you want to know, Joan, yes. Mark called me and we had coffee together. He asked me about my talk with the French professor concerning global warming. We had a great exchange. Mark is very intelligent. I was impressed by his knowledge of the subject and I learned even more about it. I like his way of relating. Clear, concise, humorous at times. We got along well and will see each other again. So, did I appease your curiosity Ms. Joan?" Mademoiselle ended with a glimmer in her eyes.

"That makes me happy, Mademoiselle! Good people getting together!" Joan beamed. "I like you both so much!"

"Thank you Joan. The universe will take care of things from now on. It always does!" Mademoiselle added with a smile. "In the meantime, I have an idea for your homework since you haven't done that much French lately. Would you write a composition on the subject I suggested and get it over to me soon so I can read and correct it before the next lesson?"

"I will, Mademoiselle. I love the assignment. I'll get to it ASAP!" Joan responded happily.

Mademoiselle left the veranda as Joan was rearranging the chairs. She was on her way to the door when she noticed Victor perched in a rubber tree silently looking at her.

"You look so sad Victor, so lonely!" Joan said to him, frowning. "I must definitely get you a mate, a nice one!"

It was early in the day yet. Since it was Saturday, her parents were gone to an afternoon meeting at the church, the same church that the Fields belonged to. Joan's parents gave up long ago on trying to take Joan along with them to these functions. She refused to accompany them every time, stating that she did not want to go, no comments, and they finally stopped trying to force her. Joan thought she would take a walk in the park, then come back and start working on her *Little Prince* assignment. She changed into comfortable shorts and walking sneakers and left for her favorite place.

How wonderful it is to walk through this beautiful place. The pond, the meadow, the woods, are all my friends. Something inside of me says that I belong here, that I am a part of it all! Joan murmured, closing her eyes as she stopped in the grass in front of a large oak tree. *This is my church, that's it, this is my church, I know! This is where I sense the presence of the infinite, a field of expanded consciousness I am a part of. I feel a sense of belonging beyond what words can express,* Joan said to herself, trying to define something which she could not put into words. It was easier to simply go inside the cave, quietly, and feel this presence somewhere in her heart. *Maybe that is why people go to church, to find what they sense is inside. Then they try to use concepts and stories to define it, accepting religion to give them explanations and guidelines,* she continued, letting her mind empty itself of thoughts to feel the space, the immensity, the field of consciousness, the belonging. *Is this where all the answers are, inside oneself and out there in the wide universe?* Shaking her head, happy and tired, Joan let herself fall softly into the grass under the tree and close her eyes. *My church,* she repeated, *my church!*

Joan remained in the quiet state of this expanded consciousness for a long time, somewhere beyond her ordinary mind. It was a place she never experienced before, though she had been close to the awe it brought, it was a place sort of like love. *Is this an essence within myself which I feel, something which has always been with me? Even before I was born?* Joan questioned, having returned to her ordinary mind. Joan started laughing aloud, as if she wanted the whole world to hear, *Well, I know now that JP Sartre was wrong, dead wrong! Our essence is here, I feel it, it is always with me and it comes before existence for sure! Wait until Mademoiselle hears about this! I have discovered my essence in the middle of the park, under the arching branches of a sacred cathedral called Nature! Whoa! This is cool.*

"This is very cool!" Joan repeated out loud, overwhelmed by her happiness. "I wonder what Mademoiselle will say!" *Oh, yes, Mademoiselle. The Little Prince, my assignment...* Joan woke from her dreamy state. She stood up quickly from her bed of grass, having recovered her dutiful mind. *I must get back! I will work on it after dinner. My parents must be home now and I'm sure they will want to spend some time with me.*

When she arrived at the house, it was totally quiet. Joan was surprised because it was already late afternoon and she wondered how long the church meeting lasted. She walked up to her room and saw that Kristin had texted her while she was away. "Where have you been? I want to tell you something important Joan. Call me."

"Hi, Kristin. What's up?"

"Joan, why don't you take your cell phone with you, so I can talk to you when something important happens? I've been trying to reach you for awhile!"

"I'm sorry Kristin. I don't like to be interrupted when I walk in the woods. It takes away my silence and connection with nature."

"Okay. Well anyway, I wanted to tell you that there was a big meeting at the church today, you know, the one your parents go to, where Mr. Field talked the other day about global warming."

"So, what happened?"

"I don't know yet, but I wanted to let you know. You probably will hear about it."

"My parents are not back yet."

"Great! I'm relieved. Now you know. Try to find out and call me later, okay?"

"I'll do my best, Kristin, if they want to talk about it. Wait, I think I hear some rummaging downstairs. Maybe they are back. Talk to you later. Bye."

Joan sat on her bed, wondering how she was going to approach her parents about the meeting at the church. It was probably about the petition and Mark Silver's status at the school. Not a discussion to look forward to with her parents! She took several deep breaths and decided she would simply play it by ear and trust her good judgment to be her guide. Then an angry voice started calling her from downstairs which challenged her resolve.

"Joan, would you come down immediately, please. We've got something to talk to you about," Susan was saying in a hostile tone that Joan recognized. The last time she heard it was a year ago, when Susan chastised her about disappearing without letting her parents know that she went to the woods, and she stayed so long that Susan almost called search and rescue!

"Yes, Mom, I'll be right down," Joan answered, taking another long, deep breath as she walked down the stairs, ready for anything!

"Mom, you upset! What happened to you?" Joan said in a quiet tone. "What happened at the church?"

Henri stood right by Susan, looking upset but sort of friendly.

"What have you and Kristin been cooking up? We have a petition started to fire your science teacher for very good reasons, and I hear that you girls organized some kind of a protest. What have you done? You are doing things behind my back and I'm not happy with you, Joan!"

"How did you find this out, Mom? I didn't know anyone knew."

"Some of the students you enrolled in your protest told their parents, that's how."

Joan was lost. Where to go from here seemed nearly impossible since her parents discovered the plot! She decided then to summon her higher self for help and after breathing deeply, she got the idea to involve her dad in the discussion to break the tension.

"Dad, do you remember the talk we had at lunch the other day, when I explained to you why I want a Prius instead of a big car that uses a lot of gas? Do you remember my reasons, my concern about carbon dioxide pollution in our environment and how global warming will hurt the planet if we continue the current use of fossil fuels? You seemed to hear what I said and didn't refute my reasoning, right? Maybe what you heard today was just a rant by someone furious about some kids trying to challenge Mr. Field's ideas. Does he really understand the science?"

"It was a rant, all right," Henri commented, puffing air out of his mouth while Susan tried to kick him in the leg. "I never saw Mr. Field so upset! He is a leader in the church and his word seems to be the gospel for a lot of people. He quoted many influential people to back him up about what he called "the global warming hoax." I had a hard time believing what he said, but he has a lot of clout in town because of his position in the church."

"Henri, I can't believe you said that in front of Joan. Here I am trying to get her to understand the enormity of what she and Kristin have done and you start questioning the integrity of this pillar of our church! What are you trying to do? Agree with what these girls did?"

"Susan, I'm just trying to understand why people want to fire someone who is appreciated as a good teacher, just because they have different beliefs, that's all. To each his own, and if Mark Silver presents his class with a scientific evidence worth examining, he shouldn't be fired for it. I don't agree with him, all right? I didn't say anything at the meeting because I didn't want to start a fight, but I'm beginning to like this Mr. Field less and less. His church meetings are starting to get on my nerves."

Susan was livid. She didn't know what to say, especially in front of Joan. She tried to quiet herself down with a drink of vodka, which she promptly poured from the bar. After a few sips and some deep breathing to regain her composure she looked at Joan, who was standing there totally at a loss about what to do.

"Don't just stand there, Joan, go tell Martha to get dinner ready," Susan said, perplexed. "Your father and I have some divergent opinions, as you can see, but I'm standing by my guns on this one. The petition will go on."

"Standing by your guns, Mom? That's a scary statement. I didn't know there are guns in the house. I don't like guns, Mom. Promise that you won't use them."

"Making fun of me, are you, miss goody-goody two-shoes," Susan said, totally disarmed and drinking her second glass of vodka. "We'll see who wins in the long run," she added aggressively. "Go tell Martha about dinner, go!"

This interaction was difficult for Joan. On one hand, she was happy to see her dad thinking about the potential seriousness of global warming. But on the other hand, she felt sorry that her mother made a scene and then tempered the problem with a drink. She wished so much that her parents would get along! Maybe this was the reason Henri said life was lousy and it was her mom's fault.

Joan left the tense atmosphere with a sense of relief. Martha said dinner would be ready in about an hour, so Joan decided to go up to her room until then. *The situation probably will clear up*, she thought. *First thing, I must call Kristin*, Joan decided. *She must be waiting impatiently to know what happened.*

"Kristin, I just had a big scene with my parents. My mother is raging mad about us countering the petition with a protest. They heard about it at the church meeting. Mr. Field ranted about the "hoax of global warming" as he called it. My dad doesn't like Mr. Field very much so I was able to get my father's help and turn the situation around by suggesting that global warming is worth looking at from a scientific perspective. Mr. Field's rant was too much for my father, I think. He said to Mom that Mark Silver should not be fired for presenting scientific opinion to the class just because Mr. Field had different views, and that the church should not have anything to do with it! We have a great ally, Kristin. My father is very intelligent and he may help us resolve this."

"Then why didn't your dad say anything in the meeting, Joan? He could have debunked all this right there!"

"My dad doesn't like to fight, as he says. It seems as if he was the only one in the group feeling this way about the petition and my mother agreed with all the others. A lot is going on between my parents that I don't understand very well. I also don't think my dad knows that much about global warming issues himself. I believe he stays on the sidelines because of his connection with the oil industry, but he may give it more thought if he sees the world climate is threatened. Everybody can see it… even if Mr. Field ignores the evidence while calling on the help of God!"

"Joan, maybe we have a chance to avoid the protest if your dad can work behind the scenes. But we should go ahead and be ready, just in case. I loved making the posters! We found such great lines! It was so fun inventing slogans!"

"Yes, it was. Let's keep thinking positively, Kristin. I have a good feeling about what my dad said and may find a way to get him involved without having to fight! I'll think about that! Now I need to do my French assignment for Mademoiselle. By the way, did you know that she went out with Mark Silver since the meeting? What do you think about that?"

"You're kidding! That's just great! Joan you are a genius sometimes. You had it all figured out! Imagine what's going to happen next. We may have a surprise. A romance that blossoms!"

"Yes we may! And you are an amazing organizer, Kristin. Such great posters! We still might need them. Good night, friend. See you at school."

Joan sat comfortably on her bed with *The Little Prince*, which she started rereading with great expectations. She had forgotten a lot of the details in the story and decided that she would scan it, looking for what Mademoiselle had asked her to find: some words of wisdom which could apply to the state of the world today. *Let's see if we can do this,* Joan said to herself smiling. *This should be easy. This book is full of wisdom, but I will only pick a few words, the ones which make the most sense to me.*

Joan liked the dialogue the Little Prince had with the king. He was an absolute monarch who ruled over everything on his planet, but the only reason why his subjects obeyed him is because his orders were reasonable. He would only demand from everyone what they could give. His authority was respected because it rested on reason. *That's true. People can relate to their leaders when what is expected of them makes sense. Perhaps this would work for taxes, for instance,* Joan thought. *Shouldn't the rich people pay taxes in proportion with what they have? That's not what I see happening in our country! What I keep hearing is the rich are getting richer while most Americans are getting poorer! Whoa! So that would not work out too well in a capitalist country, right?* She sighed. *This is much more complicated than it seems! I'm definitely not very knowledgeable about economics. I don't think I can even completely understand what capitalism is all about.* Joan decided that she would let these words of wisdom from the king rest in her mind: "Only demand from people what they can give in order to be respected." *It was a very good principle. It sounded right, but it's difficult to apply in today's world!*

There was a lot of wisdom in the way the Little Prince was put face-to-face with the drinker sitting in front of his bottles when he arrived on his planet. The exchange between the two was the perfect example of a vicious circle:

"What are you doing?" he asked him.

"I drink," he answered in a sad tone.

"Why do you drink?" asked the Little Prince.

"To forget," he answered.

"To forget what?" asked the Little Prince who was starting to feel sorry for him.

"To forget that I am ashamed," he confessed, lowering his head.

"Ashamed of what?" The Little Prince asked, ready to help him out.

"Ashamed of drinking," the drinker ended, going back to silence.

How do you stop a vicious circle? Joan asked herself. And her mind went to the growing problems of alcoholism. *Yes, alcoholism is rampant in our modern world, as well as drug addiction, even addiction to prescribed drugs. The answer to why it is such a big problem is so simple: the need to forget! There must be a lot for people to forget when they are unhappy with their present state, when they want to escape it. I guess that is also the way Mom deals with things she cannot cope with! Like she did tonight. If there are so many alcoholics and drug addicts in the world today, there must be a lot of unhappiness they want to forget,* Joan concluded. *Happiness! I asked myself that question before: what is happiness?* she continued, visualizing the meadow, the flowers, the trees, her friend Kristin, Mademoiselle, the librarian, Phillip. *Happiness is a state of mind when everything flows well from the inside and the present is just right the way it is, isn't it?*

"Joan, please come down," Henri called from the dining room, interrupting Joan's dream state. "Dinner is ready."

Joan walked down the stairs thinking of what her emotional state was at this moment. Was it flowing well from inside herself? Maybe the best way was just to go on without thinking, without fear! Of course she would have to face her parents again, but why imagine the future. She would just go with what happens intuitively, and everything would work out, everything would flow.

Whatever happened between Joan's parents when she was in her room must have been a big change from the scene she left earlier. No more fighting. There was a sense of quiet compromise between the two now, and it made Joan happy. The empty wine glasses seemed to speak of something like a peace treaty between her parents and Joan smiled thinking of what the drinker had taught her in his exchange with the Little Prince. *Well, they forgot their quarrel, and it worked with the wine,* she thought. *And all is well in this present situation, so I'll accept it gladly!*

"Hello parents," Joan greeted them joyously. "I'm starved. It takes a lot of energy to do a French assignment and I'm ready for some of Martha's delicious cooking."

The dinner was relaxed. Martha's *coq au vin* served with delicate small potatoes and then a salad tossed with a French dressing and garlic satisfied everyone.

"There was wine in that dish," Joan joked. "No wonder it tasted so good!"

Martha then brought her traditional *crème brulee*, the one Susan always must have seconds of. Everything went very well. No mention of the petition. No hard exchanges between her parents. A serene atmosphere all the way through. *Well,* Joan thought, *it looks like a little wine is good for people, it worked wonders for my parents tonight, but to go too far and become an alcoholic, that probably does not work very well! I'll have a lot to write for my French homework,* she concluded laughing.

It was already late when Joan returned to her room, but she had to finish the assignment Mademoiselle had asked her to drop off before her next class. She decided she would choose for the last one a very important quote from the Little Prince, the one she felt was the best, the most beautiful and which would solve all the problems of the world if people would only see life in a different way. "One only sees well with the heart, the essential is invisible to the eyes," Joan repeated several times as she slowly got ready for bed. *Only the heart knows the essential,* she pondered, feeling her own heart open. *It knows the essence of it all, it knows what the mind does not see… that's the secret! I must always remember that. Maybe the big dilemma between the eyes' and the heart's decisions is what is going on in the cocoon of the world right now while it metamorphoses into a new dimension of consciousness? But, why does it take so long to become a butterfly?* Joan questioned, closing her eyes, slowly

receding into a place where everything is flowing just right, peaceful
and beautiful, into the land of butterflies, and sleep.

Chapter Ten: Lunch with Mom

Susan decided that it was time to get ready for her daughter's prom. She wanted to buy Joan a suitable dress for the occasion so she decided that taking her to lunch before going shopping would work out the best. They would have time to talk, discuss the options, and have a good time together.

Yes, talk, but about what? Joan's behavior had been so difficult for Susan to understand lately. She felt that she didn't know what her daughter was all about anymore, certainly not the usual teenager she had expected to raise. She was so different from all the other girls her age! That last encounter, when Joan ended up with the upper hand in their discussion, left Susan with a bitter taste in her mouth. Joan had done this so cleverly, so intelligently, that it was hard to take! Susan bit her lips remembering the feeling. Of course Henri didn't help either. He certainly took Joan's side, and she ended up looking foolish. Overwhelmed by all these disturbing feelings Susan felt perplexed and upset, but the urgency of a social imperative, the importance of her daughter's prom in this case, took over. Susan decided to plan this event with grace and show all of their friends in town what her family was really about. Joan would be the prom queen.

Henri was out of town for a week. Susan felt good thinking that she had Joan all to herself for that time. She would not have to worry about Henri's opinion, and besides, picking a dress was a woman's thing. No problem. Susan liked beautiful expensive clothes, preferably designer quality. She had a large collection of them in her closets along with interesting shoes, boots, and jewelry which matched the outfits perfectly. The feeling she got by walking into a party all decked out, all eyes in the room fixed upon her when she made her entrance, gave her a sense of what happiness is all about. Henri often remarked that he didn't like her to be so ostentatious, but he paid the bills without complaining and Susan had continued indulging her compulsion to be the best dressed woman in town.

Susan made reservations for lunch at a trendy little café with the option to sit out in the patio if the weather permitted, and the weather did. Mother and daughter arrived, promptly ushered to a table under an umbrella in a corner of the patio near the flower garden. In spite of the latest disagreements they had, Joan loved her mother a lot, and this occasion to be out with her in these beautiful surroundings forecast a happy exchange between the two of them. She felt at ease and excited.

"Mom, what a beautiful place! I'm happy to be here with you and to relax and connect in such a lovely setting. Your new, pretty spring dress looks great on you!"

"Thank you Joan. As you know, I like clothes. They make me feel good. There are not too many things which do this for me lately," Susan added with a sigh, "but I don't have to talk about that stuff. Let's just order and have a good time, okay?"

Joan was somewhat saddened by her mother's comment about not feeling good, but she decided to avoid the obvious question, keeping it for later. The café specialized in succulent crisp panini. There were so many different kinds it was difficult to choose. Susan decided to have a turkey and bacon with onion and tomato along with a mixed greens garden salad. Joan settled on a prosciutto panini served with melon on the side and she ordered the same salad as Susan. The two wanted iced tea with their lunch.

"Good choice!" the waitress said as she wrote the order for the two women. "I see you like our café. I have seen you before," she added, smiling at Susan.

"Yes, we like your place and I often come here with friends," Susan responded in an enthusiastic tone.

"Mom, I feel so fortunate with my life! I have the best place to live, nature all around me, parents who do their best to give me their love and an education, friends I enjoy, a very smart tutor who teaches me to think for myself. What else could I want in life at this point? I want to thank you and Dad for all this! Thank you."

"You are welcome, Joan. You certainly think for yourself, girl, and I don't know where all this education is taking you! Sometimes I don't have a clue where, and I can't keep up!"

"Don't worry, Mom. I'm just trying to be in touch with what is happening around me and what is happening in the world. I'm looking for a way to understand more of what my heart says, which could help change a few things my mind sees out there."

"You lost me, Joan. Sounds like Greek to me!"

"Well, Mom, as the Little Prince says, 'One only sees well with the heart, the essential is invisible to the eyes.' Simple. Take the petition to fire Mark Silver you guys are circulating. If I look at the essential with my heart, I see our planet, our beautiful Earth being threatened by climate change caused by human consumption of fossil fuels. I feel this with my heart. I see it as something essential we have to deal with. You guys look at it with the eyes of materialism and greed. You don't want to lose what you have and you only want to save what you see with the eyes, the status quo, even if it is destructive to the planet. That is why Mr. Silver has very consciously introduced this issue of climate change and its consequences in his class. He has spoken from his heart, and Mr. Field speaks only from his eyes in his church discourse. Can you see?"

"But Mr. Field is a religious man. He speaks the truth to the community. He has studied the problem and knows God's plans for humanity and the world. Mr. Field is a pillar of the church and our community. People believe him. I do too, Joan."

"Yes, Mom, but pillars are not always that strong. Some have termites in them and they deteriorate with time. Think of it!"

"Here are your beautiful orders," the waitress said, bringing the panini to the table. "I'll bring your salads shortly, and your teas," she added, putting the plates on the table.

Susan was speechless, frowning and breathing deeply. She made an effort to reply, "Thank you miss; it looks great!"

Joan's little speech had been hard for Susan to hear, but the logic of it was sound. If she stood for Mr. Field, was she a bad apple speaking from her eyes versus her heart? *Damn Mademoiselle Giroud*, she thought, *why did she have Joan read The Little Prince?* Susan knew of the story, but she never thought further than just reading it, never putting her heart into it! Here she was, in the same place as the other day, when she argued for the petition and Joan got the upper hand. Her daughter won the argument again and there was no glass of vodka here to help her calm down!

"What else has Mademoiselle Giroud put into your innocent ears Joan?" Susan said angrily. "Any of this socialist garbage the French people revel in? I think I will have a serious talk with her."

"We don't talk politics, Mom, but Mademoiselle helps me learn how to speak for myself and in the case of the petition, I am the one, along with Kristin, who decided that it is wrong to fire Mr. Silver and that is why we are protesting. Can you see that?"

"Okay. Let's eat our lunch," Susan responded, trying to get away from the conversation as the waitress was bringing the rest of the order. "Everything looks great, let's enjoy it."

They ate their lunch in silence. Susan was obviously angry but totally at a loss about what to say. It reminded Joan of the silence her dad observed when she announced to him that she wanted a Prius instead of a white Mercedes. The panini were delicious and so were the salads. It is amazing how good food always helps calm down bad feelings, and the two relished their lunch. It also gave them time to recover, even if the conclusion was not in total accord with their opinions. The seeds had been planted for Susan and compassion had grown for Joan toward her mother who had to sit through this deluge of new ideas coming from her 16-year-old, enough to drown a confirmed Christian!

"Do you want some dessert?" the waitress asked, bringing the menu.

"I'll have the *crème brulee*, of course," Susan replied even before opening the menu. "And you, Joan?"

"Make it two. I want to see whether it tastes as good as Martha's."

"Two *crème brulee*, then," the waitress wrote down, taking the menus back. "Good choice!"

"Joan, now we must talk seriously about the main reason I brought you here today. I think I already mentioned that we must go shopping for a prom dress after lunch, right? This is important to me. We are very well known around here and I want you to be gorgeous that day. You will be representing your dad and me to the school and the community."

Joan took a deep breath. She knew it was coming. The idea of going to a store, being fitted with a fancy long gown which would probably have to be altered, trying on shoes to match, probably with heels, parading around from one mirror to another—all this was appalling to her. She kept flashing back to the little pastel green dress she loved and white lacy Mary Jane shoes. She felt trapped. How would she solve this dilemma short of getting her mother very upset? Suddenly, because of the *crème brulee* the waitress was just bringing to them, she thought of Martha and had a great idea.

"Mom, can I ask you a question? If I'm not too nosy, can you tell me how much you pay Martha by the hour?"

"What in the world does this have to do with what I was talking about, Joan? Really, you are too much, girl. I'm giving up on you!"

"Don't give up, Mom. This is important and very relevant to our conversation. Maybe you can give me an idea of what you pay Martha?"

"Well, I don't know," Susan answered totally bewildered. "Probably the minimum wage in the state. Maybe $7.25 or $7.50? I really don't know, Joan, your father takes care of all that stuff. Don't forget that Martha and her husband live in a cottage behind our house rent free and drive the house car, miss snoopy."

"Thank you, Mom. It's okay, but will you make a deal with me? How much would you spend on a prom dress for me, with new shoes?"

"Joan. this is enough," Susan answered getting totally impatient. "Okay, if you want a figure. Yes, I will spend probably around $1000 for this whole thing, and you sure don't deserve it."

"Mom, calm down. The deal I want to make with you is simple. Please, let me wear my beautiful favorite green dress with the white Mary Jane shoes for the prom. I like it so much. And give the money you would have spent on a new dress for me to Martha and Claude to thank them for their great service over the years. They deserve it. Remember the *crème brulee*? You always take seconds, doesn't that deserve recognition?"

By now Susan was overwhelmed by emotions and had pushed away the *crème brulee* the waitress had put in front of her. Her face was contracted. Joan became concerned about her mother and got up behind her, rubbing her shoulders. "Mom, I'm so sorry to disappoint you about the dress, but I don't want you to buy it for me. It isn't what my heart wants. If I accept, I would go to the prom with bad feelings, thinking of so many girls who don't even have a simple dress to wear. Besides, my little green dress is so beautiful. You will be proud of me. Forgive me, Mom. I love you so much. What can I do to help?"

Susan was now filled with the love that Joan gave to her, transmitted through her gentle hands, and she simply answered, "Nothing, Joan, just be yourself, girl. Life has taken some strange turns for me lately, never would I have guessed." She slowly savored the rest of her *crème brulee*. "Actually, you saved us a trip to the store and I'm thankful because I am really tired," she added, looking exhausted. "Let's go home."

"Thank you for the delicious lunch, Mom. And thank you for your understanding. It must be difficult for you to hear some of the things I say to you!"

"Yes, Joan. It's tough. Your generation is something else. I don't understand what is happening these days and the world is definitely changing in more ways than one!"

The mother and daughter went home, somewhat exhausted but with good feelings in their hearts.

Wasn't that better than the last time we had a disagreement? Susan thought to herself, grinning. *And I didn't even need my vodka! Jesus! What's happening?*

Chapter Eleven: Petition or Rendition?
What Would Jesus Say?

The dreaded meeting with her mother had turned into a love connection between the two, and Joan was starting to feel closer to Susan. She had not actually done anything extraordinary, only being there and keeping her heart opened. *What do you know? All the answers flowed, just like that! It felt easy! Whoa,* Joan thought. *Is that what it takes to communicate even the most difficult things to people, an open heart? Thank you, Little Prince!*

Joan decided that she would visit her cave to think over the problem about the petition. Maybe there was a peaceful solution. She had to ponder how to work it out.

She changed her clothes, took her watch because she did not want to be late for dinner, and started walking to her favorite place. It was late afternoon in the meadow and she spotted a little garter snake slithering in the grass. Its skin shimmered in the sun.

"Good luck sign!" Joan exclaimed, circumventing the little reptile. "I hope you find something good to eat!"

Some frogs were croaking on the side of the pond and a couple of magpies flew over the big oak tree that she was lying under when she had her transcendental experience. Here everything was beautiful, magical. Everything made Joan feel at home in what she had called "my church."

Joan happily entered her cave. After greeting her friendly newt with a gentle smile, she sat on the rock which had become her favorite place to sit.

The place where I talk with my soul! she sighed, sitting comfortably.

After a short time during which she cleared her mind of thoughts, Joan felt refreshed and clear. She began thinking about the petition and if she and Kristin could bring people together for a friendly dialogue.

It would take Mr. Silver, naturally, whom neither her parents nor the Fields had met, but who could work wonders with his eloquence and charismatic personality! It would take Ellen, the girl in the senior class who got so alarmed and freaked out! It would be good to hear her honestly tell what happened. Who knows if she would do that. It would take Kristin and herself, the protesters, and her parents, who were now on her side. Joan thought that maybe the librarian, Ms. Stern, who had known Mark Silver since he started teaching at the school, could also be of help with her clear mind and open approach. The Fields, of course, would be the principal actors in this play. They started the whole thing with the petition.

Next Joan wondered who could help instigate the meeting. *Would the Fields want to meet with the culprits?* She thought for awhile, closing her eyes and remembering her father's reaction about Mr. Field. Her dad had not been too happy about the way this "pillar of the church" approached the issue, evoking God as the ultimate judge regarding climate change! *Maybe her dad could ask Mr. Field to call for the meeting and Mr. Field could not refuse because her dad was a senator in D.C., right?* The prestige of power at work! *That's it,* Joan decided, *Dad can do it, I'm sure.*

Then, an amazing idea came to Joan. *Mr. Field is a man of the church, so why don't we present the facts to him with a respectful religious approach? When Mr. Silver shows him the problems, he could ask Mr. Field what Jesus would do in this situation, or what Jesus would think. That just might work!*

Joan was delighted with this idea. Jesus was a loving person of course, his opinion would be the loving answer to the problem and Mr. Field could respect that. *This is brilliant,* Joan thought as she left the cave. Of course things would have to be organized to bring all these people together. *Perhaps Kristin would take that task,* Joan thought. *She is such a great organizer. I'll call her when I get back.*

As she returned to her bedroom, Joan found a text from Kristin, asking what was going on with the petition. She was anxious to get things rolling because the prom was coming up soon and people would get preoccupied with all those plans. *That's a good point,* Joan thought as she picked up the phone.

It took awhile for Joan to explain the details of her idea about setting up a meeting between all these people to have a dialogue. It required so much coordination! Kristin thought that the idea of bringing Jesus in as a loving judge after Mark Silver presented the problem was brilliant.

"Of course, saving our planet Earth and saving the species, including human species, from destruction caused by man's actions would be right up Jesus' alley. He was a loving man who could see through the selfish reasoning of the special interest groups," Kristin agreed. The girls knew in their hearts what Jesus would have said, and it would give Mr. Field a lot to think about when he was asked!

In spite of the prom getting close and the petition being finalized, the girls decided that it would probably take a week to contact everybody and arrange the meeting. The most important detail was for Joan's dad to get Mr. Field to agree to discuss this at the next church meeting, under the pretext of urgency regarding the petition against Mark Silver. Then Mark Silver had to agree to present his case to the group, this time to a not-so-friendly group. Moreover, he would have to accept that Jesus's opinion would punctuate his presentation. What a different way for a scientist to introduce serious scientific facts! But Mark Silver's job was in the balance and he might understand this smart way to plan the encounter, considering the protagonists. Ellen might be a problem; if she is afraid of her parents she might freak out again. Ms. Stern would be happy to help and a great ally in the discussion. Finally, Kristin suggested that the Fields' best friends, who had been adamant in helping write the petition, should be involved to make sure the Fields would have allies present.

The strategy was set in action. Joan and Kristin felt that they had planned a diplomatic encounter between serious adversaries and they laughed at the idea. Is this how it works between nations when they get together, they wondered? Probably! Except Jesus may not be involved in the debate. What about Allah? Maybe all religions in the world could be present!

Now they divided the work between the two. First, the meeting would take place a week from Saturday after church. Joan would get her dad to ask Mr. Field, his wife and daughter, to come and would encourage them to invite their friends, the Smiths. Mr. Field would be told of Mark Silver's presence. Kristin would contact Mark Silver, explaining to him that Jesus would be his ally in presenting the global warming situation and he would probably laugh! Kristin would also contact Ms. Stern, explaining that since she had known Mark Silver for a long time, her opinion would be very valuable.

It had been a long day. Joan was exhausted but very happy. She went down to the dining room ready to meet her parents. She no longer felt apprehensive about seeing them for one reason or another. Something inside told her that a barrier had been broken and that love had done the trick. *Goodbye fear,* she thought, *I can see my parents with my heart! The Little Prince is quite a teacher!*

Convincing her dad to ask Mr. Field to call the meeting and invite his friends to attend was a shoo-in for Joan, and her mother went along, no problem. Kristin had success with Mark Silver, who laughed a lot at the idea of being backed up by Jesus in his presentation. Ms. Stern felt honored to join the dialogue. The date seemed to work okay for everyone, so the ball was rolling toward the following Saturday after church, and the girls were happy to have pulled it together! *It's a little over a week from now! That's a long time away!*

Everything went so well, so fast, the girls were now stuck waiting patiently for the meeting, and waiting patiently is not an easy task when you are sixteen! No more endorphins rush, strategic planning, or fancy dream expectations. Joan and Kristin went back to their daily school routine with the anticlimactic feeling of having left something important unfinished. Routine! What a drag! They went to classes, did their homework, talked to their friends and teachers, ate at the cafeteria, dealt with family obligations, but mostly they counted the days, talking to each other on the phone to strengthen their optimism for a positive result. Actually, they achieved quite a lot at school in the meantime. Things which perhaps had been somewhat neglected during their planning stage came to fruition. Joan had a successful French lesson where she exposed her love of the Little Prince's philosophy, told Mademoiselle the whole story about planning for the meeting, in French of course, and learned that Mademoiselle went on another date with Mark Silver. This time, they had taken a long walk together and Mademoiselle seemed very happy! That was great news!

Time has a way of passing quickly, however, and the day of the meeting finally arrived. Joan woke up early. The dialogue wasn't scheduled until after the church service, so she decided to spend some time in her own church in the woods. She ran through the meadow, her arms up toward the sky, singing, "Yay!"

Yay, like a little child in awe of being alive! She felt excited, thankful, and happy. She needed to say it to someone; maybe she needed to pray or something?

Pray, Really? Whom would she pray to? She asked herself, *God? Who is God? Is it someone sitting on the clouds, a man surrounded with angels and demons who personify the good and evil in humanity?* Her early days of going to church with her parents had not provided an answer. The image her mind conjured up suddenly cut Joan's joy way down. She felt that her heart needed to go beyond her mind to find the answer and she decided to go sit in her cave to find it.

Sitting on her rock in semi-darkness, Joan began to clear her mind of thoughts. Something like a meditation, she imagined, even though she had never learned how to do it. She wanted to reach a place where she would feel comfortable thanking someone or something. *Who, what?* She wanted to give thanks for being alive. She slowly let her mind melt into a field of space filled with intelligent energy and dancing clouds. She felt her heart opening until it took over and she intuitively addressed the universe, smiling from somewhere deep inside. *I am alive, this is beautiful, what a gift I have received from you! Universe, you are where everything started, you are the one who holds the secret, the secret my mind cannot explain but that my heart can feel! Everything you have created with your loving energy is amazing. The Earth, the flowers, the animals, the human beings, and here I am, a tiny part of it all, thank you, thank you, for my life and for the joy I feel inside… and, please, Universe, I pray you will help the world evolve into its next step, to get out of the cocoon. Please let humans stop killing the Earth you have made. It is so good and beautiful. Please let them stop killing each other and open their hearts.* Joan stopped for a few minutes feeling the warmth of her heart flood her body. *Thank you, Universe, and also please help us and help the meeting go well,* Joan concluded, coming back to her ordinary mind, now feeling the urgency of the upcoming work at stake.

"What time is it?" she asked, looking at her watch.

Well… the church meeting is starting in 15 minutes! Let the force be with me! she implored, resolutely walking out of the cave.

Joan walked, or rather ran, to the meeting, which fortunately was not far away. Everyone was already sitting in a circle chatting, and Mr. Silver just finished putting a poster on a board next to the door, but covered the poster with a sheet of paper.

"Joan, where have you been?" Susan asked with a big sigh while showing Joan a seat next to hers. "I guess I should know," she added, nodding. "Please sit down. Everyone has already introduced themselves."

"Thank you all for coming to this unusual meeting, prompted by the need to make a decision concerning a petition you all know about by now," Mr. Field started, "and our minister has been kind enough to let us use this facility. We will need to decide at the end of the meeting what to do with this petition. We have gathered signatures but decided it was appropriate to meet Mr. Mark Silver, the science teacher at our local high school, and let him present his side of this alarming situation before we go further." Mr. Field concluded. Looking across the room to Mark Silver, "Mark, we are here to listen."

Mark Silver came forward, looking elegant in a checkered blue shirt and tailored jeans. His sparkling blue eyes stood out, giving an impression of lightness and charm. Taking a deep breath he began speaking, "I am happy to be here with all of you. I'll do my best today to be informative and clear. Let me start with the recognition that we are all biological human beings here, and the most important thing we can do is to align ourselves with nature and with our biology. Our biology represents our limitation as humans. Although mankind can go beyond and reach illusory frontiers, we should never forget this. What good will it do to send a man to Mars in five years if we cannot resolved our problems here on Earth? Are we just trying to escape? What good is technology to save people that get cancer from polluted water and air, if we don't also address the aspects of pollution that are man-made and possibly avoidable? We are polluting the Earth is beginning to talk back to us and we need to listen."

"But before I go on, I want to ask if Ellen will participate. Ellen was in my science class and it was her concerns that it resulted in this petition. So Ellen, can you explain to us what bothered you so much that made you, as your friends said, 'freak out' and leave the science class? What was going on in your head?"

Ellen's face was white as a sheet. She looked as if she would pass out. Her mother intervened to encourage her, "Go on, Ellen. Tell him why you left class when he talked about all the horrible things that he says will happen from global warming. Please tell him what you told me."

Ellen took a deep breath and timidly answered, "I got scared by what you said and I left the class because of it. I couldn't take it."

"You know, I understand why you might react that way, because what I said is scary. I talked about the possibility of a sixth mass extinction in the world from the ill effects of CO_2 and methane gas, which some scientists predict is possible in the future. But I also made a point that it can be avoided if we pay attention to climate change, remember?"

"Yes, but my parents think climate change is a hoax! And they don't believe that global warming is real," Ellen answered blushing. "I told them that what you said was wrong so I left."

"Okay, thank you for telling me so clearly what bothered you, Ellen. So maybe I need to explain to this group why I think I said something right," Mark Silver continued, looking straight at his audience with the confidence of a man who knows what he is talking about.

"Can you give us some facts, irrefutable facts I mean," Henri intervened, "for why carbon dioxide levels and methane gas create rising temperatures and cause climate change in the world?"

"I'm a scientist in good faith and have researched this problem for years. Burning fossil fuels produces carbon dioxide and methane gas—last year in record proportions, and levels are rising more every day. The gasses create an ozone layer so thick that it traps in the Earth's heat, which would normally dissipate out in the atmosphere. The record high temperatures all over the world are settling mostly in the oceans. Ice is melting at the North and South Poles and sea levels are rising. Even the coral reefs where fish live are dying. That's not good! The oceans affect the whole planet. What we have witnessed lately—heat and cold waves, rainstorms, hurricanes, flooding, melting glaciers, destruction of coral reefs, and health problems in humans—will keep growing in dire proportions. There is also the adverse effect of deforestation all over the world, since forests create oxygen that reduce the carbon dioxide. Can you see how crucial it is to start taking strong measures to remedy these things to prevent disasters?"

Mark Silver was visibly moved and stopped talking, scanning the audience to observe. Everybody was silent including Henri, who asked the question. Thinking he may not have been scientific enough in conveying facts, Mark Silver continued by pulling some papers out of his briefcase. "Here, I prepared a list of websites you can go to and read about the research by scientists who have studied the problem. They provide lots of figures and data."

Mark passed the lists around as people were still processing the bad news and wondering what to say about this deluge of dire predictions. Mark saw the dilemma, knowing it was depressing, "But, there is some good news… it's not too late to do something if we act now. We can accept that climate change is happening and reduce fossil fuel consumption to stop destroying the Earth and ourselves. We need to start right now!" he punctuated, adamant in his assertion. "Right now, before it is too late."

The group was quiet. What do you say in the presence of a person who is supposed to be an expert when he gives you facts and hands you homework to study? Minds were running in all directions during the silence, and if someone could look inside their heads, it may have been something like this.

Mr. Field: Why did I have to schedule this meeting? The guy is smart, there is no doubt about that. Now I'll have to explain why I think global warming is a hoax! I don't even know why myself! Damn, it is so much easier to listen to a newscast give you the truth and forget about environmental experts. After all, the media knows what the score is, right? And the version we hear from most of them is contrary to what this Mr. Silver is saying. Why? I'm lost!

Mrs. Field: I wonder why Ellen is so afraid of everything. She used to freak out only at home when we told her something she didn't want to hear. Should I have her see a therapist? I thought that church would be enough help for her. She did well today though.

Mr. Smith: I'm sorry that I accepted the Fields' invitation to this meeting. I was going to get ready for my fishing trip tomorrow and now I will have to sit through this stupid talk for another hour, probably.

Mrs. Smith: What if all that this guy says is true? We could see horrible things happen in the world in our lifetime. The weather is already so terrible with the floods and the hurricanes, that's true! Okay, we have at least 20 or 30 good years ahead still. How glad I am I don't have any kids!

Ms. Stern: Mark Silver did a great job. I always knew he was a brilliant teacher. I wonder what else he has to say. I wish I knew what's behind the paper on his poster. A surprise in store?

Henri: What will happen to my BP stocks if we have to reduce or eliminate fossil fuel consumption? The guy is right though, we are moving toward a catastrophic rise in CO_2. Shit! What about fracking? Is the groundwater is being polluted by chemicals? I wish I could turn the clock back 30 years to when I was doing well and these problems didn't exist!

Susan: Joan gets us into some difficult places. I always thought she was not normal, and now I'm sure of it. She is so loving though. What a beautiful girl I have! I must remember that. That's probably the most important thing!

Ellen: Well, I didn't freak out this time! Maybe I shouldn't be afraid to think about this stuff Mr. Silver is saying! Plus he's so good looking… but I won't tell that to mom. Then she might want to keep the petition going!

Kristin: Good job, Mark! But there is even more to say. You didn't speak about the special interests groups yet, that are misleading people about all this! Maybe this poster has something to do with it?

Joan: I am keeping my fingers crossed. It should go well. Mark Silver is a great speaker and I hope he can convince everyone in the end. But he hasn't mentioned Jesus yet, probably keeping him for the coup de grace at the end!

Mark: Difficult to speak to people who are not very conscious about pollution. They are difficult to reach. I hope the poster will help do the trick. I wish Monique were here. They should have invited her!

Their minds wandered according to their subconscious programming, but there was one thing they all had in common… they would welcome a break! After Mark Silver's speech and dialog with a few people in the audience, they needed to relax their minds before hearing more. They knew something else was in store. Henri had brought some wine from his cellar and Susan some cookies baked by Martha. After all, Henri had instigated the meeting and he knew that Mr. Field was a wine lover. The young people would drink soda provided by Mr. Field, the soft drinks distributor for the county. Joan and Kristin would make an exception and ignore the sugar content.

It was a great break. A glass of wine helped the adults relax and the sodas energized the younger crowd. Global warming was gone from everybody's mind for the moment! Mr. Smith forgot his fishing trip while talking with Henri about the stock market. Ellen made friends with Joan and Kristin, who told her that she did well by talking freely at the meeting. Ms. Stern told Mark Silver that he could use the library's collection of articles on global warming any time he wanted, and the Fields felt like the gracious hosts of this very strange party which had not yet come to its focal point: petition or rendition. Would they be moved to a new interpretation of the scientific information on global warming?

After everyone returned to their seats, Mr. Field addressed Mark Silver, asking him to be brief because time was running out for use of the facility. Mark promised to do his best but that what he had to say now was probably the key to helping improve the climate change situation, which was progressing at an alarming rate.

"No one here has asked the question yet of why there is no effort to fix the climate change problem right away by getting to the root of it," Mark Silver started. "In this case, considering fossil fuels' detrimental influence, why are we not trying to limit or stop it and replace it with other more renewable sources of energy."

Now Mr. Field jumped in, "Why should we listen to people like you tell us what to do when obviously we hear others deny your 'facts' and tell us that global warming is a hoax? Those scientists have just as much credibility as you do! The news is full of facts regarding their point of view."

"I totally agree with that," Mr. Smith interrupted, nodding his head. "Ecologists and green advocates want to destroy our well-functioning institutions by threatening us with doom and making us fearful. That's exactly what you did in your classroom, Mark, and that is why we want you gone. Do you understand?" he concluded in an angry tone.

The discussion reached its apex. Mark Silver had expected it at some point and was prepared with an answer. He took a deep breath and summoned his rational voice as best he could. "Mr. Smith, I understand what you are saying. Some media outlets have presented the climate change problem in a totally different light. And what if I told you that the sponsors of these outlets are the ones who are afraid? The sponsors are afraid because they have too much to lose, so they make money the bearer of truth in our country. They are so afraid that they will spend millions of dollars to hire bogus scientists who have no real credentials to back them up in very clever ways. They hire people to misrepresent the scientific evidence and say it is a hoax. Just look at the ads! These days money is the mighty power behind it all. ”

The audience was quiet. Mark Silver's strong, vehement but quiet voice struck a chord in the room. He said something important to consider, whichever side of the political arena someone occupied. Did the sponsors of the ads pay people to say things that were not true? The girls listened, fascinated by his presence and authority. Henri scratched his head, thinking that his 1% status made him suspect. Mr. Smith wondered for a moment about his favorite newscast, if the news was affected by sponsors.

There was one more thing Mark Silver had not presented. What was on the secret poster hanging by the door? What was hidden there? Mark Silver stood up, walked over to the covered poster, and slowly revealed its content.

“I brought this poster here to illustrate a point about how long it can take for people to understand what is dangerous for their health,” he said. “I hope this climate change problem and its remedy will not take so long and that out biology can endure. This is an opportunity for our awareness to evolve and for humanity to work together to bring out our better nature.”

The poster was a replica of an ad for cigarettes, dating back to the 1920s or 1930s. It depicted a beautiful girl with a cigarette in her mouth, joyously dancing what seemed to be the Charleston, while a gorgeous man looking like Clark Gable stood in the background applauding. He also was also smoking. A camel and a pack of the brand name were visible in the corner. The audience looked at the poster, immediately understanding the analogy between cigarettes as a detriment to our heath and global warming. Some nodded, others pursed their lips.

“I won't elaborate on the time, effort, and money the tobacco industry used to deny, explain, further tempt, addict, and deceive the public and the medical establishment about smoking. We all know now where it leads—to cancer. Some companies now continue deceiving by cleverly introducing e-cigarettes as a substitute. They add flavors to attract young people to a new habit, which might revive the need for tobacco. The desire for profit motivates this industry. They want to get people addicted, although they know our biology is fragile! We fought this deception because we don't want to be poisoned anymore.

Tobacco, drugs, fossil-fuel emissions in the air, and chemicals that pollute our water; they are poisoning us. We must understand and align ourselves with nature and our biological limits. If we want to live healthy lives and survive on Earth, global warming must be taken seriously."

The audience was quiet. Mr. Smith walked out of the room waving at the group, probably on his way fishing, as his wife remained seated, looking sad and concerned. Mark Silver stopped for awhile, pensive. He looked tired, then he suddenly remembered Kristin's funny recommendation and turned to Mr. Field, having regained his composure.

"Mr. Field, I have an important question for you. You are a man of the church, so you must know in your heart that the right attitude is to save people from sickness and disaster. What interests are at stake here? What do you think Jesus would say or do if He were presented with this problem?"

The unexpected question baffled Mr. Field. He was taken aback. He first looked annoyed, then closed his eyes for a long time while heads turned in his direction, waiting. He finally said in a guttural voice, "Jesus would do what he did before. He would tip over the money changer's table!" Mr. Field had gotten the final analogy.

"I guess the meeting is over, folks. Thank you all for coming and thank you Mr. Silver for the presentation. Considering what we have learned today, I think we should drop the petition. You have earned my respect," he added, looking towards Mark Silver.

Joan and Kristin broke out is a big smile and did a high five. Ellen joined them timidly while Mrs. Field looked at her daughter with surprise. Ms. Stern teared up from relief as she said goodbye to Mark. Mrs. Smith felt embarrassed when she left, making excuses for her husband's departure. Henri grabbed Susan's hand and they went to shake hands with Mark Silver, who was happily on his way out. Mr. Field shook his head and kissed the cross hanging around his neck. The court of law had adjourned. It had been a just and honest trial!

Chapter Twelve: Getting To Know You. Getting To Know All About You!

Joan was feeling very relieved after the meeting. The difficult logistics of a full protest against the petition was avoided, with some embarrassment and some grace on the part of Mr. Field. Joan could never have guessed that the man she pictured as the pillar of the church, a pillar full of termites as she had said, was actually solid! She laughed at what imagination can do when one feels angry at someone! Taking an approach with love and understanding worked it's magic again, and she nodded in approval. *There is still so much in the world to work on and it's so hard to keep the loving cap on!* Joan thought, closing her eyes. *But I must go on, I must keep my heart open and flowing. This is the way to see and understand the essential, as the Little Prince said!*

Joan and Kristin felt like heroes when they returned to school Monday morning. They told their friends what happened during the dialogue against the petition. Mark Silver's reputation grew instantly. He probably noticed it when his classes suddenly became more popular. Ms. Stern also spread the news on her side, distributing information about climate change in the library. There was a new energy in the school, one of confident hope for the future and free speech for resolution of difficult matters. Students couldn't define it, but they felt it. Something like a triumph of progress versus old restrictions, and they walked a little straighter with their heads high as a result.

Joan saw Phillip in English class. He waved at her from the front row with thumbs up. *He heard the news of course,* Joan thought. Everybody had heard the news by now, but Joan wanted to talk to Phillip again. She was going to the prom with this young man, this poet, this guy she resonated with and yet she knew so little about him. They had talked in depth really only once at school, the day he read the butterfly poem. Maybe she could invite him to her place to visit and make plans for the prom.

Besides Kristin, Mademoiselle, and later Mark Silver, few people had ever visited Joan's place. She felt a certain reluctance to invite friends over. The ostentatious mansion with its park, woods, landing strip and hangar for her Dad's jet, indoor pool, tennis court, tropical veranda, servant's quarters—all these amenities defined a certain lifestyle she didn't want to explain. She was not ashamed of it, that was not the problem, but she felt embarrassed by her privileged status, embarrassed by the opulence she knew would shock her guests who would not know how to deal with their feelings.

Joan bit the bullet and asked Phillip to come home with her after school the next day so they could talk about the prom and get to know each other better. Phillip accepted gladly, encouraged by the friendliness of this girl he felt more and more attracted to. He was curious about her place, having heard comments about how sumptuous it was. Phillip's mother was a hairdresser in town, and women had a talent for revealing all sorts of secrets, longings and problems while they sat in his mother's chair! Phillip was told some echoes of those revelations and imagined, with his poet's mind, the fairy tale castle Joan lived in, complete with a prince riding up on a white horse. He didn't even have a horse! Shucks!

Phillip and Joan walked together to her house after school the next day. He jokingly apologized for leaving his horse in the pasture under the pretext that he preferred holding the princess's hand. Joan laughed, knowing what kind of image people painted about her residence. She answered that he would not find a dragon to fend off when they arrived, but if he wanted to offer his hand she would gladly accept it for protection! After these imaginative preliminaries the two were free to hold hands and walk with a light heart.

"Wow!" Phillip exclaimed when they came to the gate. "I saw this place from a distance but it was partly hidden by the fence. You have quite a mighty castle here, princess," Phillip concluded, very impressed. "How am I going to take you to the prom? Without a horse or even a donkey!" he continued, laughing. "I guess we'll have to settle for your chauffeur if he can drive us there."

"No problem, Phillip. Claude will be happy to take us. Wait 'til you meet him, he's a real nice guy. I've known him since I was born," Joan answered, reassured by the light approach Phillip had taken on his arrival at her place. She quickly gave him a tour of the house and surroundings, pointing to the meadow and the woods in the distance as her favorite place, stopping by the tennis court where Susan was hitting balls with her teacher to introduce Phillip. "Mom, this is Phillip, the one taking me to the prom."

"Hi Phillip," Susan said between two ball exchanges. "I'm happy to meet you. You are a lucky guy. Joan is very choosy! Sorry but we have to finish this match," she concluded, waving at the two with her racket.

"Mom loves playing tennis," Joan said in an excusing tone. "She stays very fit that way."

"I can see, and she's pretty too." Phillip complimented. "The princess has a real mother, not a cruel step mother. I like that!"

"Phillip, shall we put the fairy tale book back on the shelf, find a comfortable place to sit, and come back to a different reality? I want to take you to the veranda, the place Kristin, Mademoiselle, and Mark Silver met with me to plan our strategy to fight the petition. It is very private and warm in there and we can talk quietly."

Joan and Phillip walked to the veranda. It had been cleaned recently and the place sparkled in its tropical warmth. Victor greeted them with a long hello from the top of the banana tree. The waterfall worked its magic on the two friends with its appealing sounds and they headed for the orange seats next to it.

"Paradise," Phillip said, taking a big deep breath as he stretched out in his chair. "What else would you want in life? You do the talking, Joan. I'll enjoy the present moment!" he added, closing his eyes.

"Phillip, I want to repeat how much I was moved by the butterfly poem you read in English class. Like you, I'm very conscious of what is happening to our precious Earth and I want to do something about it in my own small way. Stopping the petition against Mark Silver gives me renewed courage. "

"It sure was a success, Joan. You and Kristin did a super job," Phillip said, sitting up in his chair, "but will we ever be able to find a way to protect our natural resources and the environment against the greed of the rich corporations who won't let go of what they have? They will fight tooth and nail to keep the status quo as they continue the destruction by poisoning, polluting, killing, and digging further into a wounded Earth. I get so sad and discouraged, Joan. It looks like a losing battle!" Phillip concluded, angry and out of breath.

"I know, Phillip, I've seen you get discouraged. The goal looks impossible to reach! I'm very conscious of this myself since my parents belong to the rich upper class. I'm embarrassed by the opulence of our lifestyle, and sometimes worry about where the money comes from. I'm determined to do something about the problems caused by putting money first. I have already started, slowly, in my own small way!"

"Joan, I know, I trust you. Do you know what my dad heard on National Public Radio this morning? They said that 5% of Americans have now have 70% of our country's wealth while the working class and the poor have only 5% of the wealth between all of them! Imagine! Isn't it a startling figure? It reveals the absolute dissolution of our democracy? We don't live in a democracy anymore, Joan. We live in a plutocracy."

"A plutocracy? What is that? Can you explain it for me?" Joan asked intrigued.

"My dad explained this term after he heard the figures. It means a country completely ruled by the controlling class of rich men. So money makes the law."

"Phillip, I'm starting to be aware of this and I can see that as long as it stays that way, chances are slim that the Earth, the environment, the species and even our own health will be a priority. So now it looks like we are either on the slow path toward a sixth mass extinction of the living species on Earth or a revolutionary expansion of people's consciousness, growing because they want to save themselves and future generations from the upcoming catastrophe. It will be do or die!"

Joan remained silent for awhile. Phillip was squirming in his chair, restless and obviously stressed. Joan wanted so badly to help calm his mind and give him something positive to hang on to. She put her hands on his shoulder, the way she had relieved her mother's stress at the restaurant. After awhile she said, "Think of it this way, Phillip. What if the power of consciousness started replacing the power of money? Consciousness is not a thing, like money is. Consciousness is a big form of energy, a powerful factor, a new dimension of our awareness just beginning to be explored and spread through people's minds! I saw it at the meeting the other day. Mr. Field had a reversal of awareness concerning the petition! Consciousness could expand and spread among us all and do the trick," Joan affirmed with a large smile. "We must not forget the metamorphosis, Phillip. Remember the butterfly?"

"Yes, but how can you expand the consciousness of the corporations? They are not people, they are entities," Phillip replied. "Entities are not humans. They don't have a heart!"

"Entities don't have a heart, but the people on their boards do. For example, My dad might be ready now to change his voice on the board of the BP Corporation! Especially since one of his friends from Texas who had a boating business, taking people on fishing trips, told him recently that his customers were appalled recently by the horrible condition of the water in the gulf. The fishermen hardly caught anything! My dad's friend was so disgusted that he sold his business and his boats, and he even told my dad that he was going to put solar panels on his roof! This kind of stuff marks a person. When it happens in your backyard it changes your awareness and becomes irrefutable. It can happen with lots of other examples of pollution which are harmful. Remember Love Canal?"

"Joan, you are a dreamer! Your optimism is contagious! A beautiful and lovely dreamer you are, so lovely that I want to kiss you," Phillip said, looking into Joan's eyes for a moment. He moved closer to her and took her into his arms. "May I, Joan?" The invitation was very gentle. Joan nodded yes, closing her eyes.

The kiss was very sweet and it lasted for awhile. How do you describe the love passing between two very awake young people who have the energy of being alive flowing through their body and the spirit of their heart flooding their mind? No one could ever describe this exquisite moment. You could only feel it.

Victor punctuated the kiss with cooing noises. The waterfall continued its rhythmic flow and the present moved to its next phase for the two young teens, whose eyes were so brilliant from their experience that anyone looking at them and those eyes would have to put on his sunglasses!

"Joan, I think I am falling in love with you real big," Phillip said, gently. "What did we say we were going to accomplish during this meeting? Anything else," he continued, stretching his arms, smiling. "besides this incredible moment?"

"I wanted to talk about ourselves and our families and how to organize the prom event, right?" Joan said, laughing. "So first, you tell me about your father, the one who listens to public radio and tells you these important things he hears. Is he a political activist?"

"No, Joan. My father is a nurse. Just a political observer, I guess. Yes, a male nurse at the Sunrise Hospital. There are not too many guys in that job! He is very intelligent and educated. He reads a lot. The patients love him because of his optimism and his way of comforting them after surgery or difficult tests. He has done a lot of research on the body and mind connection. His "thing" as he says, is that the body knows how to heal itself without drugs. Of course he cannot say that around the other medical professionals and would never interfere with their prescriptions, but he helps patients become aware of the inner power the body has to use its internal pharmacy, and of ways to use their minds to access it. Some catch on and it works well! There is naturally some psychology involved, in the belief system, but my father has a very simple way to explain the process. I love my dad and I admire him. We are great friends!"

"What about your mother, Phillip? Is she also educated and so helpful with the people she works with?" Joan asked, very curious.

"In a way my mother also helps the people she works with, yes. She has only a high school education but she is very keen psychologically! My mother is a hair dresser. She hears a lot of stories from her customers. They dump their problems on her; she listens with love and understanding and sometimes puts in a good word to make them think and maybe change their minds about something like a divorce or a child's punishment. She doesn't talk much it with us at home, except when she feels she has accomplished a miracle by helping someone turn around a really bad decision. Then she is so excited you can't help rejoicing with her! My parents give me their love and are good role models. I have learned service to others from them."

"My parents love me very much also," Joan replied, "but they mostly give me their love through things. Lots of things. Nothing is ever good enough, expensive enough, beautiful enough. Take this veranda, for instance, which my dad had a contractor build for me as a tropical paradise to escape the bad Arkansas weather! And I have really enjoyed it, I must say! My mother loves expensive clothes, fancy parties, and rich friends. Sometimes I feel like something is missing in my parents' relationship, and maybe they aren't too happy. I heard my father say that life is lousy. You know, Phillip, we were talking about consciousness. I think they live in a different kind of consciousness than me. I don't blame them for it. I would like to be a role model for them like your parents have been for you, to help them discover a larger dimension of their minds. I think they got a lesson at the meeting, seeing Mr. Field reverse his opinion the other day! I love my parents a lot, Phillip, but they belong to a different generation and think differently from me."

Joan and Phillip had talked a long time about their totally different families, and were beginning to feel tired. The essentials of what they each learned from their family was revealed. It was a good feeling and they were at peace with what they found out. Joan and Phillip also had a tacit agreement about all that they had discussed. The kiss was an important new communion for their souls. Lots and lots of new feelings and thoughts for the two young teens to integrate! Lots of new energy to process!

Soon it would be time for dinner. Phillip wanted to return home to help his mother, and Joan had to prepare a paper for her French class that evening. The two friends looked at each other with the sense that love gives to those who have crossed the barrier from almost strangers into close souls, and they smiled at each other tenderly. There was a clumsy moment figuring out what to do next, then Phillip stood up and walked toward the veranda door accompanied by Joan and Victor who was singing his strange "bye, bye" farewell. Phillip kissed Joan's hand while looking into her eyes lovingly; then he resolutely walked out without looking back. He would never forget this first visit to his princess's castle.

Chapter Thirteen: Let's Take a Break!

Joan's feelings were challenged by her interaction with Phillip. Her heart was bursting with love while her mind was trying to sort everything out. She wavered between a sense of total abandon and one of restraint. There was no question she was attracted to Phillip and the kiss had been a flight into a place of utter delight, somewhere out there, some place she had not quite encountered before. *I guess it's love*, she thought, something like what she felt for her parents, her friends, the Earth, nature, the animals: a feeling of oneness with them, of belonging, a feeling which came from her essence, warm and all encompassing. *Yes, but this time, something was different.* There was an energy in her body which made her tingle. Joan pondered for a moment trying to understand the difference. *Is this a sex-driven feeling unleased by my hormones?* Joan considered this very scientifically with her rational mind, as she started laughing. *Yes, I guess no human being can escape this part of humanity! And I am just a human being like any other one, and this nature-driven part is what causes so many problems for people in the world, right?* She pursed her lips. *The sex drive is often confused with love! No wonder it's so hard to separate. The feelings go hand in hand and the results can be disastrous, as I have seen in the movies and read in some books!* Joan frowned, putting both hands around her head, thinking of all the problems this feeling creates when things go wrong. Joan wanted to shut off her mind! *Please, Universe help me, I give up!* Joan concluded, overwhelmed by the dilemma.

Susan interrupted Joan's psychological pondering by bursting into the veranda, dripping with sweat from her tennis match. "Who was this poorly dressed kid you brought to meet me at the court, Joan? You said he's the one taking you to the prom? Why in the world didn't you pick Roger? At least he looks like a civilized guy! I guess you have some weird reason for your choice!"

"Mom, Phillip is a very intelligent and conscious person. He's a really good poet and the best student in our English class. You should hear some of his poetry. It is so beautiful!"

"Okay, a poet! That is not going to take him very far in life. Your father was writing poetry too when I met him, but I'm glad he decided to take a different direction. Poetry doesn't make money, Joan, and you need a lot of money to live on these days! It's getting harder and harder. Wake up girl. Start looking at your future and stop associating with hopeless relationships and causes! They won't take you anywhere!"

Joan felt shattered inside. She visualized the beauty of the loving moments she just experienced with Phillip drowned in a pool of black dirty oil. It was obvious her mother was in the money game. Joan could have cried, but suddenly her sadness changed to compassion for this woman, her mother, who was coming from a different place in her consciousness, like Mr. Field before he heard Mark Silver speak. Joan loved her mother. She did not know what to say, but she decided to remain silent and to walk slowly out of the room, knowing that the time had not come yet for her mother to understand her. *Some day she will get it*, Joan thought, *when she gets out of her chrysalis!*

Joan walked up to her bedroom. She needed to take a break before dinner. The events of the day had been very intense and she had a text from Kristin waiting for her! Kristin wanted to know how the visit with Phillip went. Joan threw her phone on her bed, feeling exhausted and perplexed. She didn't know if she should continue the mad intensity of the day by answering curious questions from her friend, or just close her eyes and rest her mind for awhile. She opted for the latter and sat on her chair by the bureau, relieved by her decision.

It was good for Joan to let her mind go quiet into meditation, something she had found to relieve the chaos of thoughts which often cluttered her head. After the silent break, she was usually able to synthesize what had happened into some form of a satisfying explanation for the previous uneasy feeling. It seemed to work again this time. After her quiet pause—which lasted for some 15 minutes or so—Joan felt refreshed and clear, as if she were watching a movie. The events of the past couple weeks paraded rapidly in front of her eyes, including the latest vision of what was on the news. Images of catastrophic hurricanes, floods, fires, and mud slides. People were screaming and crying, children were running toward their parents;

in third world countries wars were decimating emaciated populations and some countries fought against each other trying to decide whether they would keep their independence or revert to an old system they had lived with for a long time. It was messy and bloody. Pollution was bringing global warming to new catastrophic proportions and the world seemed upside down! Joan wondered whether everybody had this image of where things were, if they were feeling that something was wrong in today's world or if the routine and demand of their daily lives threw a veil of denial over the situation. She smiled, realizing that in spite of all this utter chaos, she also had experienced something extraordinary. Her first beautiful kiss from Phillip today! *Life is such an incredible force*, Joan thought, feeling the happiness of being alive, *Everything is stirring in the chrysalis!*

An image from *The Little Prince* came to her mind, helping Joan understand the unstoppable dance of the world in a vicious circle. It was that of the lamp lighter who could not keep up with his job of turning the lights on and off on his planet because his planet turned faster and faster around the sun. He was used to orders which he could not stop obeying and because his planet was turning now once a minute, he could not do it! Joan thought for awhile about this analogy with the way our world is now moving furiously faster with modern technology, accelerating orders which we cannot stop obeying. *What are these orders? Where do they come from? Are they dictated by our obsolete subconscious? The part of our human brain which makes up the 95% against the 5% conscious part which is only now beginning to evolve into a new dimension, with the help of our hearts? We have evolved a lot from the animal stage where we started*, Joan thought, *but there is so much more to do with our conscious mind! Will human beings be able to make that evolutionary step before they drown in orders from their subconscious? Can reason replace the outdated wiring in our unconscious brain? Can anybody see this evolution in consciousness?*

Joan decided that she was now ready to answer Kristin's curious questions about her visit with Phillip. She joked about the fairy tale fantasy which had helped him feel easier about discovering her surroundings. "It was sweet. He acted like he was entering a castle and I was the princess," Joan described.

"You certainly are, Joan. The veranda must have blown his mind!"

"It did, but he didn't lose his composure. We talked seriously about our families at length, and guess what?"

"I think I know. Phillip kissed you, right?"

"Yes, he did! And it was very, very nice. He is such a sweet guy! He even asked permission, which I gave gladly!"

"Joan, that's so great! You are catching up! It's about time. You guys are going to the prom together, and you are bonded with a kiss!"

"Okay friend, I have told you enough. See you at school tomorrow. My parents are calling me for dinner."

Joan walked downstairs. Martha was already serving some sort of cream of spinach soup with croutons. It looked delicious. Henri had just returned from D.C. and was obviously happy to be home, dropping into his seat with a sound of relief. Susan walked in, having changed her tennis outfit into a long lounge dress.

"Mom, you look so pretty," Joan commented as her mother sat down, proudly letting the dress flow over the sides of her chair.

Everybody kept silent for awhile enjoying their soup. It felt like a truce was called in an atmosphere of otherwise unrelated minds keeping their observations to themselves, tired of thinking too much.

"Let's take a break from talking tonight, I'm tired," Henri, said, looking concerned and overwhelmed. "I want to get to bed early."

"Sounds great," Susan responded, "even though you haven't noticed my new dress, Henri. I'm disappointed!"

"Yes. It looks great. Great colors," Henri said, totally involved in stretching his neck and rolling his shoulders to relax them. "But I told you, I want to take a break," he continued, "and I won't eat anymore tonight. I'm full from the noon banquet I ate before I flew back. Good night you two. Sweet dreams."

Henri walked out visibly exhausted. Joan felt sorry for him.

Susan, fluffing her dress, continued, "Thank heaven for my tennis teacher. I don't have much company these days. Your father is always away, Joan, and it's hard for me as his wife to be ignored so much!"

"Maybe you should take a break too, Mom, and think about what you said about Dad. Why do you think he is away so much? Why does he work so hard? Just think about it. Now I'm going to take a break too. Good night, Mom. I'm tired and I'm sure that you are too. We're all tired with what is happening in this household and in the world these days, don't you think? You feel it too, I'm sure."

Joan kissed her mother and left the room. Martha was picking up dishes. Mostly unfinished food was left on the plates. She wondered what was happening to the family. Martha was also surprised that the wine glasses were still half full, why? A sense of uneasiness came over her. She loved to feel that this family, which had become a part of her life, was happy. *Life!* she thought! *Maybe I need a break, too, everybody needs a break!* Martha mumbled as she carried the dinner dishes out of the room under the watchful eye of Susan, who was totally out of sorts now and walking to the bar for her glass of vodka.

Let's take a break, for sure, Joan thought, walking up to her room, relieved.

Taking a break is a good thing for people. It put things into perspective. During the next few days the unrest which everyone felt during dinner came to the surface and they dealt with it, each in their own way.

First, Susan spent some quiet days rearranging her wardrobe while giving periodic thoughts to the questions Joan asked her to answer. Why was Henri away so much? Why did he have to work so hard? Well, obviously he was away so much because he had to work so hard, those two factors were linked, of course, that was that, and Susan didn't pursue her investigation any further. However, the big question still remained: Why did he have to work so hard?

After a couple days of rearranging things, Susan began to wonder whether there was anything else. She was afraid to look deeper into the problem. Joan had suggested that Susan ask herself those questions with an accusatory tone. Why? It made Susan feel ill at ease at the time. Was there a link between working hard and her demands on Henri or was it her behavior? On top of that, she had complained of being ignored by Henri and happy to have the company of her tennis teacher, and she did it in front of Joan! What a stupid thing to say! She decided she should be more careful in the future, but her tennis teacher was so attractive! She could have jumped in bed with him any time if he had made the offer! And then what? Talk about a mess! Susan's thoughts were flying in all directions. She was totally confused now, and feeling guilty about her behavior.

The real problem was that Susan didn't feel good about her life the way it was, obviously something was missing. The only meaning she had found lately was to organize parties and to take care of Joan's needs... needs which were obviously very different from her own. The prom dress, for instance. Susan flashed back to the restaurant scene which had shamed her. To give the price of an expensive gown to Martha? What was that about? What lessons was her daughter trying to teach her? Joan had done it in such a candid way Susan could not find any reason to accuse Joan or to get mad at her.

"The hell with everything," Susan screamed after awhile, pulling a bunch of her dresses off their hangers and throwing them on the floor. "I hate this life! Henri said it was lousy and that it was my fault. What about his own life? Always away, and who is he spending time with in D.C.? How do I know what is going on there?"

Susan was crying now in anger, not knowing what to do with herself. She quickly pulled a tissue out of her pocket to wipe her tears and slammed her closet door. She ran to the bar in the dining room and poured herself a glass of vodka. "I wonder why Henri said that life was lousy. His life can't be worse than mine at this point!" she added, gulping her drink.

Joan's break was a time-out from her parents. She had a good idea by now of the reasons for their distance and inner resentment of each other. She remembered when she overheard her dad say to her mom that life was lousy and that it was her fault. It had made her so sad then, but now it started to make sense. She was beginning to understand the dynamic. Her mother filled her life with all that money can buy because she didn't have a inner sense of who she was. She was unhappy inside and material things gave her momentary comfort and illusory short-lived happiness. She surrounded herself with like-minded friends who reinforced her beliefs. As for Henri, she had probably pushed him into making money, more and more, and becoming important on the political scene because that was where the influential and rich people hovered. Consequently, he had to work harder and harder, be away a lot, and the vicious circle continued to the point that things were now beginning to break down between them and her mother was looking at the tennis teacher to give her a new illusion. No wonder her mother was drinking! She did it like the drinker in the Little Prince's story did. To forget.

Joan's father's dynamic was not so clear for her, perhaps he was a sensitive man who had been pushed into a direction in life that didn't agree with who he was inside? Joan tried to remember Henri in a situation where he seemed happy, holding her hand in the park when she was a little girl, walking along the pond, watching the ducks and showing her the frogs. Her father had been raised on a farm, maybe he missed the Earth? But his parents sent him to an expensive college so he could get a great job. *He had made money in oil, lots of money, did that make him happy?* He seemed to have second thoughts when the subject of global warming caused by fossil fuels came up. Maybe it was hard for him to oppose the petition and rally with Mark Silver's side. Joan felt that Henri was definitely asking himself questions lately, lots of questions. He was unhappy and that's why he said that life was lousy. Too much going on, too difficult to keep Susan happy, and probably also jealous and resentful to see how much attention she gave her tennis teacher! *That's why he said that it was her fault. But my father at least didn't seem to want to drown his regrets in vodka to forget his problems,* Joan concluded with some relief!

After this overview of her parents respective dynamics and behaviors, which she now understood, Joan began to visualize what her own life could be like. Happiness? Where would she find it if not in touch with her soul essence, following this inner guide who knew exactly what to do, able to see the invisible ahead, with the help of her heart! Then, things would flow well, and she would not have to worry about it, just trust what happens. In the meantime, Joan decided that she would also try this inner wisdom in dealing with her parents. She would do her best and perhaps things would change for them. The thought made her happy.

Henri's break was a couple days of catching up with work and spending hours on his computer. He hardly came to the dining room and usually did only when he could be alone and read some material for his job. A lot of that stuff dealt with what was happening in the government. It seemed as if the opposing sides would never come to a reasonable agreement and this drove him nuts. All this time and money wasted, and mostly at the taxpayer's expense. It seemed to say to him, *What's money anyway? What does this all mean? What a mess!* Henri went periodically into a reverie, imagining the world turning on a merry-go-round with its wars, violence, problems. Global warming heating up to unbearable temperatures while fracking polluted groundwater. The population exploding out of control while churches opposed birth control. The animal species disappearing one by one and human beings becoming ill with new diseases which they could not control. People without healthcare suffering needlessly. Views of doom were punctuated by the music of an organ grinding out of tune while the merry-go-round continued its mad, endless spin. This recurrent vision, which bothered Henri a lot lately, began to worry him. It was repetitious and hypnotic to the point that he thought he, too, was breaking down. *I am taking a break,* he thought, laughing to push away the reverie. *This D.C. job is driving me nuts! I give up! I wonder how many of my colleagues feel the way that I do.*

But Henri was a good man. He loved his country and his family. He felt in his heart that he could let go of his fears and start trying to change the way things were going, both in his family and in his job as a senator. He trusted something inside of himself to guide him.

His first thought toward that goal was for his daughter, Joan. Henri was amazed by her maturity and intelligence. He also was touched by the way she patiently dealt with problems, bringing in her point with irrefutable logic which disarmed him. The Prius, for example. Henri smiled remembering their lunch together. He felt proud of her. Susan was another story! He wondered whether he could ever get her out of her designer outfits and enjoy something other than parties, and then Henri got a great idea, *Why don't the three of us take a trip to a national park for a little vacation? Joan will be delighted to be in nature and Susan might remember going to Yosemite with me when we first met! She was so cute with her tight shorts and t-shirt! That's it. We'll do it this summer.*

Henri felt relieved, happy, and hopeful. The sense of overwhelming helplessness finally dissipated. The status quo of his life had morphed into a new energy: the vision of his wife in her younger years with El Capitan in the background, and Joan's happy feet bathing in the Merced River after a hike to Nevada Fall. He closed his eyes to relish the scene. There was a lot of love in his heart for the two protagonists of his dream. His burden melted away.

Taking a break was a good thing for the family. It had put things into a new perspective!

Chapter Fourteen: The Prom Is Coming Soon

Joan was becoming more and more aware of how fast her days were going and how full they were. The amount of new information she gathered from the various interactions she had with people lately was huge. *All that new software in my computer-mind,* she joked. *What am I going to do with all this? I hope it will help me make the right decisions when I need them!* She laughed.

After taking a break from her parents, Joan pretty much understood the dynamic of their relationship. Things were getting clearer and it put her mind at ease. At school there was relief in the general atmosphere since the petition, which had caused students to take sides, was dropped. But there was one person Joan had not kept up with lately because she, herself, had taken a short break, it was her role model, her confidant. It was Mademoiselle. *I have so much to tell her,* Joan thought, remembering the meeting about the petition, of the kiss with Phillip and her new understanding of her parents' relationship. *So much has happened in such a short time! And what will I do about my next French assignment which I have not prepared?* she added, scratching her head and reaching for her notebook.

Mademoiselle had asked Joan to read "The Adulterous Woman", a story by Camus which was the first in the short story collection: *The Exile and The Kingdom.* Joan took a quick look at the book Mademoiselle had loaned her. *Shucks! Twenty five pages to read and a paper to write with my comments! How am I going to do that along with my school work, the English assignment, the math problems and the science class essay on biodiversity? And the prom at the end of next week!* Joan was overwhelmed. She jumped on her bed and beat her fists on the pillows, frustrated. Taking a few deep breaths to calm down, she visualized how much she looked forward to seeing her French teacher on Saturday. She would hear what was happening with her and Mark Silver! Now Joan felt better. She opened the book, biting her lip. *So, now Camus is writing about a woman who is cheating on her husband,* she nodded. *Actually that could be interesting coming from a man who got a Nobel Prize for literature. He might present the woman's act in a different light from the usual "jump in bed with somebody other than her husband" story!* Joan's curiosity was piqued and she began reading with anticipation.

The story started with Janine and her husband Marcel riding a bus in North Africa, a country Camus was very familiar with since he was born and lived in Algeria for a long time. The description of the scene was amazing. It plunged the reader into a bus in poor shape, navigating in a hostile environment filled with Arabs dressed in djellabas trying to keep warm. It was December. Leave it to Camus to take you into the human existential pain of being by the way he described the people in the bus and their individual ways of dealing with it. You could sense the Arabs' plight by the way they bundled up, by their facial expressions, and by the way they tried to nap in awkward positions. Marcel, a cloth merchant, was taking Janine on one of his rounds. He was obviously tired, unhappy with his life, which had become routine and devoid of excitement. Janine was thinking of her own life: 25 years of married life and her lack of children. She realized she had let go of the dreams and energy of her youth to accept the reassurance of being married so she would not grow old alone. Shelter from need was what she believed she could find in the relationship, and was reason enough for her to accept it. So she lived, going on with her life and waiting. And she didn't know what she was waiting for.

The couple arrived at their destination, a village where Marcel was to do business. They checked into a shabby hotel where cold emanated from the walls. It was windy outside. Janine shivered, listening to noises coming from the street. Her legs felt heavy and she thought of the young girl she had been. After awhile they went down to dinner. Marcel tried to talk to people about his goods. They ate in a hurry because they had to leave early the next morning and Marcel had to finish his business before then. After swallowing some coffee, they walked out into the dusty and cold street. Marcel had a porter help him carry his trunk full of merchandise. Janine followed him as he made his transactions in some barely lit shanty stores along the street, where Arabs were selling their wares on a background of rugs and embroidered scarves. Janine felt alone and ignored, she didn't want to return to the hotel, discouraged by the idea of the cold room. She wanted to go up to the terrace the hotel keeper had recommended, where you could see the desert, he had said.

The couple climbed the stairs to the fort. It was early evening. The wind had stopped. It was a steep, long staircase. As they climbed, the space widened and the light changed, every noise could be heard with a distinct purity. The air seemed to vibrate around them and when they came to the terrace Janine's eyes could move along a perfect curve without encountering any obstacle. She was unable to tear herself away from the vast, open view in front of her while Marcel complained about the cold and wanted to leave. Janine was fascinated by the landscape expanding into the endless horizon. Marcel was agitated. Nothing was happening.

Joan interrupted her reading for awhile. She had eight pages to go and started imagining what was going to happen. *Would they go back to the hotel? Would Janine stay out, go back into the town, and meet someone? Would she run into the man who had looked at her very intently on the bus?* Obviously Janine was unhappy and looking for something to happen, though she didn't know what. It made Joan think of her mother's unhappiness with her life and her desire to escape it with her tennis teacher or something like that, just to take her away from her carefully disguised discontent. *It would have been a way for her mother to escape, besides the vodka,* Joan thought. *But what could happen next with Janine now?*

She had to finish her assignment and write down comments, so Joan continued her reading, trying to stop guessing about the end of the story and to give it her full attention. She also would pick out the most important things Janine said or thought, and use them when writing her own conclusions about the meaning of the story at the end. Joan's notes looked like this:

"At that place where sky and Earth joined in a pure line, something was waiting for her which she had ignored up to this day and which she, however, had not stopped missing. At the same time, in her woman's heart, a knot, which the years, habits, and boredom had tied, was beginning to loosen slowly.

"At that time Janine saw nomads encamped in black tents in the distance, and their territory was only a small part of the immense space which extended thousands of kilometers ahead into the forests and beyond. Miserable and free lords of a strange kingdom.

"She didn't know why this idea filled her with sadness so sweet and so vast that her eyes were closing. She only knew that this kingdom had been promised to her forever and that never would it be hers again but in this fugitive instant.

"After opening her eyes to the immobile sky and the rays of light, Janine felt that the course of the world had stopped and that no one in that moment would ever get old or die, life was suspended except in her heart where someone was crying with pain and marveling.

"As Janine comes back to reality, she notices that she is shivering. Her exaltation has left her and she is back in her body. Marcel is coaxing her to go back to the hotel. They come down the stairs and Janine is again in this world.

"And what would she do from now on there, if not drag herself along until sleep, until death? Janine and Marcel go back to the restaurant. She feels a cold is coming on. They get in bed in the glacial room. She has a hard time breathing. The iron bed is creaking. Dogs are barking outside. They had to go to sleep. She sees the black tents, the camels, immense stretches of land, she questions why she came here and goes to sleep on the question. Janine woke up and started questioning her life again.

"What would she have done alone? She followed Marcel, that's all, happy to feel that someone needed her. He didn't give her any other joy than feeling that he needed her, and she needed his need.

"Janine got closer to Marcel in the bed and gave him loving names that they used for each other. She was calling him with all her heart. She knew she was afraid of dying.

"'If I could surmount this fear, I would be happy,' Janine said. At that point anguish overcame her. She would die before having been freed. She wanted to be free. Janine stood up in bed hearing a call coming from the South. Where the desert and the night mixed now under a sky where life stopped and where no one got older nor died. Janine got up and stood by the bed, watching Marcel breathe. She furtively dressed in the dark, held her shoes in her hand and headed for the door. She was able to lock the door without noise, get to the hotel entrance where she told the watchman she would be right back, and run in the dark toward the fort. The cold air was burning her lungs. She climbed as fast as she could until she reached the parapet against which she leaned, out of breath, shivering. Her eyes opened finally to the night spaces. She relaxed into the night and stillness united her with her deepest self.

"After so many years fleeing from fear she had run crazily without any goal, she finally stopped. She felt she had found her roots again, sap was spreading through her body which was no longer shaking. From the obscure center of her being, Janine felt herself freed. When she returned to the room, Marcel was still asleep. He mumbled, got up, went to the sink, and drank some mineral water. He looked at Janine without understanding. She was crying, not being able to hold her tears. 'It's nothing, darling,' she said. 'It's nothing.'"

Joan put the book down. She was crying along with Janine. She understood what the woman had gone through. *A heavy trip*, she thought. *Janine had left her mind and body and contacted the part of herself which is one with the whole, her essence.* Joan knew how it felt and the emotion which the feeling induces, she recognized the place Janine found inside her core self, a place which would always be with her while her life continued. Joan knew the freedom Janine found in the experience, the promised kingdom.

Joan started to write down her comments, then she stopped resolutely and decided instead that she would write just a very short synopsis and have a conversation later with Mademoiselle about it. It would be a great exercise to discuss the story in French and ask Mademoiselle to explain some of the things which still were not totally clear to her.

Compared to this heavy story which had been difficult for Joan to get into because she lived in such a comfortable environment where she was happy to be alive, the rest of her assignments were easy. She finished her math problems, her English composition, and found online all the information she needed to understand why biodiversity was such an important factor for keeping the delicate balance the natural world needed to survive. Joan thought that Mark Silver would emphasize this crisis of biodiversity as a factor toward the dire sixth extinction scientists and biologist had been talking about for awhile.

Joan was happy. Her school work had gone well. Kristin was excited about her date for the prom, with Frank, one of the best students in her science class. Her parents seemed to return to a peaceful routine and Martha visibly appreciated the good vibes she detected at dinner, where the family resumed getting together after taking their respective breaks. Life was great!

Joan looked forward to her French lesson and when Saturday finally arrived, she met Mademoiselle in the library. She brought her notes and the short composition she wrote on "The Adulterous Woman" and was excited about seeing her teacher.

"Mademoiselle, I'm so happy to see you! It's been so long since we had that famous meeting in the veranda and so much has happened! How have you been?"

"I've been well, Joan. The days I took off did me a lot of good. I had finals at the university but I kept up with what happened with the petition. Mark told me about the meeting with Mr. Field and I was delighted to hear the result of that meeting. Congratulations to you and Kristin for organizing that so well! How did you manage to talk your parents into going, especially your dad, Joan? "

"My dad got Mr. Field to host the discussion, so that was really helpful. And he liked Mr. Silver a lot. I could tell! But my parents are going through a lot lately, especially my dad. He is asking himself a lot of questions."

"Who wouldn't like Mark?" Mademoiselle answered with a wink. "He is an amazing person. We have seen each other a lot lately, for walks and deep talks. I have learned a lot from him and we get along well. Thank you for the introduction, Joan!"

"I'm really happy about that, Mademoiselle. I thought the two of you would resonate! And you did! Nice synchronicity!"

"Now on with our French lesson, Joan. Let's talk about this obscure existential story that I asked you to read. After I did, I wondered whether I had asked you to do something too difficult for your age. You always seem so mature to me. I forget you are only sixteen! What did you think of 'The Adulterous Woman'?"

"I was curious. For quite awhile I waited for something to happen, like Janine would betray her husband with another man or something, and then it appeared that she was looking for a way to escape her boring life by connecting with her surroundings, the night, the sky, the immensity, all the Arabs in their tents with their free looking lives, she wanted to be free like they seemed to be."

"And she succeeded to free herself?"

"She was able to get away from her thoughts and into the core of herself, her roots, what it seems to me like her essence, which was always there but she had not connected with it before. It gave her a feeling of freedom that delivered her from her fear of dying. She had a wonderful physical reaction, as if sap spread into her body. Her heart was overwhelmed. It was all expressed in feelings. Nothing came from her thinking mind."

"What do you think Janine experienced? Would you know how to describe this?"

"I would say she had an altered state of consciousness, something like you find during meditation, when you leave your mind and get to something deep beyond your thoughts, the essence of yourself. I know what it feels like, Mademoiselle. I have experienced this feeling, especially when I sit alone in my cave and let go, It's wonderful. It's like freedom from ordinary daily life, it gives a sense that you will never die, that your consciousness will go on in the universe forever!"

Mademoiselle was amazed at the depth of Joan's answer. She knew this young girl had connected to a place within herself that often takes people years to become aware of, if they ever do. There was nothing more to ask her student, she had felt it in her core. "Joan, you understood the meaning of this story very well. Is there anything unclear that you want to ask me about?"

"Yes, Camus chose the title "The Adulterous Woman". I know that Janine reaches this place completely away from Marcel and is aware that he could not be with her in the experience, this is like a mystical participation. Why adulterous?"

"I think that Camus equated this state that Janine reaches as a climax of sorts, something climactic which she experienced without her husband Marcel. That was her adulterous act."

"Oh yes, I see. Also, Mademoiselle, after this reading, I don't think that Camus is an existentialist anymore. He definitely believes that essence is always inside our core and we have access to it. Why is he considered an existentialist, then?"

"He is not, Joan. That's an erroneous classification! He has been linked with them by mistake. How could Camus be an existentialist when he is so aware of our inner essence? He grew up by the sea, he loved nature, he was immersed in beauty and cosmic participation. Yes, he observed the plight of our human nature and existence and wrote a lot about it, but he was not an existentialist in the way Jean Paul Sartre and others are defined. Camus had connected with his own essence, the essential within, the part that you see with the heart, like the Little Prince does, remember?"

Joan and Mademoiselle were exhausted but happy as they hugged in silence. It was almost time to end the lesson.

Joan took a deep breath and suggested, "Mademoiselle, what do you think of giving our existential body a break and getting something sweet to eat? Martha made some delicious cookies yesterday and she'll be happy to serve us some with tea. Let's sit in the veranda and give our brains a break!"

The tea party went beautifully. The warm environment relaxed the two women who chattered about life and about finding ways to help bring awareness to the sad state of the world through a new consciousness. They also talked about the upcoming prom, about Phillip whom Mademoiselle had not met yet but who sounded great to her because of his love of poetry. They talked about Mark Silver's research on biodiversity and his writing on the dangers of fracking. Joan gave Mademoiselle a quick report on what her parents relationship looked like at this point and Mademoiselle felt sorry for Susan.

"Perhaps you can try to interest your mom in some sort of creative project," she suggested to Joan. "Ask her whether she ever had something she liked to do as a child or a teen which captivated her. She just might!"

The afternoon ended with a sense of hope. Joan felt very fortunate to have a French tutor who understood her so well and introduced her to Camus and St. Exupery. The two authors were contributing to her understanding of her own self and of philosophy. Mademoiselle felt blessed to have a student so gifted and precocious. It made her feel hopeful for the young people of today. Victor was happy to have company and responded joyfully.

It seems that everybody was happy. Joan thought it had been a good day!

There were just a few days left before the prom and you could feel the excitement among the students in the junior class. The parents reserved a large venue which Henri offered to pay for. It was located several miles away from town and instead of driving separately, people decided to meet at the high school and load the kids into seven buses to take them there. The parents thought it was a good, safe plan. Susan offered to take care of the decorations, streamers, and flowers. The parents' association would take care of the rest: the music, appetizers and drinks. Mr. Field would probably give them a good deal on soft drinks. Everything was well planned.

There was a lot of whispering about dresses, corsages, shoes, and hairdos which interfered with the usual attention to classes, as the girls exchanged tips instead of concentrating on their class work. The boys watched these chattering exchanges, looking skeptical but also excited about the upcoming event. Would they play their role well? Would their prom partner like them enough to flirt? Joan thought of Phillip and how happy she was to go with him to the prom. Would he be a better dancer than Roger? She knew Roger asked another girl to the prom, a bright student from her math class. *They should make a great couple*, Joan thought. Kristin confided that Frank offered to take her to a "wild" party after the prom and that she was very curious about it. Anyway, the few days went by fast and prom day arrived before anybody noticed.

Joan met Phillip at Kristin's house where twelve of the teens gathered with their parents. Everybody was all dressed up. Everyone exchanged flowers, corsages, and gifts while adding final touches to their outfits and taking pictures. They especially enjoyed the group pictures, some even with their parents. Phillip brought a surprise for Joan, a beautiful glass butterfly pin which he carefully attached to her dress. Joan was very touched by the symbolic meaning of his gift and gave him a big hug while his mother lovingly fluffed Joan's hair, saying, "You are such a beautiful girl, Joan, inside and out. I'm so happy Phillip is taking you to the prom today," she added, visibly moved.

Most of the teens were excited about their upcoming night, but a couple of them questioned the event because school dances have a tendency to be less than great! Joan felt happy that she chose to wear her favorite green dress. How ridiculous would she feel in some fancy long designer creation that her mother wanted to get for her! Her little green dress was just perfect. She was sure that Susan would agree had she been there, but Joan's parents had not joined the group, feeling that they had contributed enough to the preparations. Moreover, they had dinner guests that evening.

The crowd moved to the school parking lot where other families had already met and kids were starting to get into the buses. Then the procession started on its way. The bus ride was fun. Everybody talked and joked around, a long shot from the usual bus ride to or from school when the kids minds are loaded with thoughts of assignments or personal problems.

The venue was nicely decorated, attractive and welcoming. A bunch of different tables had appetizers of all kinds, enough to satisfy hungry teens. Everybody sat and enjoyed the good food and an array of colorful soft drinks. The music started with a DJ, but nobody ventured onto the floor. Everybody was waiting for someone else to go first! Two couples started to dance, but the majority were still waiting. Finally some of the girls pulled their partners out on the floor and then it became a dancing mob! The music was upbeat, aside from a few slow songs, and the teens enjoyed themselves for the most part. Some wandered around and talked or watched and didn't dance. There was a picture booth where they could take fun pictures of themselves or with friends making faces. Some had a better time than others. A few didn't participate much and by the end most were tired and just wanted to go home. The prom lasted about four hours.

The ride back to the school was fun for those who still felt energetic. Many were tired but satisfied with the long expected junior prom. Everybody got picked up and went on home or to another party. The junior prom was over.

During the whole evening Joan went through the motions. She was proud that her mother's decorations created a warm atmosphere and thankful for Phillip's company which added meaning to an event of little significance to her. But mostly she questioned the importance of customs and rites and the purpose in a person's life. She saw that she enjoyed dancing with Phillip, who, unlike Roger, was a very relaxed and at ease dancer. She felt close to the warmth he emanated. *It's good to let myself feel and enjoy the moment, without thinking of what will happen next. It is beautiful. The prom is a tradition,* Joan thought, *something to prepare, to look forward to, because it happens at that time of your life and you have to go through it. It's like Christmas in December or the Fourth of July, a celebration, some other countries have different customs and different rites at different times. Why do humans need them? Do they take us away from the monotony of life, whatever our life is like? I guess it is something like nature, music, art, a creative pursuit of some kind, something that takes us beyond the ordinary for awhile, beyond our limited selves, it gives us meaning.* Joan remembered the Camus story she had just read and she felt like Janine in search of her freedom. *But I have tasted that freedom,* Joan remembered, *and it is in me anytime I want to taste it again, beyond my thinking mind, beyond my limited self.*

Phillip's parents brought Joan to their house for awhile after the bus dropped them off. They all drank tea together and Joan experienced the warmth of a family who had taught Phillip the meaning of service in their life. Joan could feel it in the way they talked about other people in a loving way.

The group didn't visit for very long since everyone was tired. It had been a long day. Phillip borrowed his dad's car to take Joan home. It was midnight.

"Just like Cinderella," he said laughing, taking Joan's hands to let her out of the car in front of the gate. "Aren't we strange creatures of habit?" Phillip said, kissing her hand. "We just went through a ritual junior event together... but life is good, because I went through it with you," Phillip added, taking Joan in his arms and kissing her softly. "Good night my princess, my beautiful and sweet princess. I love you very much, and because you exist, I have hope for this world."

Joan was happy. She went to bed feeling love for the world, for life, for the animals, the plants, for Phillip, for being alive and feeling that she was at one with everything on this Earth, feeling free like Janine. Joan was feeling love in its purest form inside her heart. Her heart now beat softly as she breathed in, slowly, the night air flowing through her bedroom window with a scent of mint.

Chapter Fifteen: Not in My Own Back Yard

The prom was over. The effervescence of the past couple weeks had receded and the students were now looking forward to the end of the school year. There would be finals, of course, but basically their junior experience was fading in anticipation of their next and last year of high school, their senior year, finally!

Always very sensitive to what was happening in the family, Joan detected some unrest on the part of her dad lately. He looked pensive, frowned a lot, whispered bits of sentences to Susan now and then making sure that Joan would not hear what he said. Was it a problem in their relationship? It sounded as though they were talking about the property.

Henri would say, "Why do they race like hell before they know for sure, and what about the river? I don't think they realize who is living here. What about the wastewater? I'd hate to have our well contaminated."

Joan wanted to ask her dad what was going on, but she didn't dare to burden him further. He looked so concerned and puzzled. She felt sorry for him. Joan decided she would ask Mark Silver whether he could shed some light on the sentences she overheard. Who were "they?" And what was going on with the water? Mark might be able to explain.

Now that the petition had been called off, Mark Silver was more confident in presenting subjects which would have raised a lot of eyebrows previously. In his senior class, Ellen now became an ally, assiduously listening. It seemed that she had freed herself from the yoke of her mother's view and was beginning to think for herself and ask questions. The lessons on the importance of biodiversity had been a success in all of Mark Silver's classes.

Joan asked Mark Silver if she could talk to him about something important and he agreed to meet her in the library. Before his arrival she chatted with Ms. Stern who was very busy getting ready for the end of the school year. They enjoyed talking about the meeting where Jesus had been the judge who helped dissolve the petition.

"I wish it were that easy to convince the general public about the dangers of global warming and who is behind the propaganda saying it's a hoax," Ms. Stern said with a big sigh. "I think Mr. Field was very honest and conscious, I was so relieved when he dismissed the petition."

"I was very relieved myself," Joan replied, shaking her head. "Imagine the work a protest would have required! And with no guarantee of the outcome, of course!"

"And I was the one who was the most relieved of all," Mark Silver added as he entered, overhearing the women talk. "That meeting was an eye opener for me, and I'm so thankful for Joan and Kristin who organized it so well. But now you said that you had some important questions, " he said, looking at Joan. "Let's sit together and talk. You are welcome to join us, Ms. Stern."

"I would love to but I must finish filing a list of new books," Ms. Stern answered. "Why don't you use my office, it will be more private," she added pointing to the door.

Mark Silver and Joan settled down in Ms. Stern's office after closing the door. Joan jotted down some notes about the bits of sentences she heard her dad say to Susan. They didn't make much sense to her but she recorded them carefully. Mark Silver listened very intently, closing his eyes at times to focus on the words and pursing his lips when something resonated.

After Joan finished the list, he took a deep breath and quietly announced, "Joan, it sounds to me as if your dad is having a problem with the fracking being planned in his area. He must have found this out. I don't know how, but he is aware of the possibility and he is perplexed and unhappy about it. I will go over what you heard and explain it as much as possible.

"'They' probably refers to the big oil and gas companies who are racing to drill and frack more wells before the public realizes the danger it presents to their health and safety. The industry is going for any viable location, including national parks and even the most populated areas of the country. Your father sounds mad because he thinks they don't know for sure what the dangers are, so they, in your father's words, are 'racing like hell' to do it. I don't blame him, Joan."

"This is alarming, Mr. Silver, and what about what my dad referring to the water, the river, and the wastewater. What is all that?"

"Fracking a single well requires millions of gallons of water which is mixed with approximately ten thousand gallons of chemicals, Joan. Big oil and gas needs are depleting groundwater and drying up streams in some parts of the country. Wastewater treatment plants are not equipped to treat the resulting wastewater which can contain harmful levels of radioactivity. Also, the dangerous fracking chemicals are kept secret. They don't have to disclose what chemicals they use in the fracking fluid. It is a trade secret. Some independent analysts have identified cancer causing chemicals in the fluid, some of which disrupt the endocrine system. All these chemicals are emitted into the air or released underground, potentially contaminating water resources."

"But this is poisoning us all, Mr. Silver. Why aren't there some rules to prevent such a horrible outcome? I don't understand."

"Joan, it is like the problem with climate change and its causes. There is big money behind all this and big oil and gas companies are exempt from critical statutes in all the major environmental laws, including the Safe Drinking Water Act, the Clean Water Act, and the Clean Air Act. Can you believe it?"

"I'm overwhelmed. If my father knows what is happening and he is not happy, can he do something about it?"

"I think that he already thought of that. Didn't he say, 'I don't think they realize who is living here?' Meaning that when 'they' realize who he is, there will not be any fracking in proximity to his property. Do you think that people in the industry would frack in their own backyards?"

"Mr. Silver, is this the way people in leadership act? Poisoning others, and probably themselves and their children in the long run, just to keep the money-generating power in their hands alone at any cost? Why don't they invest in other forms of energy instead, which don't destroy the Earth, the animals, and the human species? This is all so sad, I don't understand."

"Welcome to Capitalism 101, Joan. An idea that looked good at the start but which has become the monster devouring the world. Until people become conscious of this race toward money that has destroyed democracy, we just have to work hard to spread the word and change the plutocracy we live in back to the democracy the United States claims to be as an example to live by in the world. But I want to do something for your dad. Instead being exempted from the fracking in his area just because he's a big shot with friends in high places, let's find a legal way for him to stop it without resorting to his name and position. This will remind him he is just one of us. I have an idea."

"Can I help, Mr. Silver? Should I talk to him?"

"No, let me investigate. Fracking has actually been a threat to the Earth when it is close to a fault and could trigger an earthquake. It is forbidden in many areas of California close to faults. I think we have faults in Arkansas and I can find out where your property lies in relationship to one of them. This would create an exemption for your dad, a legal exemption. I will do the research. Okay? You can talk to your dad later after I find out."

"I don't know how to thank you, Mr. Silver."

"I should thank you, Joan. You are the one who introduced me to Monique, the most wonderful woman I have ever met. We are having a great time together and, believe it or not, I'm even learning French! I owe you a lot!"

"She is wonderful, I know. I'm glad you are getting along so well. Life is good, isn't it?"

"Life is good, Joan, and we believe that we can save nature and our biology on this Earth if we keep it in our consciousness and work hard to spread the word. *Au revoir, Joan, à bientôt!*"

"*Au revoir*, Monsieur Silver, *et merci pour tout ce que vous avez fait pour moi et ma classe de science.*"

"Oh, I forgot, Joan. Something for the headlines that could make quite a big news item. Did you know that you could light your tap water on fire?"

"Is this a joke?

"No, Joan, it could happen if you use a well near a fracking area. When the high pressure used in fracking shatters the rock in which the oil or gas is held, methane and other hydrocarbon gases can leak into aquifers and household water wells. This gas not only makes you sick but it can explode! That would make headlines I'm sure. Imagine such a tragic event on the news! There would be a lot of attention and a lot of law suits."

"I think I see why my dad is concerned, Mr. Silver, but I hope he is not only concerned for himself and his own backyard but for all the citizens of this country. Let me know about the fault and then I'll talk to him."

Joan and Mark Silver left Ms. Stern's office. Joan's mind was challenged by the conversation but her heart was more determined than ever to bring the issue into the limelight. Maybe she would tell Phillip about this and he would write a poem about it? She wanted to help, but she didn't know where to start. *Okay, one thing at the time,* she thought, as she walked back home. When she arrived, she took a slow walk in her beautiful park to sooth her soul.

Joan looked at the pond, the trees, the river, the place she had loved since she was born. She had tears in her eyes. She felt a fierce determination to protect this place with its natural beauty and the Earth she lived on as well. Her own backyard would never look the same again.

Chapter Sixteen: Another Lunch with Dad

Henri was busier than ever, between his concern about fracking being considered in an area not too far from his property and his trips back and forth to D.C. Though he was a great pilot, the stress caused by flying his small jet was taking a toll. He kept a rigid maintenance schedule for his plane which was done by a special mechanic who came regularly from a nearby airport. It was a constant hardship and worry. Henri was also concerned about Susan. She was drinking more and more. She passed out recently and he had to take her to the emergency room in the middle of the night. The doctors questioned the amount of alcohol she regularly consumed and advised her to get some help. Henri was worried that something would happen to her while he was away in D.C.

There was a shining light in Henri's dark hours of work and stress, however. His sweet daughter Joan, whose beautiful energy and smile could take his mind away from all the rest of the bad stuff in his thoughts. The way she and her friend Kristin handled the petition against Mark Silver was a great lesson to Henri on how things could sometimes be resolved quite quickly with simple logic and irrefutable innocent arguments. He admired how the discourse developed at Mr. Field's meeting and laughed at the *coup de grace* Mark Silver gave by asking Mr. Field what Jesus would do! Try that in Congress! Henri nodded, laughing from the top of his throat.

The Prius Henri had ordered for Joan arrived at the dealer and he decided to take Joan out to lunch before going to get it. He carefully chose a pastel green color for the car, knowing she would love it. Henri was excited about the outing. He felt that he was now in a different place with his daughter than the last time they went to lunch together. He was more at ease with her, more willing to talk openly about things. Somehow Joan didn't seem like a kid anymore but like someone who understood life and was aware of some things that even he didn't know, he admitted to himself with a sense of guilt. Henri had grown not only to love Joan but to admire her.

The day before they went to lunch together, Henri received a phone call from Mark Silver which completely surprised him. Mark told him that he'd heard of his concern about possible fracking in his area and that he had some good news for him. Mark Silver did some research and found out that their property was located in a place exempt from consideration for drilling operations. The proximity of a fault line within the legal limits would stop the company from drilling in that area. Henri didn't know whether he should be relieved by the news he just heard or upset that Mark Silver had become involved in a private matter. After a few deep breaths and thinking back on the petition meeting, he realized that Mark was in good faith and just wanted to help. *Another Joan intervention,* he thought, frowning and pursing his lips, but the feeling of relief won over the resentment as Henri saw the great benefits of being legally exempt without having to call in his buddies to remedy the problem.

This Mark Silver is a very clever man, Henri concluded. *I'd rather have him as an ally, that's for sure! This was an act of friendship on his part.*

When the time came to go to lunch with Joan, Henri was ready for anything. He never knew what this girl, his daughter, was up to, but he trusted that in spite of her age, her voice was that of wisdom. He found this out before and smiled at the possibility of an interesting exchange between them. Henri picked Joan up and drove to Marius for the usual *Moules marinière,* their favorite lunch feast. This time they had a reservation and the waiter took them to their table next to the window, again decorated with beautiful flowers.

"Dad, this is great. I'm so happy to be here with you. What a treat! You are gone so much, but you are here now and I have a lot to talk to you about!"

"I'm happy to be with you in this quiet place, Joan. I told you the main reason I brought you here today is that we are going to pick up your Prius after lunch, and I'm sure you will love it. A pale green color and a GPS so you can find your way home," Henri added, smiling. "Enough to keep you wanting to come back!"

"You are joking, Dad. You know that I wouldn't want to get away from you and Mom. I'm happy at home!"

"I know, sweetie, and Mom knows it too. What will you have to drink?" Henri asked as the waiter was bringing the menu.

"Iced tea will do for me and I know what you want, Dad. White wine to go with the mussels, right?"

"Right, we are creatures of habit, aren't we?" Henri concluded as he ordered the drinks and the mussels *marinière* from the waiter. "I'm looking forward to this lunch with my smart daughter who knows everything that's going on even if she is not told!"

"Hmm… did Mark Silver call you, Dad?"

"Yes, miss snoopy. Where did you find out about the fracking problem?"

"A few sentences here and there, which I overheard you say. As a result, I got a good education in the matter, thanks to Mr. Silver."

"And thanks to you, now I'm relieved of something which was a great burden for me. I also thanked Mark Silver when he called. A nearby fault line was a life saver, if one can call it a life saver. I guess unless there is an earthquake!" He joked. "But at least the probability of fracking nearby is gone now."

Henri took a sip of his wine which the waiter brought, while Joan tasted her iced tea, smacking her lips. *So refreshing,* she concluded joyously. Henri looked at his daughter, so young, so full of life, so unaware of the load he felt weighing on his own shoulders. He thought about sitting in Congress among like politicians trying to solve unsolvable problems, all of them fighting with lobbyists, arguing about impossible laws to obey, going back and forth between their conscience and their own personal interests, campaign supporters and all the rigmarole! Henri wanted to express this to Joan but he didn't know how to talk about his feelings. He took another sip of wine.

Joan noticed the silence. "Dad, you look concerned about something, like you are carrying a weight on your shoulders. Do you want to talk about it?"

"I was just looking at you, Joan. So young, so happy, and I was flashing back to the faces of those sitting in Congress in Washington D.C. Behind the faces there is so much going on. Some look so old, so unhappy, so hopeless, others so aggressive, they don't listen but think they have all the answers. Everyone fends for themselves because they come with an agenda, but nothing gets done. What is really behind the faces? What is really in their minds? I'm so tired of the scene, Joan. I feel so useless there."

"Dad, maybe we should eat our lunch," Joan said as the waiter brought a bowl of steaming mussels. "This looks so good! I hear what you are saying, Dad, and can imagine the scene there. Maybe like some are pushing their rock up the hill and others are tired and going down the hill. I can explain what I mean, but let's eat first, Dad. It looks so good!"

Joan and Henri ate their bowl of mussels with the greatest gusto. The ritual they knew so well took over and they soaked their croutons in the sauce until the last drop. Henri looked as if he felt much better and the weight dropped off his shoulders. He was smiling now and ready to order the pear tart for dessert—with two forks, of course! Joan laughed when he did it, remembering his surprise the last time she suggested that they share the dessert!

"What was that thing about a rock, Joan? People pushing them or going downhill in the middle of Congress? What a strange description of the scene, Joan. Tell me about it. Wait 'til I tell my colleagues… pushing their rocks," Henri laughed. "They don't know what kind of daughter I have. They would be surprised!"

"Dad, your description made me think about the myth of Sisyphus. You know, Sisyphus, from Greek mythology? Camus wrote a story that describes the plight of humanity. The guy, Sisyphus, is pushing his rock up the hill until he gets to the top and then the rock rolls back down to the bottom and he starts all over again. That's what the human condition is like according to Camus. Sisyphus keeps pushing because when he does it, his life has meaning, so he keeps on trying. It seems like the people in Congress are doing their pushing up the hill to get somewhere, maybe into power or money or something, and when they get to the top, their rock rolls back down, maybe because they didn't reach their goal or it's not enough. So they try again and believe their lives have meaning by doing so. Maybe that is what goes on behind those faces you are trying to read! Some are full of meaning pushing the rock up the hill. The others are watching the rock roll down. Dad, you have sometimes made it do what you wanted, even if it doesn't have any meaning for you at this point. You don't have to go downhill and start all over again. Maybe the rock is too heavy to push, don't you think? Could you just give up your job as senator if you are tired and disappointed?… unless you want to go on fighting to make changes in the crab basket you have to maneuver in! I'm worried that your job is killing you, Dad."

Henri listened, totally overwhelmed by the analogy. He recognized himself and his life pushing the rock up the hill. He remembered reading about Sisyphus in a college class on Greek mythology without really understanding what it was about at the time. Camus made it clear. Meaning was of the essence and he had to hear this from this 16-year-old, who rattled the story off as if it were so obvious! Henri found meaning in what he was doing, but what was the meaning that his colleagues in Congress were bringing to their jobs? What were they preaching? Were they trying to improve the state of the country and the world, or were they working to improve their own selfish condition? Were they motivated by the money special interest groups were dishing out to influence the outcome? Where was the ethical meaning in all this?

"Dad, is that why I heard you tell Mom that life was lousy? Remember? I was so concerned for you!"

Henri was silent. He was thinking. Joan looked at him lovingly and respected his silence as they shared the pear tart the waiter had just brought. Henri finished his glass of wine. He took a deep breath and told Joan, just to change the subject, "Sweetie, I have something important I want to talk to you about. Let's finish our dessert and then sit in the waiting room for awhile before we go to the car dealer, shall we?"

Father and daughter sat comfortably in the waiting room with a cup of coffee. They were relaxed and happy to be together. Henri looked at his daughter, shaking his head. He had something important he wanted to share with Joan and he needed her help to make a decision, but it was hard for him to bring it up.

"Sweetie, I have been wanting to talk to you about your mom. Something happened recently that scared the hell out of me and I have to make some decisions."

"Dad, I know that Mom drinks too much. I have seen it. What happened that scared you so much? Tell me, please," Joan begged her father anxiously.

"The night after our meeting at the Fields' we had an argument— your mother and I. You were already in bed and probably sound asleep. Joan, it got pretty ugly! Then your mother drank a lot of vodka afterwards. She went to our room and I stayed in the office, reading. Sometime later, I heard some weird noises coming from our room. When I went to your mom's side, her breathing didn't sound right, and I realized she had passed out. Her hands were very cold. I called an ambulance and we went to the emergency room. The doctors told me that the alcohol had caused the episode, that it was serious, and that it could get much worse if she didn't stop drinking. They kept her a couple of hours for observation and then we came home. I was so worried, Joan. I thought we were going to lose her." Henri concluded looking alarmed. "You didn't hear anything, Joan. Did you?"

"No, Dad. I was so tired after the meeting I think I went into a deep sleep. I'm so sorry to hear this. It's such a shock for me, Dad. I knew that Mom drank a lot but I didn't realized it compromised her health to that point."

"Yes, it shocked me too. It's a long story, Joan. I'm sure you are aware that your mom loves parties. She needs to have important people around her. When I was campaigning to become a senator, she organized practically everything with groups and churches. It was amazing. She did the job for me and I was elected. Then I had to go to D.C., and now she feels left out. The parties are rare, all the important people we know live far away and your mom has very few occasions to wear her designer outfits these days. She is unhappy, Joan. Your mom drinks to compensate for her depression. I know. It is sad!"

"May I ask you Dad, if I'm not too indiscreet, what was the argument about that started the big fight? Can you tell me?"

"I think she didn't like hearing Mark Silver blame big oil money for getting in the way of constructive action against climate change. She had just planned to have a Fourth of July party at our house this summer and wants to invite some of the big shots. You would say members of the 1% club. For your mom, the richer the better. I was against it and that's what started the fight. You know, Joan, I have to be honest, if it were not for your mom I probably would not have worked so hard to make a fortune in the oil business and then run for senator. I could say, in a way, that she pushed me because she wanted it, and I went along."

"Is that why you said to Mom that life is lousy and it's all her fault because she pushes you all the time? Dad, I remember it so well. I asked you once about it, our first lunch together, remember? And you didn't want to talk about it. Now I understand. Now I see why," Joan concluded, shaking her head and looking at her dad lovingly.

Henri was shaken. Joan could see tears in his eyes. She grabbed her dad's hands, holding them firmly, and sweetly declared, "Dad, you love Mom very much and you want her to be happy. I also love Mom very much. Maybe we can do something to help her."

"I wish I knew what to do," Henri answered, letting himself cry now. "I feel hopeless at times, Joan, and I'm so tired."

"Dad, we can do it together. We can help Mom, you'll see. I want to help you do it. Can I tell you what I'm thinking?"

"Yes, sweetie, you can tell me," Henri replied, quickly drying his tears with his napkin. "If anybody can do it, you probably are the one, Joan. I must have done something right to be gifted with such a daughter. So what can we do, tell me?"

"Here's the plan, Dad. Can you do some research to find the best rehab centers for alcoholics in this country? Find one that's first class and elegant, with big name doctors and attendants, located in a beautiful, natural setting. Something like a resort but with some strings attached, like the person will leave rehab having given up alcohol permanently. Mom will stay there for a month or so. Tell her that you will throw that famous Fourth of July party she wants when she gets back. By then she will have changed her mind about a lot of things, she will be a role model for all the drinkers who are getting too far into the stuff, and she will become a hero, right? Talk about meaning in Mom's life! That could be her new vocation."

Henri had listened carefully, fascinated by the intelligence of his daughter and her sense of optimism. He was now smiling.

"God, Joan, you really can figure things out! I think that this is the best idea, but your mom has to agree to go there, of course, and I'm not sure she's ready to give up this crutch in her life. But, wait a minute, I got an idea. The wife of one of our past Presidents, Betty Ford, came out of the closet with her alcohol addiction and did so much to raise the consciousness of Americans about the problem. She became famous for her leadership! Your mother would like this! I will look into the Betty Ford Center, Joan."

"She'll like that idea, Dad, I'm sure. It will make her feel like she is important. Maybe it will give her new meaning in her life. Maybe she will be able to teach others and be a role model! Great! Also Dad, she will love the place if it is fancy enough and she can dress up for dinner every night. Remember, that makes her feel good!" Joan added, smiling, happy to have imagined the best possibility to help her mom. "Oh yes, also make sure they teach meditation there. It's a great thing! Mom might like it and it can help her discover some new dimensions she has not yet explored. Dad, trust me, this will work out. We won't lose Mom. She'll find a new side of herself in the experience and so will we!"

Henri and Joan finished their coffee. They were both smiling. They walked out of the restaurant with renewed optimism about this. They named it "Project Mom". Now they were ready to look at the Prius. Henri drove happily toward the Toyota dealership.

Chapter Seventeen: Victor Is Getting Company

The visit to the Toyota dealer was short. Joan admired the green Prius and decided that she needed some help to learn how to drive it. Henri asked whether one of the mechanics could give her a lesson and an appointment was made for later in the week. Father and daughter returned home, happy with the time they spent together. They had found a solution for Mom's problem; but now they had to persuade Susan to accept the value of going through rehabilitation. Both were optimistic.

Joan found a text from Kristin when she arrived in her room. She wanted to talk to Joan about the lesson on biodiversity which Mark Silver had introduced in his class. She was upset about some of the things he said concerning the disappearance of many species.

"It's not only the monarch butterflies, Joan. You should have heard the statistics," Kristin wrote. "Let's get together. Let's talk."

Joan left Kristin a text promising to see her at school and make plans.

Henri remembered that Joan had recently expressed the wish for Victor to get a mate.

"He is so lonely in his tropical paradise, Dad. Is there a chance that you could get him a partner?" Joan asked and Henri, who could never refuse his daughter anything, wanted to surprise her in the near future.

Victor was a gift from the company which built the veranda several years ago. They wanted Henri's little daughter to enjoy this lively addition to their masterpiece. Henri didn't have any idea where they got the parrot, but he suddenly remembered an interesting man he met on a flight once. They sat together for several hours and Henri was fascinated by his stories about animals and his love for them. He remembered that the man had a pet shop in Florida where he sold some exotic species. Henri had not kept up with the gentleman, but he knew that he had his card somewhere. After looking through a drawer full of business cards he finally found the one he was after.

"Yes, William Price, that's it. I remember him. He must be in his late sixties or more now, I wonder whether he still has a shop. I'll give him a call," Henri said with a victorious expression.

Henri called William Price. The gentleman barely remembered him.

"On a flight to Miami, you said? It must have been quite awhile ago. I don't travel much anymore since I sold my business. How can I help you Mr.…?"

"Larousse. Henri Larousse. I remember you well because of the fascinating stories you told me about animals. Anyway, I need your help."

"And how can I help you Henri?"

Henri told William the story about the veranda and the parrot, and the wish for her daughter to get a mate for the parrot. William listened, making hmmm… hmmm… noises as if this were a difficult project.

After awhile and some silence, he finally answered, "Henri, I would discourage you to pursue this project. Your parrot has been alone for a long time now, and unless you try to get him accustomed to a mate at a parrot breeder's place, I don't think it will work out. Parrots are picky creatures."

Henri and William continued their dialogue. Henri listened to the difficulties of breeding exotic animals away from their native habitat, he heard about William's disappointment with the invasive species which had spread in Florida, he listened to William's guilt about contributing to it by selling baby pythons at one point. The stories he told were as fascinating as the ones he had heard on their flight together. Henri was intrigued by the man who was still obviously close to animals and to nature, but who had a different outlook on what was happening now to their species.

"So what do you think I can do to make my daughter's parrot happy, William? And my daughter happy also in the process?"

"I have an idea, Henri. If you just get some beautiful small birds to live and fly around happily in your veranda, Victor would no longer be alone. He would have some company. I have an old friend who lives in Arkansas and whose wife passed away last week. I want to visit him. Perhaps I could get some birds from an aviary here and bring them to you if you don't live too far from my friend. They are rather expensive birds but very beautiful. Your daughter and your parrot would like them. You would have to pay for the transport. The birds may need to travel out of the cabin, you know."

"No problem, William. And when you come I want you to stay at my place for a couple days. I will make arrangements if I'm gone to D.C. Joan would love to meet you and talk to you and I'll try to be back in time to see you."

After exchanging dates and directions, Henri felt satisfied that Joan's wish would be granted. Even if Victor didn't get a mate, he would at least have the company of other beautiful birds which would also would keep the veranda alive and colorful. When Joan heard of the arrangement, she thought that it was a great idea and looked forward to meeting William Price.

Joan saw Kristin at school the next day. They not could not find a quiet place to talk there, so Joan thought of doing something she had never done before. She would invite someone to join her in her cave. It was a difficult decision. Joan's cave was her private hideout, the place where she talked with her soul and the place where she felt safe, but Kristin had become such a good friend to her! So, Joan asked Kristin to meet her at her house after school and to join her in her special retreat. For some reason she felt like sharing this private place with her best friend.

Kristin arrived with a satchel. She brought notes taken in Mark Silver's class on biodiversity, a class Joan had missed because of her lunch with Henri. It was very warm outside and the girls were wearing shorts and t-shirts. Joan led Kristin toward the park. It was a beautiful spring day, the kind which lifts your spirit up and opens your eyes to wonders.

"This is my church, Kristin. I come here to worship nature and resonate with its creation. I let go of my mind and go into my heart to feel that I'm part of nature here, that I belong with it: the trees, the pond, the river, the grass, the Earth. I listen to the birds and the frogs. I breathe, I smell, I close my eyes, and I know that God, or whatever it is in that dimension I can't think of but only feel, is there, and it makes me happy. I can forget all the bad stuff here. It's my church!"

Kristin was attentive to Joan's words which were carrying her away into that realm she described, a place where she also could feel something special which was accessible to her heart. Kristin was filled with joy.

"Joan, what a marvelous place to feel at one with nature! This is our gift from the universe. We should respect nature and it is such a pity that humans are in the process of destroying it! Imagine Joan, we have raped the Earth, poisoned the air and the water, and eliminated a lot of plants and animals. Why do we do this? Why? Why do we spit on the beautiful gift we were given? I am so sad!"

"I'm sad too, Kristin. The only refuge I find these days is to think that the human race is in a process of evolution where some consciousness will prevail and help reverse the mistakes. Remember the cocoon, and the metamorphosis, and the butterfly, Kristin? Maybe humans will become conscious of the mistakes and repair the damage. If it is not too late, of course. Sometimes I feel pessimistic Kristin. Sometimes it makes me cry!"

"I feel that way too, Joan. Wait 'til I tell you what's happening to biodiversity in the world, something which is so necessary to maintain balance. It looks like the scale is tipping slowly."

The girls reached the entrance to the cave. Joan moved a branch which was hiding it and let Kristin walk in. There was a ray of sunlight coming down through a small opening in the roof.

"Welcome to my sanctuary, Kristin, I have spent many hours in this place since I discovered it when I was a child. I'm never disappointed when I come here. It's like being in the center of the Earth!"

Kristin was speechless. She looked for a place to sit next to Joan. She remained silent for awhile listening to the slow drip of water coming from the ceiling of the cave. There was an awe within herself she didn't want to break.

Joan is the one who broke the silence. "So, Kristin, can you read me some of the notes you took in Mr. Sliver's class? Is it as dire as he said about the global warming problem?"

"Global warming has a lot to do with it, of course, because of what it has done to animal habitats, but in general terms, population growth and human consumption are the reasons for the enormous loss of species. We have destroyed their habitat and traded the wildlife. Look at what happened with the elephants and the ivory trade or the rhinoceroses killed for their horns. Look at the disappearing tigers, wolves, all the predators that keep the ecosystems in balance. The Earth needs them! Here is an example of what happens to the biodiversity balance. The sea otters' position in the food chain is key to keeping the ecosystem balanced. In Alaska the number of sea otters has dropped 90% because the orcas eat them to replace the salmon and herring which have been overfished. Sea otters eat sea urchins so now the sea urchin population has exploded. Sea urchins feed on the kelp forest, so this causes the dissolution of a complex system that supports mammals, fish, and birds. Everything is interrelated, Joan, and we don't realize it, even the insects are important. Think of what is happening to the bees and the butterflies. What about pollination?"

"Did Mr. Silver give any figures about how much is at stake for the species?"

"Here is a passage: 'Our planet is now in the midst of its sixth mass extinction of plants and animals, the sixth wave of extinctions in the past half-billion years. We are currently experiencing the worst spate of species die-offs since the loss of the dinosaurs 65 million years ago. Scientists estimate we are now loosing species at 100 to 10,000 times the normal rate, with dozens going extinct every day. It could be a scary future indeed, with as many as 30-50% of all species possibly heading toward extinction by mid century,' says the Center for Biological Diversity."

"Whoa! That's quite a loss! And we never hear people talk about this Kristin. Have you ever heard this quoted on the news? That's more important than the usual sensational items they present as if nothing else was happening in our troubled world! Why isn't this biodiversity extinction presented to the public as something crucial for natural balance, along with global warming and poisoning our Earth, plants, and water with all the chemicals?"

"Maybe people don't want to hear this. They would be afraid and think that the necessary changes to remedy the problem were beyond what can be done. They would go into denial to keep the status quo… we see this happen all the time. Remember Mr. Field and the global warming hoax? It was easier for him to accept a hoax than the difficult truth which challenges our established system. Only a change in consciousness will influence the way people think. It will take awhile, Kristin."

"So our task is to help change consciousness in our world, Joan? That's quite a task, my friend!" Kristin concluded. "Eh, look who is here," Kristin exclaimed looking at the newt crawling out of a hole. "It's so cute!"

"And slimy." Joan continued, caressing the little critter. "He is my friend. He keeps me company here. We both belong to this world, in a different form, but we both love life on our precious planet."

Kristin looked at her watch, packed her satchel, and got up. "I have to go Joan. I really enjoyed discovering your hidden sanctuary. This place will stay in my heart as a testimony to one of the Earth's little treasures. How many of these are there on this planet?"

The two girls walked back through the park silently, looking, listening, smelling and even touching the grass at times. They felt good connecting with nature, letting go of their thoughts. They stopped at the pond for a few minutes. It was glimmering with the sun's rays reflecting on the surface. School would be over in two weeks and the two friends would probably not see much of each other during the summer. They felt this loss inside. So much was happening in each of their lives. How do you stay tuned to the present when you have a past together and try to envision the future? They arrived at the gate where Kristin had parked her mom's car.

"Kristin. I'll call you as soon as I know when my dad's friend is coming. He will bring some beautiful birds to keep Victor company in the veranda. It will be in the next few days. See you at school tomorrow. Thank you for sharing the biodiversity lecture with me. So much to learn! So much to do! Let consciousness do the job!" Joan added, with a smile.

William Price let Henri know that he would arrive in two days. He had selected four pairs of beautiful exotic birds from a sanctuary for rescued birds needing lifelong homes. These had been abandoned by owners who didn't have cages big enough to accommodate them, or perhaps they moved or died, and William thought the veranda would be a paradise for these little creatures. They would no longer feel that were living in captivity, they would fly in freedom. Henri thought Joan would love the idea, of course, and he let her know when William was coming.

Joan was very excited, she jumped up and down, letting her arms fly in the air imagining what freedom would feel like for her new winged friends, and she thought that it would be a great time to have a small party to witness the release of these birds in a place which would feel more like home to them. Since it would be a weekend, she decided to invite Kristin, Phillip, Mademoiselle Giroud and Mark Silver of course, who would love to see her. Martha would be happy to bake some goodies for the group and Mom would probably show up in a veranda outfit. Joan got on the phone right away to arrange the event. Unfortunately Joan's dad would be on a trip and may not be back before William Price's departure which was scheduled the day after the birds' release.

William Price arrived at the house the day before the party. Everything was prepared for him. At first, he was a little concerned about the birds that had travelled quite a distance from Florida but after he saw the veranda, its size, the tropical plants and trees adorning it, and of course the waterfall, he felt relieved. The temperature of the place was perfect. The birds would spend their last night of captivity in the two cages William brought along and they would be okay. Freedom would be their next step.

This was the kind of party Joan liked. With friends of like mind, a beautiful natural setting, the loving presence of Phillip, Mademoiselle and Kristin, the help of Martha and probably the appearance of her curious mom who always was surprised at Joan's unexpected antics. Joan had met William Price briefly the day he arrived and told him how grateful she was that he made this effort to bring Victor some company. Joan liked William Price at once—peaceful looking, his white hair a little longer in the back, a face that reflected wisdom and kindness. She told him about the party for the release and he thought that it was a terrific idea; this way he could tell the group about each pair of birds. Joan also told William that she would join him and her mom for dinner since her dad was out of town, and that he should take a walk in the park the next morning to get the feel of the surroundings.

On Sunday, the party guests were in the veranda already when William Price arrived carrying the two cages of chirping residents, and everybody cheered when he walked in. It could have been the scene from a movie entitled *The Prisoners' Great Release*. William was honored and saluted after he put the cages down. Victor was watching the action from the top of a banana tree making some guttural noises to be sure he was noticed. William Price immediately acknowledged him.

"So here is Victor, I see, a double yellow head Amazon parrot," he commented as everyone admired the green and yellow head and the red spotted wings. "He looks very healthy. No wonder in a place like this, it's almost like his natural habitat. Hello everybody, I'm honored to see this crowd. You all look excited about what is going to take place. You must be nature lovers."

"We are," Mademoiselle answered. "I have watched this place grow for some years now and Victor is my friend. Right Victor?"

"Right... right ..." Victor repeated coming down from its perch and landing on the back of a chair.

Kristin was arranging chairs for people to sit by the waterfall and Phillip, who had given a hug to Joan, moved close to Mark Silver. "We are going to see some biodiversity here today, professor, and these birds will live a long life. It makes me feel good!"

"It makes me feel good also, Phillip, especially since I was told that these birds are coming from a sanctuary for rescued birds. They are exotic species and being caged is not what they need. They are the fortunate ones who will be free to fly again."

William Price picked up the cages and moved toward the waterfall where seats had been arranged for the group. He seemed content. "I have made a lot of mistakes in my life with animals. I had a pet shop and for a long time I didn't realize the harm we do to exotic species by importing them into our country. We remove them from their natural habitat, subject them to different climates and food, and we cage them to control their whereabouts. It is cruel. When Henri called me about Victor and the veranda, I jumped at the occasion to do something good for some birds and decided to come right away. I feel like I'm redeeming myself in a way. It's too late for the pythons I sold to some kids way back that ended up as invasive species in Florida after they multiplied uncontrollably. We always pay later for the mistakes we make when we violate nature's laws. What is happening in the world right now is telling us the heavy price of that lesson!"

"I congratulate you William," Mark Silver said, "for becoming so conscious of the laws of nature by the trials and errors in your job. Few people can reverse their thinking about what they do against nature these days, now it looks like nature has been challenged to a breaking point." Mark Silver concluded, "You are a fine man and a teacher for us all, William."

"William, I want you to know that you are a gift to us today, not only bringing these beautiful birds, but also by bringing your wisdom, something which we all need to hear," Joan interjected, smiling. "And now I can't wait to see all these precious creatures taste their freedom for the first time. Will you introduce them to us?" she added, begging.

"All these birds are different kinds of exotic finches, a species which will get along well with Victor. I brought four pairs of different birds. They all come from warm places in Africa, South America, or Australia. For example, the blue-capped cordon bleu from Ethiopia. And here they are," William said proudly, opening the side of the first cage which housed a pair of plump blue cordon bleu finches. The female hopped forward to the edge of the cage, and eagerly flew out. At first the male, distinctive with his red cheek, hesitated and stayed back, but very soon flew out following the female who was already whirling around.

William then opened the second side of the first cage, announcing, "Will you welcome now the nutmeg manikin, or spice finch, with its conical black beak, its brown and dark markings. Aren't these two gorgeous?" William commented as the female, totally lost and exited, flew toward him and landed on his head while the male flew to the top of the veranda. The group burst out laughing, but concerned, while William gently picked the female up out of his hair and sent her to rejoin her mate.

All eyes were now focused on the second cage. William opened the first side delicately. "I have a pair of Java sparrows here, black cap, white cheeks, and yellow beaks. You can see their white bellies under their grey bodies. And it looks like the female does not want to leave the cage," William continued as the male was already gone. "Maybe I can help," he said, as he cautiously took her out of the cage and placed her on a nearby hibiscus where she ruffled her feathers before flying away. "You know, these birds feel totally estranged in this new environment. Imagine if you had been locked in a cage and were suddenly presented with an open space. "What a shock," William commented pensively. "And now, for the last but not least of these beauties, the zebra finch, with its black and white body and bright orange beak," William announced, opening the last part of the second cage. "These guys are very fast. Watch them fly! Can you imagine how hard it must have been for them to sit in a cage with so much energy locked inside their bodies? I can't tell you how happy I am to witness this release, to feel the energy, the joy, the freedom they all experience."

The flock whirled and turned and landed and flew all over the veranda in spirals and circles. Victor was peacefully watching the spectacle, moving his head around, probably wondering what this was all about. The group was watching this display of liberty in silence but with happiness in their hearts. *Freedom, is this what freedom is? To be who you are without being held a prisoner, to be one with nature and the core of your being?*

William suggested that people should perhaps exit cautiously and let the flock of birds get acquainted with their new space and with each other. He brought specific directions for their feeding and care which Joan suggested he talk to Martha about. She was the one in charge and she loved Victor. He also asked whether there could be a second door added to the veranda entrance, so the birds would not escape when anyone went in or out. Something like they have in aviaries in the zoos.

Martha had prepared a tea party with pastries and *crème brulee* of course. Everybody gathered in the dining room where Susan made an appearance to greet the guests and she did a great job. She knew everybody by now, having met them at the Fields' gathering. She looked at Phillip very carefully, probably thinking of her daughter's choice for the prom. The party was quiet but very friendly. Freedom was the topic of the day. The release of the birds and what it meant to everyone present was thought provoking and heartwarming and they all talked joyously about it. They had seen and felt freedom in action, there was no need to elaborate further. They were pleased.

After everyone left and dinner was served for her mom and William, Joan went back to the veranda where she opened the door cautiously. Everything was very quiet. The birds seemed to have found their favorite niches. A couple of faint tweets were heard here and there in the branches. There was a sense of peace in the air, the peace which comes from freedom and contentment. Soon the night would descend and they would spend it in their new habitat, something close to what their original home had been. *Home is good,* Joan thought. She felt happy to have helped create this return to paradise for her winged friends. Joan closed her eyes. *Life is good.*

Chapter Eighteen: Dad, I Wish You Were Here!

Joan went to bed early that evening, still reeling from the happiness of a perfect day. The party brought her favorite people together. William showed himself to be a kind man and he fascinated his audience. Martha surpassed herself with the goodies, and she whispered in Joan's ear that she was thankful for the money Susan gave her equal to the price of a prom dress. The birds were beautiful and cheerful in the veranda. School would soon be out. Mom seemed okay and liked her group of friends. Dad would be back soon. Life was good when Joan went to sleep in her cozy bed! Life was great!

In the middle of the night, Joan awoke to some strange noises. It sounded like several cars were moving around the parking area. Some lights were flashing like those of a police car. A strong wind was agitating branches by Joan's window. She felt a sense of fear invade her and at first wanted to bury her head in the pillow, ignoring the commotion. She sat up and went to peer out of the window but couldn't see what was going on. Taking a deep breath, she put on her robe and went down to investigate. She opened the front door.

Claude got out of the family car followed by Martha who had obviously accompanied him somewhere. An officer was helping a staggering Susan out of the police car and inquiring where they should take her. Martha indicated the entrance as she walked toward the front door where Joan had just come out.

"Mom, what happened?" Joan asked very worried. "Are you hurt?"

"No, your mother is okay, she ran a red light and drove into another car, but there was little damage. Thank heaven she was driving slowly! Your mother was driving while intoxicated and she has been charged with a DWI," the police officer answered. "Will you ask Henri to stop by the station as soon as he returns? We have some papers for him to fill out." He nodded towards Martha and Claude.

Martha held Susan's arm and helped her to the bedroom where she fell on the bed moaning. She took Susan's shoes off, her jacket, and settled her under the bedspread. Susan looked like she was going to fall asleep. Martha closed the door, crying, "It's my fault! I hid the bottles of vodka after the party today because your mom looked out of sorts. I knew she would go for the bottle. Apparently she drove to a liquor store to get some. She drank quite a few glasses in the car and had an accident before she got home. I should have left the bottles alone; then she would not have gone out!" Martha continued crying and feeling guilty. "The police called the house and Claude and I had to go to the station to talk to them. They wanted to bring her home themselves because we were both so upset and worried. Your mom's car was towed away. The other car was drivable and they went home." Martha continued wiping her tears. "The ambulance came and the crew checked out your mom. They said she was okay, just very drunk. I'm so sorry Joan!"

"Martha, it's not your fault. You did something you thought was right! Mom has a big problem and we are going to do something about it. Maybe this incident is a blessing in disguise, because , she didn't get hurt, thank God, but she needs to go to rehab for sure now. Dad should return soon. He wanted to see William Price before he left. I guess the gentleman has not heard the commotion? This is strange. He must have slept through it! If dad doesn't get back before Mr. Price leaves, will you help him out Claude? The rented car is parked in the garage, I think."

Claude had heard Martha explain the situation and take the blame for Susan's escapade but remained silent. He didn't know what to say. This relieved his embarrassment. "Yes, Ms. Joan, I'll be happy to do that. You can count on me."

Everyone went to bed. It was almost three in the morning. The wind was still blowing strongly and Joan worried about what could happen if her dad came back in the bad weather. It was scary! She wished Henri had come back the day before, but she reassured herself by taking some deep breaths, remembering that the landing strip was always well lit at night and that her dad was a skilled pilot and knew his way around the area very well.

Henri still had not returned when William Price came out of his room in the morning, ready to leave. Martha prepared breakfast for him and Claude let him know that he would help him with his bag and the cages. The drive to the airport would take a little over an hour. William wanted to stop by the veranda and take a last look at his protégées, making sure they had adjusted to their new home.

When Joan walked into the dining room for breakfast, William was gone to inspect birds in the veranda. Martha told her that the gentleman was wearing hearing aids and had probably taken them off at night, which explained why he didn't hear the commotion with her mom coming home in the company of the police.

"I'm glad he was sleeping, Martha. It is better we didn't have to explain Mom's problem to him. It may have spoiled his trip. I wish Dad were back, though. He would enjoy seeing his old friend. I wonder what kept him so long on this trip," Joan added, concerned.

William Price came back from the veranda beaming. "The birds are doing their morning routine, preening themselves, singing and flying all around. It's quite a scene! Victor seems content. The whole veranda is alive with the sound of music and I will leave this place with a happy heart. I wish I could have seen Henri, though. Joan, tell your dad that I'll come back in the future to check on everything and that will make sure he can be here then."

"I will, Mr. Price, and thank you again for doing this amazing thing for all of us humans and birds. I'll send you some news about them periodically, and photos also. Dad will be very pleased." William Price left with his empty cages and the good memories of a successful trip.

A couple hours later, Susan came out of her room, feeling groggy and still wearing the clothes she had on when the police brought her back. It was obvious that she was looking for Henri. She called him several times. No answer. She walked around the house. Everything was quiet. Susan sat in the living room. She was terribly depressed. The reality of what happened was now hitting her and it was unbearable. Her whole life was at stake. Susan's thoughts were churning in the limited space of her skull, where they were too big for her mind to contain. A sense of helplessness invaded her. How could she stop the horrible sense of fear which assailed her as she felt caught in this inescapable prison? It was impossible. It was the end. Her emotions taking over, Susan burst into tears. She cried and cried, letting the healthy flow run down from her throat, her mouth and her eyes into an ocean of release and warmth.

"Please, somebody help me!" she implored sobbing. "Please!"

Martha, who had been keeping an eye on Susan, checking her room to make sure she was still asleep, could not resist the call for help. Earlier, she hesitated because of her own bad feelings about hiding the vodka bottles and therefore contributing to Susan's trip to find some and have an accident. The painful begging of the word "please," repeated by her mistress in an agonizing situation, tore her servant boundaries down and she rushed to Susan, taking her into her arms.

"Oh, Madam, I'm so sorry. I am the one who took the vodka bottles and hid them from you. I feel so bad about what happened. I care so much for you, I didn't want you to drink so much. I thought I was being helpful. I am sorry, I'm so sorry."

The two women were now crying together, arms around each other, letting the flow of their tears heal the pain in their hearts as the fence that stood between them came down. Their woman's essence was now joining on the same plane. They remained crying for awhile, having found the exquisite place of human love which is offered to people encountering a dismal life situation together. There was nothing to say. In their silence they both felt the intimacy of this delicate moment, supporting each other.

Susan took the initiative after a long pause. She sniffed a few tears and looked Martha in the eyes. "Martha, you didn't do anything wrong. You and Henri and Joan know that I have a problem. I'm sorry. I have to find a way to deal with it. I'm afraid of life, so I drink. Okay? I try to forget. I can't, so I keep doing it. I can't stop and it goes on and on. I'm tired. I am so tired," Susan concluded, taking a deep breath. "I have to talk to Henri and Joan and not hide anymore. Listen Martha, I want to thank you. You just did something big for me. Thank you."

Martha, having regained her maid's role, was looking at Susan with disbelief. Was this woman the same person—the one who ordered her impersonally to prepare dinner for the guests yesterday and the one who cried in her arms a few minutes ago? Where do boundaries start and where do they end? Is there a place where human beings can just be at ease and act from their inner sense of love for each other and feel it without creating distances that separate them? Both Susan and Martha were considering this dilemma inside and both knew they tasted the real thing during their emotional interaction. The future would tell how strong the experience had marked them.

"Martha, I would like you to call me Susan from now on. Okay? I guess it's just normal. Right? After all you have been with us for eighteen years and now we cried together," Susan said wiping the last of her tears. I'm sure Joan is going to be flabbergasted! Let's see what she says," Susan added laughing. "Oh, life!"

"Yes, Mrs." Martha paused. "Excuse me, Susan. I think that Joan will be happy. This girl of yours is the most wonderful human being I know. She throws love all around her like happy seeds which grow into flowers. We are lucky to be in her path."

Susan went back to her bedroom to get dressed. Martha went back to the kitchen to prepare things for dinner. Joan came back from school where Ms. Stern helped her do research on the Betty Ford Center for addiction treatment. She wanted to be ready to present her dad with the results. *He will have a hard enough time coping with the events of the past night, the police report and all,* she thought! Sending Mom to rehab was the most important thing to organize right now. But Dad had not come back yet… *Dad, I wish you were here,* Joan repeated to herself as she arrived home with her notes. *I wish you were here.*

Chapter Nineteen: Mom Goes to Rehab

Henri returned the next day. Claude called him on his cell phone to inform him of the situation with Susan and told him that he would need to go to the police station as soon as possible. There were papers to fill out and insurance statements to take care of. Claude reassured Henri that Susan was not hurt and that Martha was taking good care of her. He also mentioned that William Price left after a very successful bird launching and an enjoyable party to celebrate the event.

When Henri arrived, Joan was at school, one of her last days there, and Susan was moving around the bedroom, packing a suitcase. Henri could not believe his eyes.

"What in the world?" he said when he entered, carrying his own bag. "What are you doing, Susan?" he added in an incredulous tone. "Are you leaving us or what?"

"I guess I should, after what happened. Have you heard the story?" Susan said, keeping her eyes down while she picked up a pair of shoes. "Maybe I don't need too many of these where I am going," she added, tossing the pair of blue satin high heels back in the closet. "I did it, Henri, I'm going to jail, right?"

Henri maintained his composure and tried to ignore his fatigue. He didn't have any idea of what happened between Susan and Martha, didn't know if Joan had seen or heard anything and why Susan was packing and talking about jail. This was probably a scene Susan was putting up to confuse him, something she did occasionally when she felt guilty.

After a moment of silence and a few deep breaths Henri decided to go along with the game. "Yes, Susan, you are going somewhere, but instead of a jail, you are going to a place where you will be taken care of. I heard about what happened. Claude called me. All we have to do now is to arrange for you to stay in a good rehab center where you will be helped with your addiction. Maybe you have already thought of it because you need it."

"Can they teach me what I can do instead of drinking vodka when you're gone Henri? We don't have a life together. I can't do it anymore! We are just like cruise ships passing each other in the night! Life has no meaning for me at this point. My life sucks!"

"I thought I was the one who felt like life is lousy, remember? And I blamed you and said it was your fault! Well, I guess we need to look at this problem together, Susan, and do something about it. That is if we still love each other!" Henri concluded, tired and feeling mixed emotions. "But first, let's take care of you. I have already talked with Joan about you going to the Betty Ford Center. Let me see what I can do to get that set up. If you go there for awhile, you can get treatment for your alcohol abuse in a comfortable and loving environment. And when you return we'll work on my part in this, and how to improve our relationship. Is this a deal?" Henri asked, coming closer to Susan and putting his hands on her shoulders while looking into her eyes.

Susan did not know what to say. Henri had laid out and irrefutable truth, impossible to argue about. *He was so smart*, she thought, *he always had the last word*. Sure he put his arms on her shoulders but she wanted more, maybe a release like the one she felt with Martha, maybe more love from him, maybe to feel more love for him, like when they first met. He was so wonderful then. But she didn't feel like it right now. Susan could not even cry, she had already cried all of her heart out the day before. She was lost, not knowing what to say. *Where is my vodka?* Susan thought.

Joan knocked on their bedroom door when she arrived from school, happy to see that her dad was back and anxious to find out how things went between the two of them.

"Dad, I'm so happy to see you back. What kept you so long? We missed you when William Price came. You should have been here when the birds got their freedom. It was so beautiful!" Joan said hugging her dad joyously.

"That's what I also need, Joan. More freedom. Yes, freedom! Your mom was just reminding me of this, she said we were like two cruise ships passing each other in the night! Quite an image, don't you think? At least they are cruise ships… not cargo boats," Henri added jokingly. "Anyway, I know all about the car accident and the police report, and we are going to help your mom get some help. Actually, I don't want to get into details about my trip, but I had to go up to Alaska for some stupid business problem, if you want to know. I hated being gone so long, I swear. I want my freedom, too, like the birds, I want be with you both," Henri concluded, getting Susan and Joan into his arms and hugging them together. "I love you both very much."

Susan was starting to feel better. It looked as if Henri was warming up and she remembered what Martha said about Joan's presence and how she could seed flowers all around her. It sure was right! Susan thought she could add her two cents worth to the running joke about cruise ships in the night, and she ventured, "Henri, let's make sure those ships don't collide, okay? They could maybe travel together to a Pacific island and dock there for awhile, don't you think?"

"Sure, and I already know what we can do. When you get back from your rehab cruise in Rancho Mirage by the sea, Susan, I'll take both of you to the mountains. I know just the place, girls," Henri concluded, happy to see that the two women he loved were here with him, content and at peace.

The next few days were spent taking care of police papers, insurance settlements, car repairs and reservations at the Betty Ford Center in Rancho Mirage. Susan had agreed to go there knowing that Betty Ford decided to open that center because, at the time, she thought women needed a place for their special needs. Joan pointed out that psychological support was available there and told her mom to try yoga and massage to help her through this difficult time. Changing a life pattern would be hard on Susan and it would help to train her body to be in sync with her mind. Joan also suggested that Susan focus on herself, and not call or text the family too much but rather talk to people at the center, make friends with other women in her program. Maybe later she could join support groups where she could apply what she learns about addition to helping other women. It all seemed to appeal to Susan. And of course she would take her dinner dresses and her tennis racket with her, but not the teacher!

The center had advised a one month stay for Susan. She would begin in early June and be back therefore in July, just in time for the famous Fourth of July party she wanted to throw. Neither Henri nor Joan was very happy about the idea, but Henri promised Susan that he told her that he would arrange it for her return.

Joan was pleased that her mom had accepted this huge step with relative ease. Thinking of all the opposition she could have presented, it was a relief to see her almost excited about going. Was there something in her mother that Joan didn't understand that allowed this easy acceptance? Was it a need for meaning in her life other than her wife and mother roles? What was she finding in this new project, triggered by an unfortunate episode? Maybe something had to give. The status quo was unbearable for her mom, and in the process of shaking it she had felt love from her family, support, attention… she needed it. *Is that the way life proceeds?* Joan thought. *On to the next step to consciousness through suffering? Is that what happens in the world?*

Joan was silent for a long time, pondering the idea of the chrysalis of transformation with its hellish vision of chaos coming to her mind. She visualized war-like scenes and fights, hurricanes and floods, crying women, murdered babies, the Earth torn apart, and the animals gone. *Is this necessary to get to the next step in our evolution?* she wondered. Her dream-like vision ended with the image of a beautiful butterfly hovering above a rose. She took a deep breath. *Consciousness!* she murmured softly. *Love! Let the world become conscious…*

Susan finished packing. Henri took care of the aftermath of the accident. School ended in late May, and Joan planned her next lesson with Mademoiselle, who still had not covered the subject of famous French women who helped make changes in history. Kristin came to say goodbye before leaving for a summer trip with her grandparents in Montana. Phillip was getting a summer job at the hospital where his dad worked. There would be summer classes so Ms. Stern needed to stay at the library. Everything was happening like a well-choreographed ballet of people moving in all directions, some of them on pointe if they had rehearsed to perfection! Summer was almost here, it was warm and weddings were planned all around town. Life in the U.S. was going on as usual. Mr. Field had changed his view about climate change and joined the Union of Concerned Scientists. Life was moving forward and consciousness growing slowly, step by step, toward the butterfly condition.

Susan left for Rancho mirage like a big girl. Claude took her to the airport with three suitcases and a bag of shoes. Henri went back to D.C. for a very important congressional meeting and Martha felt like she was getting a vacation. Joan got her Prius and learned how to drive it from the Toyota mechanic. Summer was just around the corner. Wild irises were blooming around the pond. *Life.* Joan thought. *Life is so good!*

Chapter Twenty: Life Without Mom

Joan had suggested to her mom that she should focus on herself and her rehabilitation. She certainly did. No one heard from Susan after she left. Not even to let them know that she arrived safely! After a couple days, Joan decided to call in the evening. She was concerned. Susan answered cheerfully that life was okay, that she met a lot of other women in rehab like herself, that the food was good, the beach close by, the sessions interesting with good therapists and that the stuff they used to replace their alcohol cravings did not taste too bad. Susan cut the conversation short because of the evening meditation practice she wanted to go to. Joan was overwhelmed by the list of positive statements she heard. It was amazing to realize that her mom didn't complain. She didn't even hint at missing the family. *Weird*, Joan thought, finding it a little sad. *Somehow we are no longer needed.* But Joan's ambivalence soon made room for the happiness of imagining her mother in a safe place and content. *What did I expect? That Mom would cry and say she wanted to come back? Perish the thought! This is great. I guess I'm discovering many traits I didn't know about my mother. She knows what she needs to take care of herself. That makes me happy.*

Joan was looking forward to one of her last lessons of the school year with Mademoiselle Giroud. Mademoiselle and Mark Silver became very close since they first met in the veranda and planned to take a camping trip together in July. They would explore several of the national parks in Utah after a stop at the Grand Canyon, a dream which Mademoiselle had when she first came to the States. She had seen beautiful photographs of these wonderful places and fantasized of going someday. Never would she have dreamed of making that trip with a loving companion!

The long promised lesson on French women who helped change the course of history was the next topic for Joan's homework. She didn't know where to start and decided to go to the library to seek help. The place was empty except for Ms. Stern, who was busy organizing new books for the upcoming summer program. Her face lit up when she saw Joan.

"So good to see you, Joan. You look relaxed. Isn't it great to take a break from the school routine? I will be able to take a few weeks to go visit my sister in Wisconsin," Ms. Stern continued, coming down from the step ladder. "What's happening in your life these days and what can I do for you?"

"Well, it's a long story and I won't go into details, but let's just say that Mom was stopped by the police for a DWI. She had an accident and is now at the Betty Ford Center for alcohol addiction treatment."

"Joan! What a shock! I didn't know your mother was an alcoholic! It must be hard for the family! I am so sorry."

"Actually, I think the whole thing happened for the best, Ms. Stern. Nobody got hurt, Dad took care of everything, and Mom now has a way to deal with this serious problem of hers. It seems like the center will help her. I talked to her last night. She sounds good and is cooperating with the program. I'm very glad she agreed to go there."

"Women owe a lot to Betty Ford. Imagine the wife of a president being humble enough to reveal her own problem to the country and set an example for women in the same predicament! That's remarkable! Women can be great role models. Your mother will learn a lot by her stay there, I'm sure."

"Yes, she will. By the way, Ms. Stern, I came here to ask you a question related to this very subject... about women in history who helped change the world by their participation. Mademoiselle Giroud gave me this big subject to study! Men usually get all the recognition. History books are full of their names while women stay in the shadow. The feminine energy does not seem to be a powerful enough to make changes that are appreciated!"

"Joan, there are many women in history who have contributed in amazing ways to the advancement of the human race. Sometimes they were the forces in the shadow who inspired men with their own ingenious ideas, sometimes they were the forces in the limelight who came out and spoke a truth necessary to change the status quo. Two names pop up right now in American history: Eleanor Roosevelt and Rosa Parks. I could go on and on. Men have shown the more brutal part of masculine energy that ends up starting and fighting wars all over the world to solve problems, but women used a more feminine intuition that guides them to resolve issues and bring progress through more heartfelt resolutions."

"Ms. Stern, that's a really good and simple way to sum up the history of the world and its complex predicaments! This seems so obvious and makes so much common sense! I think we are now in a stage of our evolution where can understand these truths more clearly. Maybe brutal force often triumphs over the resistance of the powerless, but there is a little voice in the conscious mind that knows better. It can feel what the heart sees. The feeling spreads a consciousness that expands more and more in the world today."

"Joan, you said that Mademoiselle Giroud assigned you to study about women who helped to change history? What about Joan of Arc? I think she is a woman who was motivated by both the masculine and feminine energies we are talking about. She was a pioneer in her own way. Try to find the motivating factors for her quest in her history. This should be a great assignment for your French class."

"Thank you, thank you, Ms. Stern," Joan repeated, very excited by the idea. "You've been so helpful. You always talk about women in history who are great role models. Some are not recorded in books, like one we have right here in our school! Thank you again."

Ms. Stern was moved by Joan's enthusiasm about her help. She shook her head and pursed her lips. "We all are role models when we speak from our hearts, Joan. Good luck on your assignment and give my best to Monique," she added walking Joan to the library door with a large smile.

Joan called Mademoiselle to inform her that she was looking forward to the lesson about remarkable French women in history and that she had a surprise for her. She would research Joan of Arc in particular before the class. She liked the idea that Joan of Arc was a young woman like herself, and that she used both masculine and feminine energy to achieve her goal. Mademoiselle thought this was a good idea. She never thought of looking at heroines from a psychological standpoint and Joan would take a fresh look at what was behind strict historical facts. Joan asked Mademoiselle to meet her in the veranda so they could watch the birds in their new environment.

A couple days later, Mademoiselle walked into the veranda, opening the door carefully and making sure none of the residents could escape.

Joan was waiting for her by the waterfall, reading her notes. She had studied Joan of Arc's story at length on the internet, thinking how incredible it was to find everything you needed to know right there at your finger tips. *The time necessary to research such a large amount of facts in a library would be many hours or even days*, she thought! *What a miracle modern technology is!*

"Good afternoon, Joan. Our friends are happy, it seems," Mademoiselle said, observing the finches flying around the veranda. It looked as if the female blue-capped cordon bleu liked Victor. She was perched on his head as he stood still and seemed perfectly content. The zebra finch couple was busy building a nest in a hidden dark corner of the roof, bringing in twigs and debris. They were twittering cheerfully as they made their rounds. "Did your dad like the newcomers, Joan?"

"Dad was very happy with what William did. He has ordered a second door to secure the entrance to the veranda to protect them. Unfortunately Dad missed his friend, but he will invite him to come again and check the premises."

Joan and Mademoiselle sat by the waterfall, excited about the upcoming lesson. Joan loved speaking French and her vocabulary had expanded amazingly during the past year with all the reading she had done and compositions she had written in the language. Mademoiselle took out some notes she had made. "Okay Joan, now on to the French women who have contributed to changing world history. Before you start your psychological assessment of Joan of Arc and what motivated her to intervene in the war against the British, I want to mention two women I just picked who did great things to improve a situation. One is St. Genevieve, the patron saint of Paris, way back in 451. Imagine that far back! She was a young woman, just like Joan of Arc. Attila the Hun had marched across the continent to control Gaul, crossed the Rhine with his army and came in sight of Paris. The citizens were all afraid and ready to flee but Genevieve told them to stay. She gathered the women, led them outside the Paris walls, facing the enemies and their weapons, and prayed. Attila turned away. She had helped save the city and its people. Details are not very clear because it took place such a long time ago, but the fact remains that Paris was actually saved by Genevieve's intervention and the women she led. She was canonized later on and became the Patron Saint of Paris."

"Imagine the guts it must have taken to face a horde of barbaric men, ready to pillage and burn and rape," Joan said, shaking her head. "Faith versus the sword, wherever this strong belief comes from, this woman had found the strength inside herself. It is a beautiful story, Mademoiselle."

"Yes, it is, Joan, and now to a completely different story… years later and in another realm of achievement. The woman is Marie Curie and the changes she brought in the world are in the field of science. Marie Curie discovered two elements, polonium and radium, which led to the study of radioactivity. She was a physicist and chemist, the first woman ever to get a Nobel Prize. Actually she got two Nobel Prizes, one for physics and one for chemistry. She was the first woman to become a professor at the University of Paris and also the first woman to be entombed at the prestigious Pantheon of Paris, resting place of the most famous Frenchmen. Medical research centers started using radiology and during World War I, it was brought to the front lines with mobile x-ray vehicles. Actually Marie Curie became the Red Cross Director of Radiology during that war. She and her family, husband and daughter, followed her work and were very dedicated.

"But, Mademoiselle, how was radioactivity handled in these early stages? How did the workers protect themselves from radiation?"

"Unfortunately there was not much awareness about the dangers of this amazing discovery yet. People were exposed to x-rays from unshielded equipment. Marie Curie is said to have carried radioactive isotopes in her pocket! The papers she wrote in the 1890's are dangerous to handle and are stored in protective casings. Even her cook book is still radioactive! Marie Curie died of aplastic anemia caused by her exposure to radiation during World War I from the equipment she brought to the front."

"Mademoiselle, how terrible to discover something so scientifically important only to realize the ill effects later! Isn't that a lesson to learn… to look for what may be hidden behind the apparent benefits of any discovery? Radioactivity, atomic energy, their use, their results, how does anyone know where to stop and how to protect humanity? How does anyone know from the start how the result will affect nature? It is such a difficult dilemma!"

"Yes, Joan, we call it progress and continue on, but nature often rebels to tell us to stop or watch out. Marie Curie had an amazing discovery which brought the benefits of x-rays and radiation to the world, but the body said something about being careful if you want to play with fire. I'm afraid we are now experiencing some extreme conflict with the Earth in a similar way. The Earth rebels and the climate changes, water gets polluted, animal species die, and we get sick with cancer. It is important to find protection to shield us from the consequences or in some cases we have to stop. We must remain conscious and aware of effects."

"Where do we draw the line for progress, Mademoiselle? Can consciousness guide human beings to know in their core what is the right course for the future?"

"I don't know. Joan, we'll see. All we can do is our best to awaken consciousness in others and let it extend to the world. Grassroots consciousness will grow and expand as the vibrations of our minds' energy spread all around us. We are doing this right now, Joan, and so are millions of others. We must keep the faith! Like St. Genevieve when she confronted Attila, remember?"

"Yes, Mademoiselle, I know. That is also what Joan of Arc did in her own time with the situation she confronted."

"Okay Joan, it's time now to present your explanation of what you read into Joan of Arc's story about the psychological motives which prompted her decision to intervene in this difficult page of French history. Remember, the Hundred Years' War was still going on. Imagine, 100 years! Several generations of people involved in this long lasting war! What a waste!"

"Yes, Mademoiselle! War seems such a waste! I looked at Joan of Arc's story trying to understand what influenced her. It seems that she was influenced by both her feminine and masculine energies. I think the visions she had and the voices she heard telling her to go and support King Charles VII to get rid of the English came from an intuitive place in her, from a strong feminine impulse motivated by her idealistic desire to find a way to stop the war. The way I see it, Joan of Arc, being a religious person, visualized this strong urge in the form of saints telling her what to do. St. Margaret, St. Catherine, and St. Michael suggested that she support the king and help the country get rid of the English. The voices she heard were those of her conscience, of her heart, personalized by the saints in her mind. She used her masculine energy to persuade the king to give her an army, which she led dressed in men's clothing, to capture the town of Orleans. This was an immense accomplishment for a simple peasant girl. Her faith was her motivator and she followed her determination. She then helped the Dauphin be crowned in Rheims, in the cathedral where all the kings of France were crowned. Joan experienced all the insults for being a woman and dressing as a masculine warrior. She was called a whore, chastised for wearing pants, captured by the Burgundians who sold her to the British, tried as a heretic and sent to jail where she was raped. She finally was sentenced to death and burned at the stake in Rouen. The king abandoned her but France was saved and the Hundred Years' War was over. It is a long sad story but I admired the courage of this young woman who kept her faith until the end."

"Yes, Joan, it is difficult to imagine that this simple peasant girl could help accomplish such a change in history. The French have great admiration for her. You should see the beautiful church in Rouen dedicated to Joan of Arc! The church later made her a saint."

"Oh, Mademoiselle, I forgot a detail which touched me when I read it, something that came from Joan's heart. She cried often when men died on both sides of the war, and one time when a British prisoner was struck by a guard and decapitated, Joan cried and held the captive's head as he died. Isn't that a symbol of feminine energy moving into a gesture of infinite compassion? Isn't it an affirmation of the craziness of war and its stupidity? Is humanity still stuck today in that primitive phase of its evolution?"

Joan and Mademoiselle remained silent for awhile, thinking of the soldier's death scene. Images of warfare and destruction paraded before their eyes which they shut to let go of the horror. Returning to the present was the only way they could deal with what was said, and the present was good. They opened their eyes to a tropical paradise where colorful birds flew happily around the veranda. Victor was now without his head covering. The zebra finches took a break from building and whirled around the banana tree. The male spice finch searched for his mate by singing a strange inquiring tune. Life went on in motion and sound. Life was good.

"Mademoiselle, what do you think I could do to make changes in this world? Something drastic? Something like what Joan of Arc did and which would shake the status quo from its destructive foundation?"

"Joan, you are an amazing person! All I can say is… listen to your inner voice and the time will come when the answer pops out, but by all means don't let them burn you at the stake, will you? You are too precious to us all!"

"I won't Mademoiselle, I won't," Joan answered, laughing. "I have too much life left to live, and I love life, as you know. I want to live and love, right Victor?"

"Right… right… right…" Victor repeated in his best voice, happy to be asked.

And so ended the lesson on some of the French women who made changes in the world. Joan learned a lot, she was proud of this woman, her namesake, but she was also puzzled. What could she do now? She wanted to do something spectacular, like start a revolution, write a new declaration of independence or be on the news giving an eloquent speech. Working on grassroots consciousness raising was so tedious, so impersonal, so long! When will changes happen? She wanted them right now, not three or four generations from now after she died! She felt impatient.

After Mademoiselle left, Joan went to the cave for awhile to calm down. She closed her eyes and took some deep breaths, her mind was too challenged and she didn't like feeling so tense. It did not help. Letting go of her mind slowly brought her to a place where she could observe what happened. Of course, her ego visualized something spectacular because it would mean recognition and fame. Maybe she could go down in history, right? Neither Joan of Arc nor Marie Curie did what they did with this in mind. They just followed the inner voice which guided them. *I must not follow my ego voice. I must listen to the voice of my consciousness beyond it,* Joan thought, *and maybe the grassroots road is the way, no matter how unspectacular it is!* She smiled. *I will listen to my inner voice and do what it says when the time is right.* Joan repeated, totally calmed down now as she walked out of the cave into the park, breathing deeply. "I trust my inner voice," she repeated as she walked.

Dad was home when she returned. Joan hugged him eagerly. "I'm so happy to see you, Dad. Why is it that your presence brings joy to my heart? I never know where you are or when you'll return and then, all of a sudden, boom, here you are and the sun is shining a little bit brighter! Have you heard from Mom?"

"I have, Joan. It looks like the center is a good place for her. I have been in touch almost daily and I'm happy with her progress."

"That's more than I have. At first I didn't think she needed us anymore and I almost got upset, but I felt better when I realized that she was doing something good for herself and didn't need us for that."

"You're right! She has to get through this thing on her own. It will be tough but she'll make it. I should have seen this coming for a long time Joan, and understood your mom and her addiction. After she helped me with the campaign and I was elected, I didn't want to move our family to D.C. I left both of you here and was gone a lot. Maybe this was a big mistake and Mom suffered from it. No more social life for her. She drank more and more as a result! But, no regrets Joan. What is done is done, right? And Mom is on the mend now. Anyway, what have you been doing lately, sweetie? Tell me."

"Well, Dad, after I studied with Mademoiselle about Joan of Arc, I thought I wanted to do something drastic for the world. I was serious and tried to figure out what I could do."

"Well, Joan of Arkansas, I'm afraid that doing something for the world is a big endeavor these days. The world is such a mess!" Henri laughed shaking his head. "My daughter has incredible ambitions I see. Remember, sweetie, you have already started... first the Prius and then the global warming meeting at The Fields', then the fracking intervention, then the biodiversity effort with our rescued birds. So now, what else, Joan? End the war in Afghanistan?"

"Dad, don't make fun of me. I am serious. I'm so conscious of what is happening on our beautiful Earth these days that it hurts sometimes. We have damaged it so much already, and it will get worse if we don't stop what is going on. Consciousness, Dad, that's what's missing in our world today. Getting conscious, yes, looking directly at the problems so we can make changes. Even if it topples the all-consuming, heartless capitalistic system that dictates the laws in this country and stops the government from acting against the wellbeing of nature and the citizens. Even if you have to close down a big company forever. Even if we simply go back to the original tenets of our democracy which became an inspiration for the entire world." Joan stopped, out of breath.

"Hmmm. My daughter is getting into politics now!" Henri answered, pensively. "You actually are right about a lot of things, Joan, and don't quote me on this, but do you realize how impossible it is to change the system at this point. It is a big, complicated world!"

"I know, so it looks like the politicians are waiting until the point of no return, Dad. When the Earth has had enough and decides to retaliate everywhere, when the oceans flood our coasts, the hurricanes wipe out entire cities, the water is poisoned, the animal species are gone, the forests stripped, and humans are sick with cancer? The sixth mass extinction which could end this evolutionary period on our planet may not be so far away, Dad. Do you realize that? We have to do something about it!"

Henri pursed his lips and shook his head. *What can I say to answer the immovable energy of a 16-year-old whose logic disarms me and my reply could not fit the simplicity of her discourse?* Henri felt tired, confused and decided to discontinue the discussion. He smiled and asked Joan to come with him to the veranda. He wanted to see the birds.

"I'm glad we had William bring these rescued birds here Joan. They look so good in this surrounding, something like home."

"Yes, Dad. They look at peace, don't they? I can feel it when I walk in. I could sit in here for a long time."

"So could I, Joan," Henri said putting his hands on his daughter's shoulders with a big sigh. "I love the feeling of freedom the birds emanate." Henri took a deep breath and turned toward the door. "Joan, let's call Mom, shall we? I haven't talked to her today. Also, I want to tell you about the little speech you gave me awhile ago. I'll think about what you said, sweetie, I promise. You make a lot of sense sometimes, even if that sense is difficult to hear!"

"Thank you Dad, you are such a great father! I'm so lucky!" Joan answered, beaming, "I want to talk to Mom too. Let's do it."

Chapter Twenty-One: Consciousness, *Qu'est-ce Que C'est?*

Susan was progressing consistently. The intense sessions with different well-trained therapists were helpful. She'd never had therapy before and discovered where some of her problems came from. Becoming conscious of her behavior, which was triggered by her unconscious motives, was an important lesson and Susan went through some "aha" moments! It sounded simple and logical but she still missed the vodka! The habit had been anchored so long that it was taking time and effort to shake it, something inside her had a hard time letting go of the urge to drink that compensated for something missing inside. She understood it now. Talking to other women was the biggest help, and realizing what they and Betty Ford had all gone through finally gave her the courage to believe in herself. After two weeks at the center, she moved to the other side of the mountain and looked at what she could do to identify this missing need of hers.

Susan didn't want to talk too much about what was happening at the center when Henri or Joan called. The stigma of being an alcoholic still bothered her, but the acceptance and love she felt in her conversations with them made self-acceptance easier. *Life!* Susan often thought. *How long does it take to understand oneself in a conscious way?*

At this point, she also started to miss Henri and Joan and Martha and Claude! She missed her home, the *crème brulee*, the park, her tennis court, she missed everything and everyone and their love, but she had to complete what she started at the center and she was proud of her determination.

Joan was enjoying her freedom. No more school assignments. She could spend time reading about the state of the Earth in various scientific articles, driving into town in her new Prius, sitting in her cave, texting Kristin in Montana to keep in touch and visiting with

Phillip when he had a day off from the hospital. Both of her parents were gone now and she was not used to sitting at the dinner table alone. She thought of how important her parents were to her and how much she loved them in spite of their respective differences in the way they looked at life. She missed them.

One evening, thinking back to the party her mother threw before the prom, she remembered that Roger took a rain check on spending time with her and she'd promised to show him the park. Hoping that he still would be around, she sent him a text, inviting him to come and join her for an afternoon walk and tea at her place. When he could find the time, that is! The answer came almost immediately. Yes, he wanted to do this and he was free the next day! *Well, Roger must be anxious to see me I guess, or is he already bored with the summer recess?* Joan giggled. *This should be an interesting visit. We'll do it tomorrow,* she decided. *I'll ask Martha to prepare a nice tea party for us and to serve us in the veranda.*

Joan was very curious. She'd never talked with Roger about important subjects. They were just schoolmates who had trivial exchanges now and then, but his reputation as a "nerd" and his acceptance at M.I.T. were enough to trigger Joan's interest for a deeper conversation with an intelligent human being. She looked forward to the meeting.

Roger showed up dressed in a very stylish summer outfit, his tall, slender build reinforcing the elegant appearance. He brought Joan a little bouquet of spring flowers, neatly wrapped in transparent paper and topped with a bow.

"Better than the corsage I would have given you had we gone to the prom together, isn't it? I'm not fond of school rituals, anyway, and I'm happy to have some quality time with you instead," Roger said, offering the bouquet to Joan and hugging her.

"Thank you for the beautiful flowers, Roger. Let's take them inside and then we can go out to the park I want to show you. You didn't see much of our property the night of the party. The park and the forest are my favorite parts. I have spent most of my best hours there since I was a child."

Roger and Joan started to walk toward the pond which was alive with frogs. They sat on a rock on the shore, looking at the last of the yellow irises drying in the sun. The air was balmy under a light breeze which caressed their bodies. A blue belted kingfisher hovering over the water dove into the pond and emerged with a small fish in his long beak, emitting shattering cries of victory as it flew away. The perfect primeval scene went to the two onlookers' hearts. The awe was hard to resist.

"Yes, Roger, this is why I love nature so much! I grew up with it. I identify with its rhythm. Wait 'til you see the river and the forest. It's magic!"

Joan guided Roger through the meadow, then along the river into the forest. "I call this place my church, Roger. Can you see why? This is where I transcend my ordinary mind to join the part of myself out there in the field, in the big universe, in the place I cannot call by name! I just feel it!"

"Joan, you are tripping out, aren't you? And without drugs! When did you learn how to meditate?"

"I guess. I didn't learn, so to speak, I just sat quietly and followed my intuition to find that place in my mind, or rather, beyond my mind. It is by being alone with nature that I slowly discovered a dimension which feels like something that has always been in me, even before I was born. Kind of my essence, you would say, which resonates with nature. That's how I knew that the existentialists were wrong to think that there is no essence; there is an essence in everything."

Roger was baffled by the statement Joan made so clearly. He never heard transcendence explained in such a clear way and higher consciousness demonstrated with a simple equation!

"Joan, we have come a long way in our evolution as human beings, our minds show superb possibilities that modern technology affirms more and more, but what you are talking about is a dimension computers can't match. Shall we go back to square one and talk about consciousness, where it starts and where it goes? Actually, what it is all about."

Joan and Roger reached the forest and walked silently in the woods, smelling the pine trees, walking on beds of needles and hearing a few birdsongs now and then. When they arrived by the rocks Joan hesitated about bringing Roger into her cave. Kristin had been the only one she had wanted to show her private retreat to, but it seemed to her that Roger would be open to the experience, so she smiled as she pulled aside the branches which concealed the entrance.

"Here Roger, now let go of all your preconceived ideas and go with what develops. This is my cave. This is where it all started for me."

"Really, a cave Joan? I never would have guessed! So you sit in that place like a hermit, trying to understand the mysteries of our human condition by meditating? Do your parents have any idea that you are going through this process? Do they practice something like what you do?"

"Not exactly. They know of the cave and the fact that I played in it when I was a little girl. My mother likes to say that I'm weird and not much interested in 'normal things' for my age group, but I let them think what they want and still love them! My parents are very good to me. They do their best with what their life is all about and their understanding of it. Let us say with their own consciousness, they don't know much about mine. We live in different dimensions."

Roger entered the cave respectfully. Thinking of all that it meant for Joan and what she was able to uncover within herself in that place gave him a sense of awe. He was eager to get closer to this girl's mind. "Joan, let's talk about consciousness. It sounds like you made a personal study of it, sort of a trial and error on the job type of learning about it!" Roger summed up as he found one of the rocks to sit on. "It's amazing how comfortable it is in here and how light." Roger noticed, pointing to the ray of sun shining from the left part of the ceiling. "And what is this little critter?" he said indicating a small line moving along the wall.

"That's Newty, my friend. He keeps me company," Joan answered, laughing. "He is always happy. No big decisions to make. Just enjoys life!"

Joan sat next to Roger and took a deep breath. "Yes, consciousness! That's a biggie! Probably more complicated than we can imagine. They don't teach us about this in high school, yet it should be a major subject to investigate, don't you think?"

"I think that with the introduction of computers, it is easier to understand how our minds function," Roger declared, shaking his head. "Obviously our minds are programmed and the hardware we come equipped with is what we have to use. Of course we added a lot of software to modify the output over the years and our progress is amazing!"

"Here is a techno-logician for you," Joan answered, laughing. "A computer expert who thinks in programs and software. I like the analogy but I think that our minds are more complicated than machines."

"I agree absolutely, Joan. Consciousness is the part of the human being which, over the years of evolution, is capable of transcending man's animal instincts. It happened slowly and is accelerating in our lifetime, when everything seems to be falling apart!"

"Yes it has! Imagine, Roger, only a century ago Indians were exhibited in some zoos in cages, and in the fifties the lynching of blacks still went on in the South! It's hard to believe some people were still programmed, as you said, to view this as normal!"

"It's all in the subconscious of the person, of course, both the personal subconscious programmed by what the child was raised to believe and the collective unconscious from eons of ideas programmed by the countries where people grew up, the customs which were prevalent and the religious beliefs they were taught to make sense of their plight on this Earth!"

"Why don't they explain in school that the mind is like an iceberg in the brain, with 90% of it subconscious and only 10% conscious? That would help kids see what happens when they do things without thinking consciously and instead of feeling that something is not quite right, they would understand and change their behaviors?" Joan continued.

"That is the task of the therapist, Joan, but you are right, it should be explained in the schools. There would be fewer problems and more ways to get things out in the open as a result, so kids would evolve by understanding consciously what their programming is!"

"I have a theory of what our next step in evolution could be about the mind, Roger. It seems like we are stuck in the conscious stage, noticing what is wrong but incapable of correcting things because of the fear of changing the status quo. Look at the destruction of the Earth and the species on this planet? Look at the increasing number of wars, the proliferation of guns, the serious health problems, overpopulation and utter chaos. I think we reached the place where the mind has done its part and discovered everything we need to survive, but the dimension we must look at now is beyond the mind, a dimension we can reach in meditation to take away our fear of dying. We'll know that our essence belongs to the whole, to the eternal part of the universe, and we will feel it. That dimension is the next one in our evolution. Just like evolving from the chimpanzee to the new Homo super-sapiens!"

"You are a dreamer, Joan. A beautiful dreamer. This sounds quite idealistic but may be a logical next step! However, how can we stimulate this drive away from subconscious programming to this idealistic dimension? It looks hopeless to me," Roger asserted.

"I think we can do it by enlisting the help of the heart in our evolution. As the Little Prince says, 'One can only see with the heart, the essential is invisible to the eyes.' Consciousness is only whole when it adds the heart to the equation. Don't you think Roger? Perhaps the universe wanted us human beings to get to that point? Perhaps this is the next step of evolution? Perhaps it is what the seers and avatars were transcending to in their search for the God dimension?"

"I guess you are right, Joan," Roger answered, shaking his head. "The heart adds the feeling of belonging to nature to our brain, the part we felt when we walked by the pond, the one you also transcend to in your meditation. The heart and the core of oneself must be close in our human bodies. We are not machines!" Roger concluded pensively.

The two friends remained silent for awhile, breathing quietly in the peace of the cave. Joan interrupted Roger's thoughts with an enthusiastic offer.

"Great talk, Roger, and now, what about some more down to Earth attention? I'm all excited! Martha prepared a great tea party for us in the veranda. I want you to see that place and what we did with the birds. You are in for another surprise!"

Joan and Roger left the cave satisfied by their mutual understanding of the question they first asked. It created a feeling of acceptance which resonated between them. Resonance is close to oneness and they intuitively walked back holding hands. Roger told Joan about his future plans to study computerized robots for medical surgery, Joan still didn't like the idea but accepted the fact that technology was a big factor in furthering evolution, in the right direction that is! It was a lovely walk back, enjoying the forest, the river, the meadow and the pond. Joan was giggling inside, thinking about texting Kristin about her outing with Roger. No more stiffness this time. Roger was very relaxed!

Roger was amazed at the veranda. He had never seen a tropical greenhouse except in the zoo. Every winged beauty was in full motion, grazing Roger's and Joan's heads when they flew over them. Victor sat in the middle of the air show. Martha did her best to satisfy these two teens and their appetites. Her traditional *crème brulee* was one of the goodies displayed on a tray. They ate with gusto, they laughed, and they talked about life seriously. It was not a humorous subject, as their future and that of their possible children was at stake, but they mostly exchanged youthful energy and shared plans for the summer. The afternoon was a success. Joan was happy she had invited Roger. *He actually is a nice guy*, she concluded after he left. *It's interesting how different he is from Phillip but pleasant to be with. I wonder how many more nice guys I will meet in the next few years*, Joan considered, perplexed.

When she arrived in her room, Joan found a text from Kristin, who could not wait to hear about her visit with Roger and if he had kissed her and what else? Joan laughed so hard she could not contain herself. When she finally calmed down she started to text Kristin back. "Hi friend, sorry to disappoint you but nothing sexual happened. We got quite a way into the evolution of consciousness, though, and it brought us closer than a kiss would have, I'm sure. We got very close on the resonance level that is, and yes, we held hands walking back from the park! It was a great visit!"

It did not take long for Kristin to answer. She was probably sitting in her Montana paradise with her cell phone, waiting for something exciting to happen to her friend. "Joan, you are too much! I don't think your story would mean anything to anyone but crazy nerds like you guys. I'm disappointed."

Joan smiled. She had been called a nerd for the first time. "Kristin, I felt close to Roger on a core level. It was a very satisfying climactic encounter. Probably beats sex in the long run. No birth control needed."

"Joan, you are too much in your head, but you are my best friend, have fun with your consciousness, I'm returning to my book. It's a love story. Bye."

Joan closed her eyes and reflected on Kristin's reaction to her visit with Roger. She imagined her friend in a Montana landscape, sitting under a tree reading a love story with her cell phone next to her. Joan thought about what happened and asked herself why Roger and she never got to a place where they exchanged a kiss, the way it happened with Phillip. Maybe there was something more going on with Phillip, something physical in her body, something dictated by nature?

So, nature is a big influence like the heart and the mind. All this mixes up in my consciousness. Maybe I'll just stay with my intuition and trust and flow with what happens, what feels right! Things felt so right with Roger, but also with Phillip. God! But that kiss felt so good!"

Chapter **Twenty-Two: Mom's Great Party**

In spite of the unusually strong weather disturbances all over the country, and Arkansas was not spared, life continued as usual. It looked as if the climate change effects of hurricanes, floods, drought, water pollution and diminished biodiversity now became an accepted reality. Some of these events began appearing on the news. The repeated earthquakes in Oklahoma may be due to fracking, for example, something that surfaced as a question on network news. Very little was covered on national news. Were they afraid to look at the truth? But everybody started to feel inside that there was a correlation between man's indiscriminate abuse of the Earth and the extreme natural disasters happening in the world. It looked overwhelmingly impossible to question that the money giants, who fought the increasing awareness with more and more dollars, played a role in the equation. Some people reacted to the phenomenon by developing a new kind of depression: an eco-depression, a feeling of helplessness inside that there is total imbalance in the Earth and the environment. It was some sort of rebellion in their human nature and biology against something trying to poison and destroy it. It was subtle at first, but soon it spread throughout the population, and sensitive people were the most affected. Eco-therapy was coming into the picture.

The end of June was almost here and Susan would come home shortly. Her stay at the Betty Ford Center had been very beneficial; she was feeling strong. The therapy sessions were most helpful and she understood herself better at this point. She was ready to move on.

Henri kept in touch with Susan and remembered his promise to put together a big Fourth of July party for her. He was busy rallying important CEO's he knew through previous contacts, asking them to come to the celebration at his place. Organizing the reception took a lot of work, though his secretary in D.C. helped figure out places to stay, schedule flights, and record RSVPs from those invited. Henri knew that

Susan would be delighted. She relished the company of wealthy and famous people; she loved to mingle with well-dressed women talking about their travels around the world and their children educated at famous universities. She felt a kinship with this group of people who had made it to the top and flaunted their power and wealth with a superior air. It always gave her a feeling of belonging. She had missed this mingling since Henri opted to go to D.C. alone and she remained home alone most of the time. This party was something she looked forward to for a long time and Henri knew it.

Joan was perplexed. She didn't like her mom's parties very much in the past. The company of the wealthy guests felt phony. Would she find someone she could even talk to in a genuine manner? She decided to ask her dad if she could invite some of her friends. She knew Mademoiselle would be welcome, and of course Mr. Silver would have to accompany her. *What about Roger and Phillip if they could make it? Kristin was away. Ms. Stern perhaps?* Well, she would try to invite them and see.

Mom arrived home and looked great. She got some sun in California and favored her sports clothes while there. She admitted that she didn't open her shoe bag the whole time and took way too many dresses for the stay. They didn't look right in the company of simple, relaxed, summer-dressed ladies who had fun at dinner instead of showing off. It was a lesson for Susan! Joan felt that her mom came back a new person and she wondered what would happen now.

She couldn't help but compliment her mom, "Mom, you look terrific! It looks like the center agreed with you."

"I guess it did. Lots of hard work though. I was never so busy in my life, Joan! You just can't change things in yourself overnight, but it helped me to look at things in a different way instead of relying on vodka to make me feel better! I feel better physically too. No more headaches."

"Mom, I'm really happy to hear you say that. It is balm to my ears and heart!" She paused with a sweet smile. "Martha will be relieved that her intervention triggered events and brought a good result for you! The universe has secret ways to make good things happen, don't you think? Even if they look really bad at first. I think all this helps to increase consciousness in the world. I trust the ways of the universe, Mom; it works!"

The next few days were devoted to preparing for the party. Susan felt strange when she decided on the drinks, knowing that all the alcoholic beverages would be off limits for her this time. It gave her a sense of estrangement from a group she had so looked forward to feeling at home with. How would she handle this so soon in her recovery? What would they think about her? Susan felt a lot of apprehension now, instead of looking forward to the event, but knew she had to move on.

The weather report was good so the reception room would open onto the park to allow guests to roam around outside if they so desired. The band would play inside, mostly country music and patriotic tunes celebrating the Fourth of July. Susan supervised the elaborate decorations—everything in red white and blue, of course. The buffet was catered by a renowned chef who specialized in seafood dishes and the desserts were flown from a fancy New York pastry shop along with cases of champagne. A lot of extra help was hired for the biggest party ever held on the property and probably in the whole county. Martha felt almost inept in this deluge of luxury. It overwhelmed her. The incessant landing of small jets bringing in supplies from all sorts of places disturbed her sense of peace. Claude had never been so challenged by the demands of the suppliers asking where and when and what. An amazing and chaotic scene unfolded as the morning progressed, and everything had to be ready by 4 o'clock when the guests would begin to arrive.

Joan decided to stay away from the preparation. She took a walk in the park, plagued by mixed feelings. Her mom had come a long way, working on her addiction and understanding herself. She looked radiant. Was it also because she was about to indulge in another craving she had? The desire to feel rich, powerful, special, and beautiful and to show it to the world? Joan loved her mom and wanted her to be happy, but wondered about the things that made her mom happy. It didn't resonate with her own sense of happiness. It didn't feel good to criticize, but something seemed awkward in her mom's behavior. Was it because her mom wasn't looking at life with her heart? Was she missing the essential which only the heart can see? Joan walked over to her cave and sat quietly, thinking about the question she had just raised.

What would Susan see if she looked at the upcoming event with her heart? Perhaps she would be stricken by the outrageous difference between the very rich and others, between the 1% or even the 5%

and the rest of the people in the country who have so much less? Could her parents throw this obscenely expensive party for a small exclusive group if they were conscious of the pain a young working couple endures, for instance, trying to make ends meet, working two jobs and raising a family? Would her parents feel good if they saw with their hearts the hardship of the poor and the struggles of the middle class these days, would they forget everybody else's woes while they ate their desserts flown in from New York and drank a glass of the $70 bottle of champagne? Joan thought about the money coming from the dirtiest energy processes that are affecting the Earth so badly, polluting and poisoning the environment we live in. Some people from those wealthy corporations, responsible for that harm, will be at the party. Joan wondered how she could handle that in the best way possible, using her essence and consciousness.

Henri agreed to let Joan invite some friends, remarking that they probably wouldn't have much in common with the guests. Joan agreed that was probably true, thanked her Dad, then proceeded to go through her list. Mademoiselle and Mark Silver had just returned from their enchanting trip through the parks and were available. They were curious to see what this segment of the human race is like. Roger was still in town, before he would leave for a workshop in the East later in the summer. Phillip didn't know yet whether he could take the time off from his job. He worked in the emergency room with his dad, and since the Fourth of July is a busy time at the hospital, he probably couldn't come. Ms. Stern should be back from her trip and would come.

Great, Joan thought. *At least I have four people I can talk to and feel good about.* But she would miss Phillip's presence. *Four friends*, Joan repeated as she walked back from the cave. *My friends will help me keep my mind in the right place. I will do my best.*

Of course, Joan decided to wear the pastel green dress! Mom didn't say anything about what she should wear for the occasion. This was something new. Susan didn't even offer to buy Joan a new designer dress to present her daughter in her best light at this special party! That was surprising. *Things are changing*, Joan thought, happy to avoid a discussion with her mom and happy to put on her favorite dress.

I just love my little green dress, Joan thought joyfully. *It's symbolic of being myself in the flow of do and don't. It makes me feel good! Oh yes, and the butterfly pin from Phillip. I'll wear it thinking of him when I talk to the big company CEOs. This should make an obvious point!*

It looked like the morning and early afternoon chaos had morphed into the best organized party Susan had ever put together. The weather was perfect, the decorations impressive, and the reception room looked elegant with the silverware and bouquets of flowers on each table. The musicians had a comfortable platform for their instruments and the dance floor would attract those who wanted to move to the music, while others could walk in the park and discover nature. Susan thought she had foreseen every single wish her guests could have. Of course, she hadn't forgotten the bar. The bartenders would serve anything the guests wanted, including vodka. She sighed, looking at the bottles. *Would anyone choose the non-alcoholic punch like she would? Well, maybe someone would*, she thought, resigned.

Everything was now ready. Susan put on one of her designer dresses which showed a lot of cleavage. With her California tan she looked healthy and sexy. The red dress was adorned with a white and blue bow, discretely displayed on her left shoulder. Henri wore his white summer tuxedo, an elegant linen outfit perfect for the weather. Joan, who had to be in the lineup for introductions, first met her own guests in the veranda. They would appear later and join the crowd. In the meantime they enjoyed talking with each other and looking at the birds. They all wondered what they were in for, maybe like joining a party at Buckingham Palace? This would be interesting!

Shortly after 4 o'clock limos and taxis began arriving. Claude, who had donned his best butler outfit, was kept busy opening doors and bringing people in, while the parking attendants directed the drivers toward their arranged stations to wait for their passengers. It was a well choreographed entrance to a well organized celebration. It looked like something out of a movie that could be entitled *La Grande Illusion*.

Susan, Henri, and Joan were smiling, greeting, shaking hands, complimenting, thanking, and pointing out places where people could sit down and relax. Joan's guests joined the group at 4:30; almost everyone had arrived by then. Henri looked as if he were pleased to see them come in and to see Joan's face light up. The band played a country-western version of *America the Beautiful*. Everybody was smiling. It was the Fourth of July!

During the introductions, Joan memorized the names and functions of the guests and their spouses or dates. Most men were CEOs of big companies, the ones who make all the important decisions concerning energy production and fuel supply, the ones who dictate where, how, when, and especially how much projects will cost and yield, the ones who indiscriminately rule the entire world of business that also affect the stock market. To Joan's satisfaction, the CEO of Monsanto company was present, along with others in the food industry and one from a pharmaceutical company. *All these human beings make the world go around in constantly changing circles*, Joan thought, *and have become the new powerful kings which the government bows to in fear. These people, how distant do they all seem? Up there, somewhere? And yet, here they are in the flesh, with us today!* She nodded.

Things started smoothly in the pleasant warmth of this beautiful afternoon, as couples walked from the bar to a chosen table or out into the park with their drinks. The band alternated country-western tunes with popular favorites. Some people sat together in groups of four, having heated conversations with expressive gestures. Joan's friends gathered at a table near the band after they picked up their drinks, and Mademoiselle and Mark Silver gave an enthusiastic account of their trip. Arches National Park was a highlight for them. Susan flitted from one table to the next, enjoying the guests' compliments on her beautiful table settings, decorations and of course her looks. She beamed. Dinner would not start for another hour.

Henri was conversing with some of his former friends from the oil and gas companies. From a distance Joan could detect occasional frowning and lip biting. One of them shook his head repeatedly. She wished she could hear the conversation. Had her dad mentioned the aborted fracking project which had concerned him recently?

The hour passed very pleasantly. It was time to introduce the speaker who would give the Fourth of July address. Henri had asked the CEO of Monsanto to do the honor, and he had accepted. A handsome, tall gentleman, probably in his late sixties, approached the podium with a dignified air and ascended like the President climbing the steps of Air Force One.

"Ladies and gentlemen, I'm honored to address all of you, my friends and citizens of the greatest country in the world. This Fourth of July date should remind us that this is, indeed, the most wonderful country on the face of the Earth and in spite of all that is happening today, we can celebrate the occasion with pride and thanks for our part in its wonder. The United States has always contributed to help other countries. We have spent money and lives to make the world a better place. We have shown the example of our democratic principles to be a road to happiness and success and we will continue with this belief.

"I am proud to say that Monsanto, with the help of science and technology, has developed new ways to transform agriculture so that farmers can grow a more sustainable yield of healthier foods, better animal feeds, and more fiber, while reducing agricultural impact on the environment. Our scope extends to foreign lands all around the globe. We know that, with the world population expanding at alarming rates, our new found ways to increase the yield of food is the only answer to the population problem facing humanity. We will save the world from hunger! Happy Fourth of July, all my friends, let's drink to the United States of America, the beautiful!"

The band played the Star Spangled Banner as he descended proudly from the podium, drinking from the champagne glass which was offered by a bartender standing by. The crowd applauded, glasses clinked, and some people stood up, transported by the emotion. The mood was high. Henri, who remained close to the podium, climbed up after the applause subsided.

He tapped the microphone. "I thank our friend from Monsanto for his proud speech about our country. We should indeed admire the role our democracy plays and how it has been admired by the entire world. There is no other country like ours, and we all know it. Allow me now to give voice to another speaker to say some things of current interest. He is a science teacher at the local high school and I had a chance to discuss his wholehearted thoughts on some important issues in our country. In the name of the right to the freedom of speech that our democracy endorses, let me introduce to you Mark Silver, a scientist, a teacher of our children, and a keen mind."

Mark Silver, baffled by Henri's introduction and trying to quickly assess what he was going to say, took a deep breath and got up from his chair. Mademoiselle was already applauding, encouraging him while also aware that his heart was probably beating fast and his mind churning. Mark was such a handsome young man with his black hair, blue eyes, and elegant beige summer suit, that the audience couldn't help applauding when he climbed to the podium. He definitely looked from a different generation than that of the previous speaker and a healthy young energy emanated from him which immediately seduced the audience.

"When I was in high school," Mark started confidently, "I belonged to a speech and debate team. It taught me the value of rebuttal, so in the art of debate, I will address the speech we just heard. But first I want to honor the altruistic goal to save the world from hunger. This is a noble ambition which we all can relate to. The world population is indeed growing at an alarming rate! We all know it and we Americans always want to save everybody! I support the goal to prevent hunger for world populations, but want to debate the means to reaching that goal. First consider that attempts to increase food production through patented, genetically engineered crops and using herbicides to kill insects can affect the balance of nature in a destructive and permanent way. The pesticides not only kill weeds, but decrease biodiversity. Genetically modified foods are confirmed to harm farm animals and the environment, killing off some plant, insect, and bird populations. Second, a recent study through the National Institute of Health found that herbicides cause damage to human genes and threaten human health. Like a drug which is at first seems to be the answer to curing a disease, these chemical products can have side effects worse than the disease itself. As human beings, our biology is linked to the natural world around us. Adding poisonous chemicals to our environment can destroy the fragile equilibrium of our DNA and of our biology. Chemicals like Dioxin cause cancer and can kill us over time. Just as disturbing, large companies also want control over the seeds, which are the first link in the food chain, the source of life. That means corporations control our sustenance for life and the lives of the farmers who depend on seed. Thousands of Indian farmers committed suicide when they were forced to buy unwanted seeds they could not finance. It's a sad story. At this point, however, I join the altruistic goal to save the world by suggesting that company executives consider a different approach to the problem of the growing population. Even a child can do the math. Why not focus on decreasing this rate of growth? Why is the world getting over populated? We could implement international programs on family planning, teach important concepts of birth control to children in the schools, and spread the knowledge to third-world countries. Instead we justify the burgeoning world population by hiding behind obsolete religious myths and selling people a bill of agricultural goods that will poison nature. Let's find an intelligent and viable remedy for this problem. Let's think about logical, sustainable solutions!

"I am honored to have this opportunity to open my heart and express my thoughts to this educated audience. My generation is beginning to join in with new ways to help save the world. We want to live healthy and happy lives for generations to come, and America can lead the way once more to a democratic example of noble principles and viable solutions. Happy Fourth of July, my friends."

The audience was silent for a few seconds. Eyebrows were raised and some men grabbed their chins. The direct and logical aspect of Mark Silver's speech had struck an chord which no one wanted to challenge. It was an awkward moment and no one knew what to do or say. Mademoiselle got up, and then Roger, then Ms. Stern, then Joan, who walked toward the podium. All four applauded bravely, and soon were joined by some daring souls who resonated with Mark's approach. The Monsanto CEO nodded with a bemused expression, knowingly to a fool who had just spoiled the party! Encouraged by the few people who joined the applause, mostly women, others started to clap as well. Susan was quite upset. Why did Henri put the audience in such a dilemma? She tried to walk around smiling but her heart was not in it. The band attempted to lighten the mood by playing an uplifting tune. The waiters offered more drinks. A feeling of discord invaded the previously happy crowd. At that moment, Joan decided to do something drastic to try to change the strange ambiance which prevailed among the guests. She climbed up and grabbed the mike.

"Hello everyone, and happy Fourth of July! I am Joan, Henri's and Susan's daughter. I'm proud of my father today, who showed a wonderful democratic way to illustrate what our country believes in: the freedom of speech and the value of debate. My father grew up, like many of you here, in the Sixties and Seventies. From what I have read and heard from my parents, those years were full of new ideas the youth introduced to the world. It was a revolution in the consciousness of people at the time. Can you remember the excitement of breaking taboos? Of seeing things in a new way? Of challenging old worn out ideas that were obsolete, too old for those times? Do you remember the Beatles, the Rolling Stones, Bob Dylan and all the songs? Shall we close our eyes for a moment and imagine what the world would be like today if we could listen to John Lennon sing again? If we look at the mess the world is in now, can we imagine new ideas to bring back life to old institutions? A world where we use our hearts to change to the way we think? Can we bring a loving revolution change to some obsolete ways of thinking? My generation is ready to do this! Maybe I'm a dreamer, or maybe it is what we have to offer to world..."

At this point one of the younger women, probably a girlfriend of one of the CEOs, was transported by her emotion and memories and started singing "Imagine" by the Beatles, a song she memorized a long time ago. The band joyously joined in and some of the women in the audience hummed the tune. There were actually a few wet eyes among the guests. Some people stood up, listening to the words. The crowd had obviously found a common denominator. Joan stepped down and joined her friends. The waiters started to bring food to the tables, and the bartenders got very busy as everybody wanted a lift after the emotional episode. The humming stopped and the conversations resumed. Many of the guests remembered the Sixties gone by, and saw the resemblance to this moment in time. People were both perplexed and pleased. Susan felt better. Henri scratched his head and smiled at the same time, thinking that this party had turned into a very interesting sort of experience. Did all these people need this kind of emotional release after hiding from their mounting fears in the past few months about the state of the world? Was an eco-depression being sublimated in this moment of challenge and participation? It was a special moment that everybody felt deep inside in their own way, in that place which reaches beyond the mind to a dimension that only the heart can explain. It was good.

As everybody finished eating the delicious dinner and the fabulous dessert flown in from New York, which the French champagne complimented, the evening slowly descended. The sun would set soon. The band switched to dance music and some couples headed for the floor. The Monsanto CEO joined Mark Silver at his table with an offer to engage his intelligent mind. He asked Mark to walk with him to the park and they were involved in a serious conversation when Joan briefly joined them.

"I want to give you this poem," she interrupted, handing him Phillip's "Killing A Butterfly" poem and pointing at her pin. "We are very concerned about the butterflies dying, sir, and very sad! Perhaps you would consider doing something about this? You must have loved butterflies when you were a little boy? Do you remember?" She continued, looking him in the eye, and then left graciously, walking toward the pond.

Roger was talking with one of the oil and gas company CEOs discussing the dangers of fracking. He introduced himself as a future M.I.T. student who was very interested in technology and in sources of renewable energies for the future. For him, wind and solar were the clean and healthy solution, even if they cost more to produce in the beginning. Coal was obviously the worst avenue to continue. He argued that money is not always the most important factor to consider but that health and the environment should come first. His listener was shaking his head politely, agreeing timidly with some of his remarks. Mademoiselle found a woman in the group who had spent time in Paris at the Sorbonne. They exchanged memories of the city, of the university, and of how fortunate French students were to go to college without paying tuition. It is free for all those who have grades good enough to qualify them to attend, even medical students. Mademoiselle seemed proud of the way French students were treated.

Ms. Stern found a captive audience in one of the wives who was concerned about her autistic grandchild. They discussed the increasing percentage of autistic children nowadays and deplored why this was happening more and more. Ms. Stern listened compassionately to her and said that the cause of the increase was still a big question, but that some scientists were studying some pregnant women who had been exposed to pesticides to see if it could be a factor. Research in that direction is important, she added. Both women nodded, agreeing, "Yes, pesticides… chemicals… where is this going?"

The band had now rallied at least half of the audience. Henri and Susan were enjoying a Sixties tune, dancing at a happy tempo, soon joined by more baby boomers who nostalgically danced their memories away in style. Joan found Roger to be a more relaxed partner this time. Mademoiselle and Mark were dancing cheek-to-cheek in a loving embrace. Helped by the champagne which flowed generously, everyone had reached a mellow place, even Susan, who had to make do with her non-alcoholic punch. Actually, she had found two other guests who joined her in abstinence and whom she commiserated with about the difficulty of quitting alcohol. One of them had gone to the same program at the Betty Ford Center.

More guests decided to walk into the park as the sunset was nearing. It was a beautiful place to watch a sunset in the romantic cool of the evening. The man Henri was walking with toward the pond exclaimed in admiration, "Great place to have a hunting party, Henri! This park and forest must provide a lot of game. You should have thought of it!"

"Well, my friend," Henri answered. "It would not happen here on my property! First, I don't like guns. And second, I don't like to kill animals. Moreover, after a few drinks people do crazy things! Remember what happened at that famous hunting party which a well-known member of our government attended? He accidentally shot his friend in the face! Fortunately the man didn't die, but he could have. A hunting party would not work for me, my friend, so let's just enjoy nature without destroying it!"

Henri went toward the reception room, inviting people to walk outside into the park. The musicians and waiters joined the crowd. The sun was slowly descending to the horizon. Henri brought the mike and addressed everybody in an appreciative tone, "My friends, I'm so pleased you joined me and my family today for this extraordinary party. I must admit, I feel all our hearts are in unison. Now I present to you the most beautiful fireworks nature can offer us on this Fourth of July, the magnificence of a sunset. Enjoy the awe of it, my friends, and thank you all for coming.

The orange disc slowly descended behind the assorted dark shapes of the mountains rising at the end of the immense plateau. As the sun peacefully faded, the clouds in the foreground darkened, became in turn grayish, then coal black, leaving only a few small areas of blue which soon weakened. Then the action shifted to the mountains, a strange show where the stage lights came from behind the set and accentuated its outline as they slowly dimmed, morphing into a powerful show offering surprises of orange, pink, red and purple hues playing hide-and-seek behind the mountains. At that point a rosy tip dotted the edges of the dark clouds, bringing in a parade of colors, changing, blending, and combining their tones until they slowly faded into the evening twilight.

There was no applause. No "ooh" and "ahh," only a religious silence prevailed as the sun slowly disappeared. Some people were holding hands, others were hugging. Nobody wanted to move away from the feeling of completion the sunset had created and yet no one knew why they felt that way. *One only sees well with the heart*, Joan thought. *The essential is invisible to the eyes.*

The crowd dispersed slowly after awhile. There were goodbyes, thanks, promises of getting together again, and departures to the waiting vehicles and their drivers. Martha and Claude, who had remained away from the party, joined the guests and helped organize their exits. It took awhile to get everybody going but the hosts patiently helped everyone, smiling. After the last guest had left, Henri escorted Susan and Joan to the living room where they dropped happily into their seats. It was time to rest and assess the eventful party.

"Did I keep my promise, Susan, and was your party a success?" Henri asked cautiously.

Susan took a deep breath. "It was a very different kind of a party for sure, Henri! I would never have expected a confrontation between people in high places and Joan's friends! I felt very nervous at times. I didn't know what to say to their wives. You have quite some guts to challenge the head of Monsanto, I must say… but it ended okay, I guess. Everyone seemed to have a good time."

"People in high places need to be confronted when they take advantage of their high places to start going off limits, Susan," Henri replied. "The world needs to confront the abuse of power backed by the money put in the wrong direction. I think Mark Silver did a great job! People needed to hear what he said. I'm beginning to see that a lot of what is happening in the world is caused by the wrong people setting the rules and I hope to make amends for it. Something has to change."

"I guess there is some truth to what you said, Henri," Susan continued. "I liked what Joan said about the Sixties and Seventies. It made me feel young again. I was rebellious in those days and thought it important to tear down the establishment! Trying to imagine new good ways to deal with the world, you know! But the establishment made us rich, Henri, and I enjoy that very much. I guess I forgot all the principles of my youth! Perhaps I started to drink because I wanted to forget, to forget that I was ashamed, then ashamed of drinking… the vicious circle, Henri."

"You sound like the man the Little Prince met on one of the planets he visited! Mom, at least you found a way out of the vicious circle. You stopped your drinking. I'm so proud of you, Mom. It must have been hard."

"It was, but I got a lot of help from you and Dad. Your love did it for me! Thank you, you two. I may even find the principles of my youth inside somewhere, buried under the gunk!" Susan added, laughing. "Don't ever lose your wonderful spirit, Joan. You are on the right track!"

"And I know just where you might find your youth back, Susan! Remember our trip to Yosemite, when we were young and idealistic? We had such a great time. I think Joan should visit that place with us, so I made reservations at the Ahwahnee Hotel for a week in the park. The three of us need a vacation, don't you think? Let's go girls. I'm ready for a break from the crazy life in D.C. I want to spend time with my girls!"

"I'm ready too, Henri. That's such a great idea. I love it! God, this was an amazing day. Thank you for creating it for me. Good things happen sometimes when you least expect them."

"The universe did it, Mom!" Joan concluded with a witty smile. "All we need is to continue to imagine!"

Chapter **Twenty-Three:** A Tribute to John Muir

Henri was excited when he came back from his last trip to D.C. before the Yosemite vacation.

"Susan, guess what? I found this quote by Theodore Roosevelt in a colleague's office. It's from a letter addressed to John Muir and it said, 'I want to drop politics absolutely for four days and just be out in the open with you.' Imagine, in 1903, a president who got fed up with politics and wanted to get back to the real thing—nature and beauty! Theodore Roosevelt felt this need to heal his soul. I can understand. That was just before he posed with John Muir on top of Glacier Point and camped with him in a hole, waking up in the morning with five inches of snow! There is a famous photograph about their encounter."

"Yes, I saw it somewhere," Susan answered. "Isn't John Muir the one who founded the Sierra Club which became a role model for conservationists around the world?"

"Yes, and he did an unimaginable number of things to promote and preserve the wilderness. We'll probably hear and see more about him when we are in Yosemite. By the way, are you and Joan ready to go? We are leaving early tomorrow morning you know. I'm anxious to get there and have a real break," Henri added, jumping for joy like a kid.

Joan had visited several parks in Arkansas. She also had been to Yellowstone and the Grand Canyon, but had never seen Yosemite. She heard the story about her parents going there when they were young, camping and hiking and visiting the Mariposa Grove, her mother walking in the Merced River with her tight shorts was legendary and she laughed at the idea.

"I have to remind Mom not to forget her shorts," she kidded. Joan was excited to go on this trip with her parents.

The family flew from Little Rock to Fresno where they rented a car to drive to the park. Henri had planned to go this way so that they would enter the park through the Southern entrance and then drive down to the Valley without missing the spectacular view right after they exit the Yosemite tunnel on the way down. After the long drive through Oakhurst, the park entrance and beautiful Wawona, they finally entered the long dark tunnel which Henri had told them about. Though it was already 5 o'clock, the trip was worth the wait. The tunnel opened onto the most stunning view they could have ever imagined. Majestic El Capitan, puzzling Half Dome and the graceful Bridal Veil Falls were all there in front of their eyes, probably one of the most beautiful landscapes in the world, so amazingly put together that it was hard to imagine a more striking design. They stopped the car and stood on the ramp, speechless, overwhelmed.

"I can see why you wanted us to start our visit to the park with this view, Dad. There are no words for its beauty," Joan said after awhile. "Thank you for the foresight!"

By the time they arrived at the Ahwahnee Hotel, after getting their first look at Yosemite Falls on the way, it was 7 o'clock This superb landmark, built in 1927, with its granite façade and log-beamed ceilings was a welcome end to their long trip. They settled in their rooms facing Half Dome and Glacier Point, and appreciated a restorative dinner in the elegant dining room. They had arrived in Yosemite Valley, an iconic place in the United States.

During their flight to Fresno, Henri had talked to Susan and Joan about the hikes they could take in Yosemite. Susan agreed to stay with something easy and spend time at the Visitors' Center and photo shops. Joan wanted to get to the top of everything and Henri laughed about her enthusiasm, but he thought that climbing to the top of the Half Dome would probably be an experience she would remember for the rest of her life, so he proceeded to make arrangements with a guide to take them there toward the end of their stay. The guide would help them get the permit, carry camping equipment for an overnight stay above Nevada Falls, prepare their meals and guide them up the cables to the top of Half Dome the next day. Making the round trip from the valley floor in one day would be too strenuous. They were not used to the 16-plus miles it would take to do it and they would enjoy the excursion better this way.

Susan was still asleep when Henri came back from the park center, having made the arrangements for the projected trip. He drew the curtains as Susan slowly opened her eyes on a beautiful sunny view of Half Dome.

"Joan and I will be on top of this rock in a few days," Henri proudly said coming to the bed to kiss her. "We never did this one when we were here, years ago. I wonder why?"

"Well, Henri, we were only students who went camping. We spent a lot of time making love, didn't have much money and our car broke down on the way to the tunnel one day. Remember?" Susan laughed as she got out of bed heading for the bathroom. "You have a way to forget things. You and Joan are one of a kind, the dreamers of this world!"

Joan had slept longer than usual, tired from the trip and long hours sitting in planes and car. She also woke up to a beautiful view of Half Dome and noticed a quote by John Muir on the wall she had missed when she arrived, "Keep close to Nature's heart and break clear away, once in awhile, and climb a mountain or spend a week in the woods. Wash your spirit clean." She pondered on the importance of being near nature and thanked her good fortune to have been so close to it since she was born. *What a difference it has made in my life*, she thought. *I'm grateful for having had the chance to never lose my natural connection.*

Their first day was spent resting and touring the valley at a quiet pace. They walked to the bottom of Yosemite Falls, of course, encountering a crowd of people from all over the world speaking incomprehensible languages, but who probably all agreed with the beauty of the site. Their expressions said it all. They sat in the grass later on, at the foot of El Capitan, watching climbers ascend the sheer wall, most of them roped in and knowing that it would take several days to reach the summit, sleeping in hanging rest baskets on the way there. With binoculars you could see clearly their slow search for cracks with their picks and placement of pitons or using the ones already there. It was an awesome spectacle. How could anyone do this, especially the overhanging passages when the climbers were suspended in the air?

"People are doing more and more challenging feats these days to test their limits," Henri remarked. "I, myself, could not do it," he concluded, nodding.

The Merced River was nearby, running clearly between trees, probably some of the dogwoods which flower so beautifully at the end of spring. Henri took Susan's hand and led her to the bank where she took her shoes off and started walking into the water.

"I knew you would want a photo of this Henri," she said, laughing. "And I have my shorts on," she added showing off the pink outfit. "See, I don't look too bad still?" she posed as if she was doing a magazine cover.

"Mom, you look so cute!" Joan commented, "I'll join you. It looks like fun." The two frolicked happily for awhile as Henri took several shots for remembrance. "When you did that the last time, Susan, we didn't even own a camera. I had to do with my memories! This time, this memorable image will end up on the wall."

The walk from the Ahwahnee to El Capitan and back had been quite a stretch and the family came back tired but very cheerful. It had been an exhilarating day. They ate dinner early and decided to sit out in front of the hotel for an herbal tea drink. The air had cooled down and they were wearing light sweaters.

"I just want to express the joy I feel to be here with you two," Henri began, "in this incredibly inspiring place which lifts my spirit. A family! There is nothing that can replace the feeling!" He stopped, much moved, as if something was in his heart which he could not say. Joan felt her dad's hesitation.

"Dad, you speak of the joy of our family together. What about your family growing up? I have heard so little about it."

"There is not much to say anymore, Joan. It's an old story. Both my parents died in the fire at their home, as I probably told you before. They were asleep. I never knew much about my grandparents either, who died in the early part of the last century. I never dealt well with these traumas and just kept going on with life the best I could."

"Didn't you say that your grandparents had immigrated from France to become farmers in the U.S., Dad?"

"Yes. That's why I was named Henri, the French way to spell Henri with an "i." They died before I was born. My parents died in the fire when I was in college and I inherited all that money from them because I was an only child. The rest is history, right? But you see why this family of mine is now the most important thing I have on this Earth? I love you two girls so much. Let's enjoy our stay in Yosemite!" Henri concluded, toasting his tea to Susan.

Joan didn't know how to respond to his emotional revelation. "Dad, I love you so much! Thank you for bringing us here. It's perfect!"

The next few days were spent hiking and enjoying the park. Henri and Joan climbed to the top of Yosemite Falls, which was quite a hike but very rewarding when they reached the top of the upper falls. The view was breathtaking. Susan had opted to spend her time discovering the whole collection of Ansel Adams photographs. They were the most beautiful rendition of the park's beauty at the time. There was something special about the black and white photography, though she could not define it, but there were also some beautiful shots of the park's features in color by more recent photographers like Howard Weamer, for instance. She liked his work, so she bought one of his photos of Half Dome for the library.

Joan and Henri took another hike, four miles to the top of Glacier Point, the place where John Muir and Roosevelt slept one night. Susan took the easy way up, getting to the top of Glacier Point on a mule. She commented on how vertiginous it felt, though, when they went down and the mule would turn a switchback. "I was sitting on the butt of this creature perched directly over the precipice! I ground my teeth, wishing I had gone up with you guys on solid ground! I took a deep breath when we went back to the corral! But… it was beautiful anyway. I can imagine the climbers of El Capitan, what they must see when they look down!"

They became accustomed to spending some time after dinner sitting in front of the hotel watching the mountains and drinking tea. It was a restful place to talk. One night after they had all discovered the beauty of the park and the effect nature had created for them, they gave a long grateful thanks to the founders of the national parks and the idea which prompted them to create these amazing places for the people of this country. Already in the 1870s, incredible stories had surfaced about the natural wonders explorers had seen all over the country, like in Yellowstone for instance. This gave birth to the idea of establishing national parks to preserve these wonders. In 1890 an act of Congress created Yosemite National Park, followed by Sequoia, Mt. Rainier, then the Grand Canyon, etc.

"What a wonderful idea!" Joan exclaimed. "Imagine if, instead of preserving all these areas, it had been left to developers who brought their money and destroyed the landscape? The trees would have been cut, a bunch of expensive houses built for the rich, and there might be a fast food restaurant at the foot of Half Dome!" she added, laughing in horror. "I have heard also that the idea of national parks was copied all over the world after that. Great for the U.S. to have contributed to save beauty! I hope no one will ever change any of these incredible parks and we will open many more. I think that John Muir also said…" Joan took a little piece of paper out of her pocket, "'Everybody needs beauty as well as bread, places to play in and pray, where nature may heal and give strength to body and soul.' The national parks are treasures and a gift to all of us," Joan continued with a lot of emotion in her voice.

After dinner that night, it was Susan's turn to talk about her family and reminisce. Her parents had died rather young—not in a fire but in a car accident—and it was the death of their parents in difficult circumstances which had brought Susan and Henri together when they met at the university. Susan didn't inherit a fortune from them, but enough to go to school while also working on the side as a teacher's aide. She hated being poor and had encouraged Henri to go for it and make a lot of money, which he did when he joined the oil company as an engineer first, then worked his way into upper management for the corporation.

"So, both you and Mom were only children, and then you had me, an only child also! Were you thinking of the population explosion at the time?" Joan concluded, laughing. "I wish I had a brother or sister! But I guess it's too late now. Anyway, I love my life the way it is and the universe has a way of putting us in situations where we grow and learn how to be happy with what we have in the present. The present which is all that we have, right? And look what we have now!" Joan concluded enthusiastically. The evening light was slowly descending over the mountains, obscuring the tops of their peaks as some clouds formed in clumps of black cotton. One lightning bolt zigzagged in the distance. It was awesome and peaceful.

"Shall we go in, girls?" Henri proposed. "I'm tired and we have a big program tomorrow. Joan and I will climb Half Dome after we camp at the top of Nevada Falls. You've got two days to yourself, Susan."

The guide picked Joan and Henri up early the next day. They walked together to Happy Isles getting acquainted. Michael had worked for the park for ten years and knew all of its secrets. He had prepared three packs, one for himself which carried most of the camping equipment they would need and one for each of the two, carrying individual supplies like water, snacks, and rain gear. They would also carry their own sleeping bags. The weather was predicted to be perfect and the three were excited to get going on such a beautiful day.

The Mist Trail, which follows the Merced River, climbs up to the top of Nevada Falls past Vernal Falls and Emerald Pool. The elevation gain of 1900 feet represents quite a hike up rocky trails, steps, some difficult passages under leaking rock arcades, and a gentle blow of mist comes to refresh you as you ascend close to the falls. It is breathtaking and you can't help stopping to drink in the fabulous views which are offered as you climb. A sense of happiness, transcendence, and exhilaration overtakes every cell of your body. Something you can't define and which is probably what every climber experiences when working his way to the top of a mountain, a sense of the impossible becoming possible, a sense of reaching the infinite. Joan and Henri followed Michael, gleaning here and there a comment on the rock formations, the flora, or stopping to catch their breath. It was not El Capitan, but you could read a sense of accomplishment and joy on the faces of all the hikers going up, especially the children enjoying the challenges of another step up or bypassing a rock too hard for them to climb over. How poorly an amusement park tries to recreate this inimitable feeling which only nature can offer to the soul! How do you copy what the imagination does for us in such a setting? And where "the power of imagination makes us infinite," as John Muir said. It's impossible.

The group decided to stop for lunch at a place where they could admire Nevada Falls, the huge water formation descending straight down a large rock wall. They ate their tuna sandwich and tomato garnish silently, remembering that their bodies needed the energy from these nutrients to continue the hike, and then there was a delicious dark chocolate bar. Why is it that food always tastes so great after a physical effort?

Little Yosemite Valley, the campground upstream from Nevada Falls, would be their stop for the night. Camping there would give them two or three hours ahead of the crowds climbing Half Dome the next day. Their water bottles were empty by the time they arrived and Michael helped refill them using the water filter he had brought. They organized their camping site by a large tree, took their hiking boots off to rest their feet, and looked forward to a quiet evening in the wilderness.

Having a few hours to spend in this beautiful site, Joan asked her dad if he wouldn't mind walking with her to the river and sitting on its bank by the cascading waters. Henri, who had scouted the area as they were walking up, accepted readily. They walked together to a small beach and sat on some well-polished rocks, comfortable and dry. The negative ions were energizing to their bodies.

"Dad, I'm so happy to be here with you. Thank you for bringing us to Yosemite. No wonder John Muir always said that Nature was a great teacher and thought that it is where one finds oneself in the presence of the divine. Something special happens here, don't you think?"

"Yes, Joan, and how fast we forget the feeling when we get immersed in all the other stuff of life, the daily planning for the next step which will make us happier or richer or more self important, but which never satisfies us completely! Here you can just be present to what is, without thinking, and be happy!"

"Dad, I wanted to tell you about a dream I had last night before our trip. It sounds silly, but it was so real! I dreamed that I was dressed in men's clothing, riding a horse and going to The White House. All the security guards bowed as I passed the gate and let me in. They unbridled the horse and led me to the Oval Office where I sat in a huge chair in front of the President, who was staring at me. I didn't know what to say but I put my hand on my chest and pointed to my heart. At that point I woke up much shaken and my heart was beating a mile a minute. Can you make anything of this, Dad?"

Henri was taken aback and quite moved by the dream Joan had just told him. He remained silent for quite awhile, trying to get over the emotion. "That heart thing is the most important, Joan, it seems to me. It looks like you would like to talk to the President about something which comes from that part of yourself. Sounds like a dream, baby. A beautiful dream. Something like the 'Imagine' song of John Lennon! Are you serious about doing something like this someday? You'd better have something convincing to say to the President and you may have to use more than your heart to get the message across!"

"Dad, you remember the story of Joan of Arc? She helped the king of France end the Hundred Years' War. She was determined and only 17 years old! Would you help me get an audience with the President? I would like to speak to him. I'm serious."

Henri took a deep breath, shook his head seriously, and waited for awhile before answering this startling demand. "Okay Joan, I'll do my best to get you an audience before the President leaves for the summer recess, but I will take you there myself. No horse or bowing guards, and you need to have a good speech prepared. I'm not sure the President would understand your heart pointing gesture. Washington is not too keen on seeing things this way. They don't use much of their hearts in making decisions these days, weapons are more like it, Joan. You are very Pollyannaish, my sweet daughter, but very wonderful and innocent. Who knows, you may get to the President's heart with the amazing eloquence of unspoiled youth. There is something about the logic of a young woman which is very convincing. You proved it to me! Okay, I'll try to help you make your dream come true, Joan."

In the quiet cocoon of little Yosemite Valley, the three campers spent the night closer to the divine, each one reaching that place in their own dreamy way while the sounds of the cascading river accompanied their flights.

After a solid breakfast in the early morning, the fearless hikers were ready for the big venture, reaching the top of Half Dome. Michael had warned them about the difficult climb up to the start of the cable. It was indeed tricky; they had to use their hands to help themselves up over the rocks and crawl up a steep incline on all fours. The climb took a long time and finally they arrived at the foot of the cable. Two vertiginous, vertical metal lines were inviting them to hold on while walking carefully up to the top between them. They started cautiously. When the guide books talk about the ascent being extremely difficult, they are not exaggerating. It was extremely challenging and our intrepid climbers were happy when they reached the top. Half Dome—the summit—they had done it, reaching a view out of this world which they enjoyed like a well-deserved reward.

It is harder to come down than to go up the cables. Looking down creates vertigo for people who are not used to this type of exercise. Joan and Henri had never done anything that scary and it took a lot of courage to descend the cables. Michael, who had left his heavy pack at the bottom of the climb, was positioned between the two, reassuring them or helping by an occasional hand touching and they finally got to the bottom of the cables where the descent to the other part of the trek started, this time mostly on their hands and butts, sliding toward the bottom. That was it. They had climbed Half Dome up and down and they had done it well. They now had a little idea of what mountain climbers endure.

The threesome came back to the bottom of the mountain, exhilarated by the experience but also tired. The effort had been sustained and exhausting, except for Michael who seemed to be accustomed to this type of mountaineering. He probably would repeat the performance very soon. They took the shuttle to the Ahwahnee Hotel from Happy Isles instead of walking this time. They could not wait for the bath they had been dreaming about all the way from Vernal Falls.

Susan was sitting at the café when they arrived, all rested and cheerful. She welcomed the two tired hikers with compliments and encouraged them to get bathed and changed.

"I thought of you guys up that Dome, and tried to imagine how you could ever get there! What a challenge! Harder than going through the Betty Ford rehab, I bet! Only shorter time, but I could not have done it. You are my heroes."

It took a day to recuperate from the Half Dome climb. The family visited the Ansel Adams gallery, relaxed by the Merced River, stopped at the gift shop for photos and souvenirs and the book store which carried a lot of John Muir writings. They also watched a video in the visitor center about National Parks. It pointed out what a great treasure Americans have in this institution. A great treasure indeed.

Getting back home was to take a couple days as Henri had planned to stop at the Mariposa Grove before driving to Fresno where they would sleep over before flying the next day. Joan had never seen giant sequoias and she was delighted at the idea. She also wanted to stop before the tunnel for the striking view which had amazed them so much the day they arrived.

After bidding goodbye to the Ahwahnee and Yosemite Valley, they drove the winding road up to the tunnel. It was a beautiful day again, clear and sunny. They stopped before the entrance and looked at the now familiar landscape in front of their eyes.

"Dad, imagine, we were on top of that dome a couple days ago! Remember the cable? It seems like a dream when you see that mountain from here! I'm so proud we made it, Dad. I'll never forget as long as

I live!" she exclaimed enthusiastically. "This has been quite a trip! Thank you!"

"And wait 'til you see the giant sequoias, girl. You have never seen trees that size I'm sure," Henri continued.

They drove again through lovely Wawona and its historic hotel, just a few miles from the entrance to the Mariposa Grove, an amazing redwood forest saved by Abraham Lincoln who signed an act of congress ceding it to California. What a foresight it was, considering what happened to most redwood forests in Northern California which were subject to cutting and destruction.

The giant sequoias are the largest and tallest trees on Earth. Logging and agriculture have wiped out nearly all of the 2,000,000 acres of forest that once covered California. The state must have been quite a sight at one point in history! Some 20 houses could be made out of a single one of the giants and a lot of the wood was used for railroad ties at the turn of the Twentieth Century. They disappeared fast. Thirty of these giant trees still remain in Mariposa Grove and many are very old, over 2000 years.

The family started their walk into the park with a sense of great respect. Being in the presence of a living thing which has been standing there, day after day, way back even before years started to be counted on a calendar, is an awesome feeling! It makes you feel small and your life just a flick of time! Susan touched the bark of one of the giants standing on the side of the trail, nodding her head.

"Were you born before Christ was?" she asked, moved by the experience. "You have been here so long and you are so wise in your silence. What can you teach me?" she questioned, smiling.

The family stopped for a long time before the Grizzly Giant surrounded by a fence, admiring its enormous size yet its graceful limbs. They kept walking further encountering more giants, the Bachelor, the Three Graces, and many others, nameless. They spotted baby giant trees, recently born, wondering what the world would be like when they reached maturity or whether they ever would, the Earth having taken a different form in its evolution and the destruction that humankind was imposing on it.

When they walked out of the park, the three explorers left with the sense of humility which they had felt before the majestic giants but also a sense of responsibility for doing all they could to preserve this gift of nature which was so little respected today.

"I wish nature could speak," Joan said, moved by the experience. "I heard their voices clearly, perhaps is it because I listened?" she added with a tear in her eye. "Nature is so eloquent these days, the plants, the butterflies, the Earth, the birds, the trees and the sea. Why can't we all listen with our hearts? Why?"

Henri put his arm around Joan's shoulders and directed her toward the car. Susan followed quietly, having sensed Joan's emotion and feeling strongly the impact of their visit. This part of Yosemite Park had brought the most emotion for the family, and it was not only an aesthetic one.

When they reached the park gate, it was time to come back to what is called "reality," that is driving, freeways, gas stations, ugly signs on the side of the road, fields and fields of irrigated culture, crossing small towns you soon want to leave behind, moving on, moving to get to Fresno to sleep and tomorrow catch a plane to go home. The three were going back into their minds, their own plans, their fears and questions about the future. The ride back was anticlimactic and long, unlike the ride to Yosemite which had been full of promises, but if they let go of their churning minds for awhile and go into their hearts, the outside would disappear. They could feel the cool of Mist Trail, the exhilaration of Yosemite Valley. They could hear the voices of the sequoias in the silence of the forest. They could feel all that had registered in their essence to bring in more beauty and love for nature which was theirs and which they had felt so strongly during the past few days. A unity with nature and a trip home to it, where they knew they had come from.

"Dad," Joan said, interrupting a long silence which only the engine had broken. "It's hard to say anything, words don't do it, but thank you, Dad. Thank you for bringing us closer inside of ourselves in such a beautiful way!"

Chapter Twenty-Four: Joan Goes to Washington

The return home went smoothly. Connections at the two airports worked well and Claude welcomed the travelers happily back to Little Rock. He and Martha had a good break and took advantage of their free time to go south and visit some relatives. A guard was hired for a few days to watch the house and take care of the birds during their absence. The welcome home dinner was delicious as Martha made a special effort to get some fresh wild salmon for the occasion, which she served with a spinach soufflé, a salad, and a *crème brulee* for dessert, of course.

"Dad, did I hear you say once that life was lousy?" Joan joked around after they finished their meal. "When was that?"

"That was… I can't remember, Joan," Henri hesitated. "Perhaps that was before my daughter made us look at things with new eyes, like being grateful for the life we have in the present. Right Susan?"

"Yes, Henri, shall we celebrate with champagne?" she added joking.

"No, but I will settle for a kiss," Henri replied, taking Susan in his arms, "Remember walking in the Merced River with your little shorts? You did it again beautifully, this time," he added, kissing her gently. "This trip was a success for our family. Where shall we go next time, girls?"

"I want to go to Glacier Park," Joan answered, "before the glaciers are totally gone," she added sadly. "I have heard it is a very beautiful park."

Henri returned to D.C. to work, planning to organize an audience with the President for Joan. He wanted to make sure it would be possible before the summer recess in August. There was not much time left. Joan was starting to be a little shaky about what she was going to say. The responsibility felt huge. Now that she was committed, she was getting cold feet. Where would her supporters be? Mark Silver and Mademoiselle? And Ms. Stern and Phillip? Kristin was going to tease her about her guts to do such a crazy thing and Roger probably thinks that it is a lost cause. Where would all of her friends be when she needed them? Many defeatist thoughts were running through Joan's head as the days were going by, especially the thought of being alone in the presence of the most important man in the country, but Joan of Arc did it, didn't she? Joan decided to have a short conversation with all these friends who supported her and ask them some of the important things they would want to mention to the President. It would give her some confidence and then she would put her hand on her heart and go and do it. She knew the words would come easily out because they were the voice of her consciousness speaking.

Mark Silver told Joan that global warming, fracking, and their destructive results had become so evident by now that the President would probably agree. He said not to forget to mention the influence of special interest groups which had poured millions in trying to deny the damage and hide the name of chemicals or pesticides used in critical processes. Mademoiselle encouraged Joan to be herself, the bright and conscious girl who, like Joan of Arc, had to keep her faith and be brave in pursuing her goal. Ms. Stern said that they needed to add her name to the list of famous women in history, women with a mission to do what they could to change the state of the world. Phillip was very moved when he heard of the project. He thanked Joan for her courage and gave her a sweet good luck kiss. He also said not to forget the butterfly pin. Kristin, who had just returned from her grandmother's place, was the most verbal.

"Well, friend, I can't believe all that happened when I was away. I missed the party with the exciting speeches, right? Too bad! Now you are on your way to The White House! It takes a lot of guts to even think of doing such a thing!"

"Actually, I had a dream about it when I was in Yosemite, just before climbing Half Dome!"

"Well, if you climbed Half Dome I think that you can do this also, Joan! But don't forget what happened to your namesake. She ended up burning alive after saving France and I don't want to lose you."

"Don't worry, Kristin. I will just be talking, not leading an army. Sometimes words can be powerful. I'll do my best. I feel so committed to this Earth we live on and to all its residents. I'm sad to see our blue planet be raped to its core. I will speak from my heart."

The last friend who had been supportive was Roger, and he was away when Joan tried to call him, so she texted him, telling him of her request. Roger answered that he was skeptical about this big mission of hers but that if he had something to say to the President he would emphasize the subject they had talked about on their walk together in the park, consciousness, and the evolutionary step humanity must take in that direction if they wish to survive the insanity of what is happening. Joan thought that this was probably the key to the whole problem and she was happy Roger reminded her of it.

Joan spent a long time in her cave after she read Roger's message. She was no longer vacillating between defeatist thoughts concerning her audience with the President but was feeling the reassurance that her consciousness was instilling in her heart. She left her mind and entered the field of divine energy the universe bestows on the natural world. She felt at one with it, and she was going to speak for it.

Susan had stayed away from the whole thing. She was not too excited about Henri encouraging Joan and facilitating her crazy venture, but that girl of hers had proved before that she was smart and able to show great judgment in making decisions, so she just nodded and encouraged her when the time came to go to Washington at the end of July.

And the time came on July 29th! Susan took a deep breath when Henri and Joan left the house and walked to the jet which was roaring on the strip after the mechanic finished his thorough inspection and started the engine. Martha and Claude were standing by her, ready to wave goodbye and to bring Susan back in, as she looked in need of support which vodka could not provide for her this time. Joan's horse had turned out to be her dad's jet, and she was on her way to meet the "King" in Washington. To be true to the image, Joan had decided to wear men's clothing, if you can call men's clothing a pair of pants and a tee-shirt, which is today the standard outfit of both sexes in her age group. She thought it would mean something regarding equality.

How times have changed, Joan sighed, thinking of the romantic image of Joan of Arc going to meet King Charles VII in the 1400s! Over 600 years ago! Really? It was hard for her to imagine the 17-year-old riding into the unknown, confidently following the strong incentive the saints of her vision had given her, toward a fate which would change history. *What an amazing woman, she was!* Joan thought. *Will I find that courage in myself, without the help of the saints? Will my heart be able to voice what the essential is? Be with me Little Prince!* she murmured, smiling.

Henri had decided to let Joan go by herself to The White House. After all, she was a big girl and she had an appointment with the President. He dropped her off in front of the entrance with her pass in due form and he kissed her with his best wishes for the audience. She could contact him when it was all over. Henri was visibly shaken, but he tried to conceal it the best he could.

"I love you, baby. I know you will be great," he added quickly as he left Joan walking into the entrance, holding her pass.

The security guards immediately stopped her, checked her pass and called in to verify the appointment. One of them apologized for the delay and then escorted her. The Oval Office was a welcoming room and Joan immediately liked the painting of Abraham Lincoln adorning the wall. This great legend of American history had done so much for changing the consciousness of the country toward the humanity of all its citizens as equal. It was comforting to her.

Joan took a seat in a wide comfortable chair facing the President's desk. It didn't take long for him to walk in with a big smile on his face. Joan stood up to meet him.

"So, this is Ms. Larousse, the daughter of one of my favorite senators. Welcome to the Oval Office, Joan. Your dad told me a lot about you. He is very proud of his daughter and I'm happy to meet you."

"I am much honored to meet you, Mr. President, and very happy you agreed to this meeting. I feel blessed that you have consented to see me. Thank you."

A morning light, emanating from the large bay window, was bathing the room in a diffuse warm glow behind the President's shoulders. It made the man look friendly and receptive. Joan felt immediately at ease and ready for the meeting.

"So, you want to speak to me, Joan? Your dad said that your generation was concerned about a lot of issues and that perhaps I should hear what you had to say."

"Mr. President, a young woman my age went to see the King of France, some 600 years ago, and her intervention helped to save the country and to end the Hundred Years' War. It was a big achievement and I'm sure you know the story. Something very strong encouraged her to do it, some voices she heard and a vision which she had. She was compelled to follow them and she did.

"Something very strong has compelled me to come here to see you, Mr. President. Two weeks ago, my father took my mother and me to Yosemite. We were camping at the foot of Half Dome and I had a dream that night, where I went to see you. I was so shaken and I could not talk, all I could do was to put my hand on my heart and I woke up. I told my dad about the dream and he arranged for me to come here to see you. The voice which brought me here today, Mr. President, and the vision which I have are not coming from an outside driving force. They are the voices of my own consciousness. I'm here to speak to you from my heart about what is happening to the Earth, to the plants and animals on our beautiful blue planet and to our humanity. I'm here to ask you to do what you can to help stop the escalating destruction of our natural world and its biology."

"This sounds like a very ambitious goal, Joan. It will be harder to deal with than the Hundred Years' War! We live in different times now, and the ball is rolling on a larger scale, but I will be very happy to hear what you have to say."

"Mr. President, imagine for a moment that the Earth stopped turning around the sun, took a pause and said, 'People, I have had it! Look at me and wake up! Can you see the gashes in the bowels of my oceans, spurting dirty oil which will spill and burn? That oil which was the blood of past dinosaurs, creating gases which will poison your environment and bring weather changes everywhere, with floods and hurricanes destroying your cities? Do you realize the fish are disappearing and the ice is melting? Can't you see? People, look at the ways they dig my entrails now, with machines which frack them raw, injecting unknown chemicals which bring diseases, and waste my water supply by the million gallons? People, look at the sides of my beautiful mountains, scraped to the bone into ugly black crevasses to dig up more material which will burn into poisonous fumes? People, can you see my forests being cut? They provide healthy oxygen for you and they are almost gone now! Can you see the species of mammals and birds disappearing every day, along with the fish? Will a computer generated image ever replace the beauty of a bird in flight or the exquisiteness of a monarch butterfly? I could go on and on naming all the beautiful creatures which you destroy with your lust for money and material things. People, can't you see that you are next on the list of extinction if you don't stop this insanity now? People, are you blind? I created for you a paradise through which you could emerge into existence, and what have you done with it?'"

The President was visibly shaken, tears were running from his eyes. He remained silent for awhile, unable to find words. The heaviness of the world was weighing on his shoulders. He looked at this young woman, totally identified with the Earth she had spoken for, and coming from a place which, he knew, resonated with the core of every human being who sees what is happening in the world today. He blotted his tears and switched to a teasing mode.

"So, Ms. Joan, did the Earth stop talking after this heavy reprimand? I can see that she was defending its integrity, but was she aware of what it took for humanity to continue existing on the planet, to keep living in difficult conditions, to find ways to generate the energy we needed and the means to feed millions with ingenious agricultural inventions? Is the Earth blind to what humanity has accomplished in its science and technology while evolving to where we are today?"

"The Earth is not blind, Mr. President. She is aware of the incredible progress humanity has made to get where we are today, she has generously cooperated in giving lots of resources to help humans make a better life for themselves and she continues applauding the amazing discoveries of science, but something is happening now to the balance of nature, and what worked before no longer does, and the Earth is crying. The scale is sliding toward chaos and insanity that we witness today, while people try to deny it, consuming more and more of her resources to make them feel better. The Earth is not blind, Mr. President, but she doesn't understand why humans have arrived at a technological point where they are contemplating putting a man on Mars very soon when they are not even able to find a way to fix things at home! It does not make sense! Mr. President, I also want to quote F.D.R. who said that, 'Men and Nature must work hand in hand. The throwing out of balance of the resources of Nature throws out of balance also the lives of men.' Do you think that he was predicting what is happening today in our country Mr. President?"

"You are very convincing, Joan, and your arguments sound irrefutable. I agree with you about the imbalance. The Earth is in a dangerous position. When there is imbalance, the solution is to reestablish the equilibrium in some ways, right? But that is the problem! You like metaphors Joan, so here is a good one for you. Today, the world is running ahead full speed, like a mad long freight train heading into a tunnel, seeking equilibrium. In the tunnel are all the possible changes which would improve the balance. It is dark, smoky, unpredictable and scary inside. It is a trip of transition, a step further toward our evolution as human beings. The freight is heavy and it rumbles around with unimaginable bouncing. To restore a semblance of equilibrium would entail a complete transformation of that freight. Like power, truth, money, belief systems, the right and the wrong, God, education, science, biology, and evolution. And everything else which ever came to the human mind that creates some Tower of Babel style concepts. The task is seemingly impossible but, as one says, there is always a light at the end of the tunnel, Joan."

"I like your metaphor, Mr. President. It is somewhat like the one I visualize of the chrysalis before it changes into a butterfly. That entire gunk in its interior turning into beauty, just like the freight in your train going through the tunnel! Can you see the light, somewhere at the end, Mr. President?"

"Some days I can see it, Joan, and I believe in our human intelligence to solve the problems. But intelligence is not sufficient. It can be very adept at distorting the truth, whatever the truth is, so things get mixed up and there is no agreement and we continue to run around in circles. So to answer your question, Joan, no, some days, I can't see the light at the end of the tunnel."

"Mr. President, do you think that there are many people in this country and in the world who feel like I do, that we are close to our natural heritage, our biology, our environment, people who cry with the Earth at all that is happening to her and the biodiversity on this planet everywhere? Are their voices important enough to you, Mr. President, to call for a stop to the destructive practices of the oil, the gas and the coal industries which are destroying the Earth and our biology, and try to find other means of fostering energy from more natural, non-destructive sources? We have wonderful scientists who could find the way to do it! Are the special interest groups too strong to be confronted; will they keep silencing our voices?"

"Joan, you have entered a forbidden territory here. I wish it were simple. Remember, we are in the tunnel and that freight train might take awhile to reach the light. The train may even get stopped in the middle of the tunnel! You have to be patient, Ms. Larousse. It might take awhile!"

"Yes, Mr. President, but if the train stops too long, our species may not survive and my generation and the ones to come would like to live long and fruitful lives. Mr. President, forgive me, but I would like to ask you a direct question. Is this all about money?"

The President bit his lip. He thought for a moment and took a deep breath. Joan's question had dug into the core issue of the problem and there was no metaphor he could invoke to bypass the answer. "Yes, Joan, it is about money, and about will. Though we are a country that endorses capitalism, it's hard to look it in the face and explain problems such as the one you presented. This is America the beautiful and we have functioned very well with the system as it is since we established our democracy."

"Mr. President, I'm so sorry to confront you so directly, but being sixteen, I question a lot of things just trying to understand how the government works. I'm not educated in politics or constitutional rights, but it seems to me that the democracy our country was founded on is very different nowadays from the one this man endorsed. He was an ethical man I deeply admire," Joan emphasized pointing at the portrait on the wall. "Lincoln is one of my heroes as he seems to be one of yours," she added, humbly, "and he wouldn't like to endorse the plutocracy we live under now I'm sure."

"Yes, Joan, he is my hero also and I'm trying to keep his example in mind when I make decisions. There are things a president has to deal with that you could not understand, Joan, but I am happy to see that you are interested and that your generation looks forward to a long and happy life. We'll try to make this dream come true and hopefully, come out of the tunnel!"

Joan felt that the President was beginning to get tired, answering questions from a teenager about issues which he probably had a difficult time dealing with. She felt sorry for him and his difficult role as leader of a country which had to confront so many problems and difficult decisions. She felt compassion for the man, he looked tired and perplexed. How could she bring some positive element into a view for the future which he could relate to and didn't involve making a judgment on his peers or the corporations which were obviously the special interests he had not addressed in his admission to the capitalism issue.

Joan then remembered what Roger had recommended to bring up to the President about the importance of consciousness in looking at issues. She lit up and asked.

"Mr. President, would you say that in that rumbling in the tunnel, looking at the differences of opinions could help understand and repair the damage? Would you say for example that looking at the plight of the Earth simply from a greedy standpoint as the corporations do, is opposed to looking at it with the heart of those who see the Earth abused and destroyed? Where does consciousness stand in the equation, Mr. President? Or has consciousness disappeared from the souls of people who have grown accustomed to being brainwashed for economic growth, profit and the capitalistic way of running the country? We are looking for balance here, Mr. President. Do you see some form of balance in a society where 5% of the richest members of a country own 70% of the wealth while the poorest 50% only own 5% of the nation's wealth? Has consciousness been lost and does the rumbling in the tunnel mean that the majority of the people are starting to feel this gap? It's as if they were subjected to a new Middle Ages regime of powerful kings or emperors who usurp the country's resources while the others labor overtime in the dark and feel the injustice. Should consciousness be taught in the schools as a key principle of life in looking at the way the mind functions as well as how the body does? It seems that computer programming has taken over the role of our minds and of our biology in school programs, Mr. President. I'm concerned and I'm asking you to consider what I'm saying here today, because the future of my generation depends a lot on what happens to the freight train stuck in the tunnel."

"You have been very eloquent and explicit in your request, Joan, and I've taken note of all you said. It makes sense to me, but as I explained, changes don't happen fast, especially when the freight train is loaded and moves slowly. Remember the light at the end of the tunnel, Joan, which will come someday. It's all that I can work toward as president, and I will do my best."

As the President finished his sentence, Henri walked in accompanied by a guard. He shook hands with the President who had gotten up, smiling, and shaking his head. "You have got quite a daughter here, Mr. Larousse, a very bright and conscious young woman who can explain things in such a clear way that you get taken by her logic and heartfelt approach. Sixteen? Incredible! Where did she get all this knowledge?"

"She was brought up in the middle of a natural setting with plants and animals. She spent a lot of time in a cave, contemplating things and going beyond her mind, as I'm told. She reads a lot. She studied French and philosophy with a French tutor. She's very concerned with the state of the Earth and of the world but, mostly, she is a loving and sweet daughter whom Susan and I admire for her young wisdom and whom we love very much, Mr. President!"

"You are very fortunate, Henri. Joan has given me a fresh look at her generation and its concerns, and I admire her for her courage. Be well my friend and have a safe trip home," the President said while shaking Henri's hand. "And you, Ms. Joan, thank you for your concerned vision and intelligent participation in this difficult discussion. This has been the most stimulating audience I've held this year, I must say, and I loved our metaphors! I wish we would use more of those in Congress! "So, *au revoir*, Joan," the President said in his best French accent, and added, "A *bientot!*"

"*Au revoir, Monsieur le Président*," Joan replied, with tears in her eyes.

The emotion of the audience had been too much for the 16-year-old who quickly grabbed her dad's hand as they walked toward the exit of the Oval Office. She looked tired. She was very quiet and silent. Joan's dream had come to an end.

Chapter Twenty-Five: I Love, Therefore I Am

Henri was aware of Joan's feelings. After they left The White House, he decided to take some time and talk to her before they flew back to Arkansas. There was a small park he used to walk to when he wanted some quiet time between congressional sessions and he thought it would be perfect to sit there with his daughter. She obviously had gone through a lot.

Encouraged by her dad's positive suggestion, Joan started to relate in detail what had gone on during her conversation with the President. She admired his kindness and cooperation with what she had expressed to him, his willingness to go along with metaphors and listening to the Earth speaking through her voice. She was excited to tell her dad that the President even had tears in his eyes after she had spoken on behalf of the Earth. Joan continued with the freight train in the tunnel metaphor and the hypothetical coming out into the light at the end. Henri could detect a combination of excitement and strong disappointment in the way Joan felt about the outcome of her audience. She was perplexed.

"What did you expect to happen, Joan?" Henri asked gently. "Were you disappointed because the President could not promise to take immediate measures to take care of the environment and of the reasons for climate change?"

"I don't know, Dad. He just said he would look into it as if there was no big rush. I'm so worried about the time frame for what is happening."

"Joan, did you expect the President to give you an army to head toward the bad guys and fight the chemical companies, the oil, gas and coal corporations? Do you think that he would have the power to make that decision? I think that the President's reaction to the Earth talking was powerful and it will sit deep in his heart. The best way you can achieve a reversal of consciousness in the hearts of people, Joan, is just what you did, keep bringing images like that one into their hearts and their minds. Soon they will resonate with what is happening and see who is responsible for the damage."

"Dad, but what do you think about the millions which are spent to deny the damage and to continue it? Isn't it more powerful than the voice of the Earth?

"It is powerful, Joan, the corporations own the media who speak to the people these days, and they even have bought the federal court system. It is a disgrace to our democracy. However, don't forget that great injustices never last. Sooner or later, people will see that the essential is invisible to the eyes and they will look at what is going on with their hearts, as you told me the Little Prince said, sweet daughter, remember?" Henri said, hugging her. "You must keep your spirit up, Joan. It is a beautiful spirit."

"Thank you for arranging this meeting, Dad. I was so hopeful when I came here! But the dream I had in Yosemite didn't end with a resolution, it just told me to show my heart to the President, and I did, so I accomplished my mission, right? I have done well. Let's go home, Dad. Mom must be wondering about us."

"Yes, let's go home, sweetie. Mom called me when you were in the meeting, she was concerned about you. We should arrive for dinner if I have calculated right."

The flight home was smooth. Henri was a seasoned pilot and landing was almost unnoticed by Joan who had dozed off during the flight. Claude welcomed the travelers. Martha was waiting with dinner which she served on the patio so they could watch the sunset. It was a well orchestrated return.

"Well, look who is back!" Susan said when she saw Joan walk toward the table. "I'm so happy to see you, girl. Come, let me look at you!" Susan examined Joan from head to toe, smiling. "Did you ask the President to start giving more attention to women in the country and give them more jobs in the government? Men have done such a pitiful job lately, always fighting against each other! Women are the ones who understand the Earth the best. They are closer to her and they are the ones who give birth remember?"

"No Mom, I didn't ask him that. I didn't have enough time. But I did my best to speak on behalf of the Earth and I think he was touched.

I'm happy to see you, Mom. Did you start the project you told me about before I left?"

"I started. It involves getting an organization going for better nutrition in the school lunches around here. Mostly organic foods and non-GMO of course. I also have joined the local AA."

"Mom, you have been busy, I didn't know how serious you were! This is great, great! I'm so proud of you!"

Joan was happy to be back at home. The familiarity of her surroundings felt soothing, Martha was beaming when she saw her and hugged her. The park was beautiful in the sunset, the air sweet. It looked like life was good again, but Joan was already thinking of something important she could do to put a closure to the way she felt about her visit with the President. A piece was missing for her.

Joan decided that Mademoiselle would be the best person to help her to find this piece. She had been her guiding light many times. She would know what to say. Joan called her the next morning, asking her to come as soon as she could. Hearing the urgency in Joan's voice, Mademoiselle answered that she would be at the veranda in the early afternoon.

Mademoiselle walked into the veranda looking radiant. *She really is in love*, Joan thought as she offered a chair to her tutor next to the waterfall. The birds were all active, flying happily around the place. Victor was sitting on his favorite banana tree, looking alertly at the action.

Mademoiselle greeted Joan with a hug. "So, Joan, I'm happy to see our spokeswoman back from her mission. The Earth needed you, miss Joan of Arkansas, and you accomplished your request. I'm proud of my wonderful student who went all the way to The White House to achieve this."

"Yes, Mademoiselle, I'm happy I was able to do this and the President was very understanding. He listened and he was even moved at times, but..." and Joan started crying, not able to finish her sentence.

Mademoiselle took both her hands in hers and held them for a long time, respectfully letting the young woman's tears flow softly down her cheeks.

After awhile, Joan blotted her face and continued, "I felt that there was no hope, that the President could not do anything against all these powerful corporations, these dinosaurs who are devouring the Earth and its resources. I still feel that they don't care about what will happen to the Earth, to the animals, the plants, to humanity and the generations to come, possibly heading for the sixth mass extinction! I'm angry at them, angry and hopeless. So much that is happening in the world right now is tied up with this lack of balance with our natural world. I feel it so strongly, and I don't know how to reconcile myself with it!"

Mademoiselle kept silent for awhile, allowing Joan to calm down. She was very moved as she resonated totally with what Joan had just said. She had been feeling the same anger and hopelessness about the state of the natural world, and had shared her feelings with Mark Silver who was adamant about the causes of the imbalance. What could she do to help her young student accept what is, while working on raising consciousness? That is such a difficult suggestion for a young person, full of energy and dreams, who is looking at life ahead with the eyes of beauty, love, and anticipation of happiness, as time is of the essence! Mademoiselle decided that letting Joan find her own answer to the dilemma was the best solution for this very conscious and bright young woman, that she would simply suggest some quotes to help and guide her.

"Joan, I'm not you, and I can't tell you what to do to reconcile this dilemma within yourself. Remember the Little Prince? One only sees well with the heart; the essential is invisible to the eyes. Maybe your heart will tell you how to do it; it will show you what the essential is! I'll name two wise people who can guide you if you need help. Their names: Nelson Mandela and T.S. Elliot. When I get home, I'll send you two famous quotes by email. The first may help you with your anger, the second with our place in the universe. You are growing so fast, young lady, and this is but one passage in your life. Bless your beautiful consciousness. Now, Joan, I must say goodbye. Mark and I are leaving for France for three weeks. I want him to meet my family!"

"I'm so happy for you, Mademoiselle! Going to France! You can show Mark your beautiful country! And thank you for all your guidance. Now I'm on my own, right?"

"Yes you are, Joan, as you were in Washington. And you did well!"

Life returned as usual for Joan. Her exchanges with her parents, her friends, especially Kristin who wanted to know everything about the trip to Washington and Phillip who was curious about the way the President had taken her view about the Earth and biodiversity. Roger was happy that she talked about consciousness and Ms. Stern complimented her on her courage. Joan was also glad to have again found the solace of the meadow, the pond and the forest. Everything was oozing with the richness of summer there, and the animals were plentiful, showing out of furrows, swimming in the pond, and the birds singing in the trees. Of course, Joan was also anxious to sit in her cave and she decided to do just that after she received the email from Mademoiselle about these two sages she had mentioned. She walked through the woods to her peaceful retreat one quiet afternoon and sat on her rock.

Yes, my anger, Joan thought. *My anger at the culprits for this rape of the Earth! What is it that I feel inside?* Joan tried to answer for herself, as she let go of her mind to focus on what was happening inside her body. A lot was happening. Something like an inner rage was twisting her guts and making her heart beat faster. It was moving all over and painful. The mere thought of anger at the corporations had morphed into an organic realization and she was stuck with it. She stayed in it for awhile, not knowing how to get out of the feeling, when the little newt distracted her trip inside herself and made her laugh, and she began to ask more precise questions. *Is this feeling a rejection for these people? Rejecting is just saying no…it is not strong enough. So, what is it? I hate them. I want them to pay for their crime. I want them to hurt as bad as they are hurting the Earth!*

Joan stopped, afraid of what she had just said. The feeling was so strong! Joan remained pensive for awhile, tired and afraid, but she soon decided to take out the little paper with the quote by Nelson Mandela which Mademoiselle had said would help her with her anger. It said: "Resentment against someone is like drinking poison and thinking it will kill your enemy."

Whoa! So, it is resentment I feel. So I am drinking poison when I do that! Sure felt like it inside! Maybe Nelson Mandela survived his long prison time by not resenting what his enemies had done to him? Maybe he was doing something inside to ward it off! What is the opposite of resentment?

Calming herself down after this very difficult attempt to understand her feelings from inside her body, a word popped up in Joan's mind: acceptance, which she decided to feel inside as she had felt the anger.

Acceptance, she repeated several times, as she again went inside to feel what it was like. The trip, this time, was amazingly peaceful and soothing. Every cell in her body responded with a sense of letting go which spread further and further until her whole body floated in a sea of well being and release. It was wonderful. *Are feelings that potent?* Joan asked herself, thinking of what they create in the body. *What a discovery I have made thanks to Nelson Mandela! I cannot continue to feel resentment for these people! It would poison me! Just accept what is, since I can't do anything, and it does not mean that I agree with them, of course, but just continue to help people see what is happening to the Earth, without resenting the culprits.*

Joan was already feeling better. Her trip into anger had given her a sense of what she didn't want to hold against the bad guys, she would hurt herself in the process. She took a break for awhile, quiet, but she knew there was something else she had to understand further or maybe meditate upon. She leaned against the wall of the cave and closed her eyes, trying to remember. Overwhelmed by the fatigue, Joan fell asleep, her head hanging over her lap.

When she woke up, Joan took a deep breath and rolled her head around. She felt that she needed to move out of the cave and stretch her body in the sunlight. She got up and walked out toward the river. The energy of the running water was a tonic, refreshing after her long nap. She sat on a rock near the edge and put her feet in the cool water. It was the perfect place to continue processing her thoughts.

Where was I? Joan asked herself, tapping her feet in the water, making little waves. *I guess there was something important I understood after my body was able to help me see that there is a difference between a concept, straight from the mind, stark cold, and the meaning of that concept when it is felt from inside! That's how I got to see that I couldn't resent but had to accept the bad guys, lest I poison myself with the feeling!* This was an amazing realization!

How does the mind make decisions anyway? Joan continued. *Is it with a cool rational thinking motivated by profit-taking, for example, bypassing the connection with our nature, like in the case of the corporations? Did they ever feel what the results would be for the Earth, the environment and humanity simply by looking inside of themselves? Are they totally cut off from their relationship with the natural world, with their biology, with the voice inside that says that they are part of the whole and that they should care for* the Earth? Maybe we have arrived at a stage of our evolution today, where we now have to go beyond our mind to decide, to feel again our essence and where we come from, and go with its wisdom. Maybe the time has come to involve our body wisdom and our heart to help us keep in balance with the natural world and the Earth which sustains us. Is this the next step in our evolution as human beings, after what all the trial and error that following the mind only, has done to humanity? Maybe we will not survive if we cannot do this? Maybe the time has come to go back where we came from and go beyond our mind to understand where that place was?

T.S. Eliot was right, Joan decided after she read the quote Mademoiselle had sent her. *We shall not cease from exploration, and the end of our exploring will be to arrive where we started from and know the place for the first time. Maybe the time has come to see with our hearts.*

Joan felt complete, a great love for humanity and its long struggle toward consciousness flooded her being with quiet compassion. *This life is an amazing trip,* Joan thought. *The mystery which the universe holds will continue bathing us in its field, until we rejoin the whole, someday, and we all will be one again forever.* Joan felt complete, a great love for humanity and its long struggle toward consciousness flooded her being with quiet compassion.

Discussion Guide for Joan of Arkansas

TS Elliot: *Maybe the time has come to see with our hearts.*

Read each group of questions and discuss what you learned fom the book.

Character and Values

1. How did nature influence Joan and help shape her beliefs? What events show how Joan's values are different from her mother's? How does Joan resolve her conflicting feelings toward her mother? Describe how conversations with her father were different from those with her mother.

2. Joan had a French assignment to study existentialism (a person's essence comes from worldly experience). But another assignment quoted the Little Prince *"One only sees well with the heart, the essential is invisible to the eyes."* Which did she come to believe—that a person is shaped from worldly experience (existentialism) or instead that a person's essence comes from the heart? How did she experience this and use it in her life?

3. The librarian discussed the evolution of human consciousness with Joan. When Joan sat quietly in her cave she could expand her mind and feel her pure essence. How did she apply this to solving problems and resolving conflict? How would you define consciousness? What are the benefits of expanding your thinking?

4. When Joan reads about Joan of Arc, how was she inspired by the French heroine? What qualities do you admire in Joan of Arkansas? Who are your heros and heroines? What are your best qualities and what qualities would you like to develop further?

5. Both Philip and Roger asked Joan to the prom. How was Roger different from Phillip? Why was it easier for Joan to relate to Phillip? What admirable trait did Joan learn from Roger's response when she turned him down? How were Phillip's and Roger's families different economically? Did this matter to Joan?

6. Both Joan's mother and father drank at dinner and social events, but what made Joan realize that her mother had a serious drinking problem? How did her father's job contribute to their problems? How did Joan and her father support her mom to get better? What made the Forth of July party difficult for her mom after being in rehab? What important memory did the party bring back to her mom and dad, and how did the trip to Yosemite remind them of the aspirations of their youth?

Socioeconomic Status

7. Why was Joan's dad driven to make a lot of money and run for Congress? How did Joan's mom feel about money and how did Joan's attitude differ? Why was Joan reluctant to invite people to her home? When her mom took her to buy a prom dress, what did she ask her mother to do that demonstrated Joan's concern about economic inequality?

8. Joan's father wanted to buy her a Mercedes. What were her reasons for wanting a Pruis instead? Why was it so hard for her father to understand? Did he respect her decision?

9. How did Joan define the 1% club? How do you think rich people and money influence social issues in the United States?

Environmental Concerns

10. The science teacher, Mr. Silver, taught a class on global warming which scared a student and her parent started a petition to fire him. What might he have done to be less alarming? Why do you think global warming is controversial? Do you think teachers should be fired for teaching subjects that are controversial?

11. Why were Joan and her friends motivated to stop the petition? At the community meeting, Mr. Silver pointed our that human biology counted on nature, and that special interest money was preventing action against pollution. What point did he want to make when he showed a poster of a beautiful woman smoking a cigarette? What did Joan suggest Mr. Silver say to relate specifically to the church people that made them reconsider the petition?

12. In Phillip's poem, what was the significance of chemicals killing over 80% of the milkweed in the Midwest? How was the metamorphosis of a butterfly used as an analogy in his poem? How did Joan embellish on the same analogy later to lift Phillip's spirits?

13. Joan asked her father to get a companion for her parrot Victor. An animal conservationist proposed a better solution. What did he propose and why was it better for Victor?

14. The Scientific Method uses observation and research to form a hypothesis, or state a theory. That hypothesis is then tested with a structured experiment to collect data and draw scientific conclusions. Based on this, how is science different from beliefs? Is evolution a scientific theory or a belief? Is creationism a scientific theory or a belief? Should both be taught at school?

16. Environmentalists say fracking pollutes the soil and ground water. Joan's dad believed fracking was important for oil drilling, but he reconsidered when a nearby land was on a list for drilling. How did the Mr. Silver find a legal way to abort the drilling without her dad having to pull strings in Congress?

EPA and Role of Government

17. The Environmental Protection Agency (EPA) was formed to identify, measure and protect human health and the environment. How does their mission rely on science?

https://www.epa.gov/aboutepa/our-mission-and-what-we-do

18. Why are carbon and mercury emissions from coal-powered energy regulated? Why is renewable energy called clean energy as compared to coal?

19. The President agreed with Joan that money from corporations made it harder to make changes in legislation. Why do you think penalties are generally not imposed on companies for polluting the environment? If a company does something that damages human health or the environment, who do you think should pay the cost? What role do you think government should play?

20. EPA standards limit carbon and mercury emissions from power plants, which science says lead to heart attacks, asthma attacks, and premature deaths. The coal industry opposes any regulation, and says the cost to convert to clean energy will cause coal-powered plants to close. If the regulations are repealed, are we trading public health for corporate profits? Do you think it is more important to save money or protect human lives?

https://www.nytimes.com/2018/04/24/climate/epa-science-transparency-pruitt.html

21. National Geographic tracked the EPA rules that were reversed under President Trump beginning in 2016. Pick one of the rules at this link and discuss the pros and cons of maintaining the rule.

https://news.nationalgeographic.com/2017/03/how-trump-is-changing-science-environment/

Political Process

22. A plutocracy is a country or society governed by the wealthy. Phillip believed that corporate control creates a plutocracy in America, so the political process is controlled by money. Do you think the United States government is controlled by corporate interests? Do you think the United States is more of a plutocracy than a democracy?

23. Before Joan met with the President, she was nervous about which questions would be best to ask. What did she do to prepare? What did she want to tell him? How did the meeting affect Joan, and what was her main lesson?

24. An activist is a person who campaigns to bring about political or social change. What motivated Joan to take action against the petition, and later to meet with the President? What did Joan learn about speaking effectively and using the political process? When Joan became overwhelmed by her mission to save the world from pollution, what was her French teacher's advice? What did the President encourage her to do? If it seems hard to reach one of your goals, how could you apply the advice given to Joan?

25. What would you want to say if you had a chance to meet with the President of the United States? What current concerns do you have? What are you passionate about?

About the Author

Madeleine Herrmann was born in Lyon, France, on March 17, 1930. She lived through the World War II years in Nantes, which was bombed repeatedly by the Americans.

After the war, Madeleine became a competitive athlete who won French national track and field titles and participated in the University World Games in 1949 in Budapest. She studied in Paris for two years at the Ecole Normale Supérieure d'Éducation Physique then received a Fullbright scholarship to study at the University of Iowa. There she met Fred Herrmann, a German linguist and gifted violinist.

Madeleine and Fred defied the age-old hostility between the Germans and the French and married. They lived in California, built two houses, and raised four children. Madeleine pioneered physical fitness classes for women and children in California and graduated from UC Berkeley in 1962 with a master's degree. She taught French at Del Valle High School, then at Diablo Valley College in Pleasant Hill, California. Fred Herrmann committed suicide in 1969.

In 1983, Madeleine went back to college to study Transpersonal Psychology in the master's program at JFK University in Orinda, CA. She has lived in Taos, New Mexico, since 1992.

In 1986, her book of poetry, *L'Envolée Magique* (Editions Saint-Germain-Des Prés), was published in France. In it she explored "the essence of the feminine and the masculine." She has continued writing poetry, plays, short stories, and a children's story. This is her third novel. She published *Partita, A Psychological Mystery* in 2009 and *Isabelle's Dream* in 2012.

madeleineherrmann@msn.com
575-751-1051

www.ingramcontent.com/pod-product-compliance
Lightning Source LLC
Chambersburg PA
CBHW070455120726
47910CB00003B/1048